The **women** *of* CORONATION ST.

The *women of* ·CORONATION ST.·

Daran Little

Coronation Street **is based on an idea by Tony Warren**

B⬧XTREE

Published in association with

 GRANADA TELEVISION

Dedicated to the memory of my grandmother
Edna Morgan who first introduced me to the
Women of Coronation Street

First published in the UK in 1998 by Boxtree,
an imprint of Macmillan Publishers Ltd, 25 Eccleston Place, London SW1 W 9NF and Basingstoke
Associated companies throughout the world

ISBN: 0 7522 2443 3

10 9 8 7 6 5 4 3 2 1

Inside page design by Maggie Aldred

Printed and bound by New Interlitho

Reproduction by Speedscan Ltd

A CIP catalogue entry for this book is available from the British Library

Picture Acknowledgements
All photographs © Granada Television Limited 1998, except:
page 154 – estate of Lynne Carol
page 156 – estate of Violet Carson
page 183 – estate of Doris Speed

CONTENTS

"The women in this street are capable of anything!"

DES BARNES

Who are the biggest names in British television? Who are the best-known creations? Probably the names that come to mind are women, and chances are, they are characters from *Coronation Street* – Ena Sharples, Bet Lynch, Hilda Ogden, Elsie Tanner – for during its thirty-eight-year history *Coronation Street* has brought into the homes of millions of people characters who have become institutions. When Violet Carson travelled to Australia in the mid-sixties she was mobbed by a crowd of fifty thousand. Harold Wilson posed with Pat Phoenix on the steps of No.10, certain that in being seen as friendly with the nation's sex symbol he would romp home in the general election. Sir Laurence Olivier maintained that Jean Alexander's portrayal of Hilda Ogden was the only thing worth switching on for, and Sir John Betjeman called Doris Speed the Queen of British television.

The person who started it all was Tony Warren, a one-time child actor who wrote the *Street's* first episodes. Then aged twenty-three, he called upon memories of his matriarchal background that changed television for ever. He created the three monumental characters who influenced generations of writers and actors. He wrote the following character sketches for casting purposes:

Ena Sharples – seventies. Small, with a crabby walnut of a face and flashing eyes. Doomsday in woman's clothing! One minute she is a poor old woman, the next a screeching fiend. She is wicked, wicked, yet never defeated and somehow one can't help admiring her.

Annie Walker – late fifties. A publican's wife and looks it. Brisk, well corseted, well permed and a bit overdressed.

Elsie Tanner – late forties with the very battered, and much painted over, remains of good looks. She is easily raised to anger but has the proverbial tart's heart of gold.

Although Tony Warren laid the blueprint for *Coronation Street,* many writers and producers have followed him. For many years Adele Rose was the sole woman on the writing team and she fought hard to flesh out the female characters who followed Annie, Elsie and Ena. Bet Lynch, Rita Fairclough, Deirdre Langton, Gail Tilsley – all strong, passionate women whose highs and lows have kept, and still keep, viewers glued to their television sets.

Over nearly four decades *Coronation Street* has survived while other series have died. Critics, students, reporters and analysts have struggled to work out why it is so successful and most pick up on two aspects: the mixture of comedy and drama, and the strength of the female characters. On 24 April 1994, the *Sunday Times* said,

'This is matriarchy that Pauline Fowler of *EastEnders*, with her whingeing and cardigan, can only dream of. While the men skive and simper or simply stand about like latter-day Andy Capps, the women of the *Street* are reincarnated in ever-stronger models. Landlady Annie Walker has mutated into the camp parody of Bet Gilroy (née Lynch), Ena Sharples has come back as marauding Maud and, as Vera said only the other week, as far as

men are concerned, Elsie Tanner hadn't got a thing on that Denise Osbourne.'

The content of this book follows a similar line; that each character falls into one of several types. This is not an analytical grouping worked out after hours of calculation, merely a common-sense approach to the variety found in the characters. Over a twenty- or thirty-year period many characters have changed and could be said to transfer from one grouping to another, but for simplicity's sake they are found in the category for which they are most commonly known.

Don't be tempted to think that the groupings prove some theory that the Street is full of stereotypes. Rather, remember that Elsie, Ena and Co. were the first of their kind ever seen on British television. If later characters are stereotypes, it is because they are from the same original mould. It is the hundreds of programmes that have followed which have copied *Coronation Street*.

WOUNDED

"All I wanted, all I ever wanted, was to be loved..."

ELSIE TANNER

They're known as 'the tart with a heart', 'a good-time girl', 'a lively sort' and are loved by many men. Blessed with beauty, passion and sex appeal, they bluster through life like little boats buffeted from one rock to the next.

They are shrewd and share their hard-earned wisdom with other women who find themselves in the romantic situations so common to this kind – but when a pair of tight jeans or bulging wallet walks by they forget everything they have learned about men. An early marriage often leaves them with children who grow up with a succession of 'uncles' and become, in their mother's eyes, sexually active too early. They are no strangers to the divorce courts, the beauty parlour or the unemployment centre – many a good job lost because of a jealous wife. If a neighbour is burgled, feels suicidal or has a broken heart they're round like a shot, offering comforting words and a shoulder to cry on.

Unlike their Gad-about sisters, these women enter every relationship with wedding bells ringing in their ears. So desperate are they to catch a man that they give their all straight away. Their hearts drive these women to extremes, encouraging them to sacrifice everything for their man – careers, families, self-respect. They are viewed by older women as 'trollops' or 'loose pieces', and by women of their own age as a threat, when all they want is a home, children and, that most valuable of commodities, a man.

Character Name:	ELSIE TANNER
Date of Birth:	5 March 1923
Husbands:	Arnold Tanner (1939–62)
	Steve Tanner (1967–68)
	Alan Howard (1970–78)
Children:	Linda (1940)
	Dennis (1942)
Parents:	Arthur and Alice Grimshaw

"I've always been a sucker for a hunk o' man in a uniform, ever since I was a little girl on holiday, walking behind a big blond with Lifeguard written across his chest."

ELSIE TANNER

Elsie Tanner was the Queen of Coronation Street for the first twenty-three years of its history. She first appeared in Episode One, gazing into her compact mirror and telling herself she was 'fit for the knacker's yard'. She was a struggling mother with a son just out of prison and a daughter who had run away from her husband. Her own husband, the ''Orrible Arnold', had left her and the kids in 1945 to reappear in 1961 only because he wanted a divorce.

Elsie had moved into the Street in the days leading up to the Second World War as a sixteen-year-old bride, heavily pregnant with her Linda. The local women had her marked down as a threat straight away and during the war she gave fuel to their opinion by entertaining the GIs from Burtonwood, and starting her lifelong feud with Mission caretaker Ena Sharples, who never ceased telling Elsie exactly what she thought of her: 'We all know what your war work was. During the years 1942 and 1945 No.11 Coronation Street was like Liberty Hall, it always surprised me that, come VJ Day, them Yanks didn't take it down brick by brick and transport it to the United States of America!'

After Arnold left her, Elsie moved a succession of men into the house – and made certain they came and went using the front door in full view of Ena's twitching curtains. When she wasn't sitting at home on the lap of some sailor or butcher, she enjoyed slipping into a tight little number for a dance in Manchester. Little Linda and Dennis grew up on a diet of fish and chips, and the knowledge that a new pair of braces hanging over the banisters meant an opportunity to extract bribes from an eager new 'uncle'.

In twenty-three years Elsie entertained a total of twenty men, of whom she married two and kept returning to three. Some were of little consequence, picked up in a pub, good for a few nights before they disappeared. But a handful are worth a mention.

Elsie had one rule and that was not to mess with another woman's chap; she'd lost a man to a fresh tart more than once before, and she wouldn't wish the pain and anger on anyone else. In 1961 she started a Big Romance with Chief Petty Officer Bill Gregory, a tall, dark, handsome man in a naval uniform: 'I've always been a sucker for a hunk o' man in a uniform, ever since I was a little girl on holiday, walking behind a big blond with Lifeguard written across his chest.' Bill was generous, kind, strong, and swore he loved her. The only problem was that he was married. As soon as she found out, Elsie dropped him, although she loved him deeply.

The next married rat was flash Laurie Fraser, a theatrical agent who wore the first camel coat ever seen on the Street. He enjoyed throwing his money about and bought Elsie a fur wrap. When he opened a casino Elsie stood up for him against Ena and her Bible-bashing cronies, and even became a croupier at the club. Her first night at the job was also her last as one of her customers was Rosemary Fraser, Laurie's wife up from London for the grand opening. She didn't see Elsie as a threat, knowing that she easily outclassed her. All she had to do was order Laurie to drop his 'bit of rough' and Elsie was at her bedroom window, throwing all his presents down into the cobbles. Ena picked them up and advised her to keep her investments: 'No doubt you worked hard to earn them.'

Bookie Dave Smith was another flash businessman – 'Stick with me and they'll bury you in a silver casket' – who made no pretence about his wife, Lillian, in London. He actually invited Elsie and Lillian to dinner where, after discussing their pending divorce, Lillian gave his new relationship her blessing. Dave made Elsie manageress of his florist shop, the Pink Posy Bowl, and introduced her to horseracing, but Elsie knew that he would never marry her so she finished with him.

One regular boyfriend who never stopped proposing was builder Len Fairclough. He was the man next door, always there to pick up the pieces, always available for a night on the town. As Annie Walker once said of the pair: 'They seem to act like blotting paper, soaking up each other's woes.' To Len, Elsie was all a man could ask in a woman – a good laugh, a loyal friend and a sexy lady. Unfortunately for him, Elsie viewed him as her best mate, and refused to marry him for fear of losing his friendship. As a result of their unique relationship, Len saw sides of Elsie that she hid from everyone else: 'Elsie's a sparrow in a dirty street. She couldn't survive in an aviary with birds of paradise.'

Steve Tanner was an American who had fallen for Elsie during the war. When he returned to Weatherfield twenty years later Elsie refused to meet him, fearing he would think she had aged too much, but he wore down her defences. Before long, their reminiscences of the past had turned to love in the present. Before Elsie had time to blink, Steve had proposed. He was rich, good-looking, sophisticated, and had an accent to die for. They married in September 1967 and that Christmas flew away to a new life in the States.

Three months later Elsie was back, having sold her wedding ring to buy her airline ticket: her Prince Charming had turned into King Rat, drinking, gambling and refusing to let her out of the house for fear she'd run off with another man. She set about starting her life again, but Steve followed and begged her for a reconciliation. Before she could decide what to do, his body was found at the foot of a flight of stairs – Elsie, Len and even Dave Smith found themselves suspected of murder. Eventually a verdict of 'murder by persons unknown' was reached, although the romantic in Elsie believed Len had killed Steve out of jealousy. Two years later another American GI, Joe Donnelli, confessed to the Tanner murder, by which time Elsie was married to her third husband, garage owner Alan Howard. When he had arrived in the Street all the local women had fallen at his feet, but

Relaxing after a hard day selling frocks. Elsie still manages to look glamorous in the midst of a grotty existence.

Elsie won his heart. He, too, was rich, charming and handsome, and it seemed that Hilda Ogden was right when she remarked: 'Elsie Tanner's heart is where a feller's wallet is – and the bigger the wallet, the more heart she's got.'

It was when they returned from honeymoon that Elsie discovered Alan was insolvent, had a drink problem and a son from a previous marriage. Nevertheless, she gave up her plans for a life of idle leisure, and took a job selling cosmetics door to door. Despite his financial misfortunes Alan had a natural flair for business and soon had bought shares in a local garage and nightclub. While glad of the security provided by the garage, Elsie hated Alan's involvement with the club because of the potential for exploits with the hostess, although she was a formidable foe when faced with a rival. She tolerated Alan's flirtation with dolly-birds like Deirdre Hunt as she knew he was frightened of young girls, but his keeping company with singer Rita Littlewood was a different matter: she was more Elsie's age than Deirdre's and, like Elsie herself, a flaming redhead. Elsie went for the jugular, only to have Rita tell her that it wasn't other women that were a threat to her marriage, it was the bottle. Elsie couldn't stop Alan's drinking, which grew worse as their three-year marriage slipped into a daily routine of accusation and conflict.

After being knocked unconscious by a taxi in a London street, Elsie lay unidentified in hospital for two weeks. When Alan was traced he assumed that Elsie had been in the capital with a lover, but in fact she had been visiting her son Dennis in prison. Alan brought her home to find all the neighbours gossiping about her 'little trip', but rather than cause her pain by telling them about Dennis he allowed them to continue to assume the worst about her bruises. The Howard marriage became a public spectacle, especially after Alan assaulted Stan Ogden for referring to

Elsie as 'an old slag'. When Elsie was offered promotion in Alan's native Newcastle the couple didn't think twice and quickly packed.

For three years Elsie stayed away from the Street, watching her marriage die. When she returned to No.11, in 1976, it was as a wife separated from her husband. She divorced Alan but even those celebrations turned sour: out on the town she was mistaken for a prostitute. The incident forced her to reassess her life and she hated what she saw: 'When I get meself done up shall I tell you what I look like? Like a clapped-out old tart! Too much makeup. Too much cleavage. Too much scent. Too much everything. Lookin' worn out and a bit desperate. I walked through them streets last night in the pourin' rain and cried . . . for a girl who once 'ad guts, and hope . . . only she's dead now. And I'm not sure just when it was she died.'

Elsie could never rid herself of the need to be loved and protected by a strong man and it came as such a blow to her when Len married Rita Littlewood that she couldn't bring herself to attend the wedding. She had a long-term affair with Irish taxi driver Ron Mather but that broke up after they took domestic jobs in Torquay. Elsie became housekeeper to a retired tycoon while Ron was his chauffeur but within a month Elsie was back at No.11: Ron had not protected her from the old man's advances.

Working as manageress at Jim's Café, Elsie had ample opportunity to flirt with muscular lorry drivers over plates of black pudding. She decided to offer bed and breakfast in her back room and took in Dan Johnson as her first customer. As soon as he arrived, Elsie wanted him in her bed rather than the spare one and chose to ignore his string of other 'landladies'. When she found him kissing barmaid Bet Lynch, though, Elsie threw out his gear and flew at Bet across the Rovers' bar: 'If you lay your mucky hands again on a feller that has owt to do with me then I'll knock that

"Elsie Tanner's heart is where a feller's wallet is – and the bigger the wallet, the more heart she's got."

HILDA OGDEN

over-painted head of yours from off its shoulders. You foul-mouthed, cheap floozy.'

As she reached her sixtieth birthday, Elsie found herself alone in a grotty little house in a grotty back-street, working at a sewing-machine in a grotty sweatshop. Just when she had decided that her life would continue downhill to the grave, a face from the past reappeared. In Weatherfield to offer condolences to Rita following Len's tragic death, Bill Gregory was amazed to find Elsie still at No.11. He had retired from the Navy, his wife was dead and he ran a successful wine bar in the Algarve. Without hesitation he urged Elsie to come with him to Portugal, saying that he had never stopped loving her. Elsie grasped what she knew was her last chance for happiness and left England.

As well as sharing her home with various husbands and boyfriends, Elsie also enjoyed having young people around her. After Linda married a Pole and moved away, Dennis remained with her for another eight years. He blamed his mother for his spell in prison and his inability to hold down a job, and accused her of making him feel insecure as a child. She tried hard to steer him into the path of a normal, quiet girl who'd look after him but he was drawn to a type she knew only too well – her own: 'I can't be normal, can I, Mother dear? Becos I 'aven't got a normal mother, 'ave I? Do you think I'd bring a decent girl in 'ere – do you? Don't forget I've 'eard the way you talk to our Linda – "tell us about them Yanks at Burtonwood." – Is that the way a normal mother talks to 'er kids? I tell yer, I'll start respectin' you when you respect yerself!' In private, though, he was glad that his mother was lively and vivacious rather than a stay-at-home like Ida Barlow. The girl he married was just like the young Elsie: full of sexual confidence and not knowing a butter knife from a carving knife.

Elsie also kept a motherly eye on young girls. When they were involved with older

men, she urged them to walk away before their hearts were broken. Of course, they never listened and neither did the men, whom she tried hard to frighten off: 'You put the kettle on, love, whilst I have a nice chat with your friend. I'm sure we've got a lot in common. Tell me, what did you do on VE night?' After the affair was broken up (normally by a vengeful wife), Elsie was there to mop up the tears and offer words of encouragement, which normally included an invitation to a night on the town to 'fight back'. In a club or pub, Elsie would forget her own advice and make eyes at a businessman at the bar. She never learned.

Setting off for a new lifestyle. After her fairy-tale marriage a new world beckoned but within three months she was back home licking her wounds.

Character Name:	SUSAN (SUZIE) BIRCHALL
Date of Birth:	3 May 1958
Husband:	Terry Goodwin (1982–83)
Parents:	Bob and Margaret Birchall

O ne of the girls taken under Elsie's protective wing was Suzie Birchall. She ran away from a violent father to lodge at No.11, sharing Gail Potter's room. At first Elsie didn't want her around naïve Gail: she recognized herself in the young redhead and didn't want Gail led astray. However, Suzie and Gail became firm friends, although they remained poles apart when it came to men and romance. Gail was looking for a future husband in every lad she met while Suzie saw

men as notches on her bedpost: she'd watched her downtrodden mother strive to keep her husband happy and the blows he rained upon her.

The two girls clashed a few times over lads, normally because Suzie threw herself at any guy even if Gail had confided to her that she was falling in love with him. Suzie was amused by Gail's intensity, saying that men were around only to give a girl a good time. French student Roger Floriet caused a few waves in the house when the girls let him stay in Elsie's bed during her annual holiday. Suzie was attracted to his accent and while Gail cooked his meals and left love notes under his plates, she put on her shortest nightie and crept into his bedroom. The same thing happened with Steve Fisher, a young local lad whom Gail fancied. Suzie thought him a wet joke but Gail's infatuation with him made Suzie lure him

Elsie shows Suzie the door after her failed attempt to ruin the Tilsleys' marriage.

upstairs during a party at No.11 where she took his virginity, devastating her best friend.

But Suzie was most attracted to older, more experienced, wealthier men, using her body and looks to get what she could out of them. When her boss Mike Baldwin complained about her bad time-keeping Suzie kept him sweet by agreeing to a night out with him – she kept returning to him over three years when younger men failed to show her the same, expensive, good time.

Suzie tried to trade on her looks by joining a model agency but the only assignments she was given involved demonstrating fancy foods in supermarkets. However, the job had its compensations: fifty-two-year-old Paul Stringer, who ran the agency, took her out and bought her clothes and perfume. At first she lapped up the attention and ignored Elsie's warnings, but she made the mistake of thinking she was special to him and it came as a shock when he said, 'Come on, love, paint yer face on an' stop getting stroppy. You come from a big pool o' tarts, darlin', an' if you don't want what's on offer I can soon find another o' you who will.'

In 1979 Suzie decided to take her chance of a new life in the fast lane in London. She thought a big modelling house would snap her up and propel her to stardom. Instead, she ended up working in burger bars and pubs. For a laugh she even got married, to a sales rep called Terry Goodwin. All was well for the first two weeks and then he started to use his fists on her. Appalled that she had followed in her mother's footsteps, she broke free and returned to Weatherfield and Elsie. Terry came after her, but Elsie protected her and made him see that there was no future in the marriage.

Suzie took a job as barmaid at the Rovers and approached Mike Baldwin again, but was put out when he told her he wasn't interested in her any more. It seemed to her that, in her absence, life on the Street had stood still, and

she despised Gail for having found the happiness that had eluded her. Gail had married her sweetheart Brian Tilsley and had an infant son, which she felt gave her the moral high ground and she infuriated Suzie by belittling her lifestyle – so much so that Suzie attempted to seduce Brian. The plan backfired when he resisted her and told Gail. Elsie was disgusted with Suzie's tactics and threw her out of No.11. Suzie called her landlady a hypocrite: 'Come on, Elsie, maybe I did go a bit over the top but it's not like you to take this high moral tone. I mean, Elsie Tanner, she used to be the biggest slag of the lot!' She stormed away from the Street, this time for good.

Character Name:	FREDA (IRMA) BARLOW
Date of Birth:	28 September 1946
Husband:	David Barlow (1965–70)
Children:	Darren (1969)
Parents:	Stan and Hilda Ogden

Another young, high-spirited redhead to live on Coronation Street was Irma Ogden Barlow. She arrived in 1964, when she moved into No.13 with her parents, Stan and Hilda, and held down two jobs: assistant at the Corner Shop and barmaid at the Rovers. Living next door to the Ogdens, Elsie Tanner took an instant liking to the girl, who enjoyed a laugh with her: although Elsie was the same age as Irma's own mother, she was the complete opposite of Hilda. Irma was often embarrassed by her parents, and tried to keep her family and social life separate.

Shortly after moving into the Street, Irma fell for footballer David Barlow and was thrilled when he proposed marriage. She accepted him but warned that she would

United in grief following Valerie Barlow's death, Ken reaches out for comfort from an old sparring partner, his sister-in-law Irma.

waking hour with him so she took a job as a welder in the PVC factory across the Street. Irma enjoyed spending time with her sister-in-law Valerie's twins and longed for a child of her own. In 1967 she became pregnant but miscarried and fell into a depression, feeling she'd never have a child. David didn't lose his interest in football, though, and without telling Irma, he tested out his knee injury in a local game. When a doctor confirmed that it had miraculously healed itself, David told the stunned Irma that he intended to return to playing and had been offered a place in an Australian team. Irma had no wish to leave her parents or start afresh on the other side of the world, but when she realized she was pregnant again she had to agree with David that Australia would offer their child a better life. The couple emigrated in 1968, selling the shop to the Cleggs.

Darren was born five months after they arrived in Sydney but while David had the time of his life with matches, parties and fame, Irma had little but a screaming baby to occupy her. Rows were commonplace and Irma found that she was becoming as much of a nag as her mother. She felt trapped and longed for release. Tragically, her prayers were answered: a family outing ended in a car crash in which David and Darren were killed.

Irma Barlow returned to Coronation Street to her parents and David's family as a widow in her late 20s. She told David's brother Ken of how their Australian lifestyle had pushed them apart and was staggered when he forced her to face truths she had tried to hide: 'You can only live for yourself, that's all you're capable of. When you married David I thought you were wrong for him but this goes deeper than that. You'd be no good for anybody! If you have to spend the rest of your life living alone, then that's the best thing for you. You've got two graves to prove it. That brands you, Irma, that brands you for life!'

Irma shrugged off what he and the neigh-

never settle for respectability: 'I'm goin' ter be swappin' rude jokes wi' Elsie Tanner an' slangin' Mrs Sharples an' battin' me eyelashes at the fellers till they carry me out in me box.'

After a quiet wedding, the Barlows settled into a luxury flat and Irma gave up work, but almost immediately David was injured in a football match and had to retire from the same. He used his savings to buy the Corner Shop and set about learning the art of shopkeeping from his wife. As much as she loved David, Irma had no wish to spend every bours thought of her and entered into partnership with Maggie Clegg, running the shop. She moved into the flat above it and resumed her life as a bachelor-girl. She gave the gossips ammunition by going out with bookie Dave Smith, Elsie's old flame, and showed off the clothes and jewellery he bought her.

After she and Dave split up Irma fell for American Joe Donnelli, who had served with Steve Tanner. He was on the run from the Army and confessed to Irma that he had murdered Steve. Then he imprisoned her in the flat and threatened to stab her if she tried to escape. Luckily the residents discovered what was going on and freed Irma but Joe shot himself.

It seemed to Irma that she was turning into another Elsie Tanner, waiting for a chap, any chap, to buy her a gin at the Rovers. In an attempt to break free and leave the past behind, she ran off in the middle of the night for pastures new. The last Hilda heard of her, she was living with a dentist in Canada.

Character Name:	ELIZABETH THERESA (BET) GILROY
Date of Birth:	4 May 1940
Husband:	Alec Gilroy (1987–)
Children:	Martin Downes (1956)
Parents:	Patrick and Mary Lynch

While working at the PVC factory, Irma had befriended fellow welder Bet Lynch. She was amused by the way Bet reigned as top dog in the factory, fighting the other girls when they crossed her and keeping the foreman company at night. When she moved into the Corner Shop flat, she asked Bet to come, knowing that with Bet around her spirits would never get too low.

Bet was a native of Weatherfield, brought up by her religious mother after her father walked out when she was six months old. She'd had a child of her own - a boy named Martin – who had been taken from her when she was just sixteen. Since then she had built up a reputation among the local men as being available and willing, although all she wanted was a pair of protective arms around her.

On the surface Bet came across as a bitter realist, worn down by disastrous love affairs, but as soon as a new man entered her life the little girl within her took over and led her into shark-infested waters. Her first true love was Frank Bradley, an ex-Borstal teenager who, although Bet was ten years older, decided she was ripe for him. She, in her turn, saw herself as the person he needed to help him reform.

'I'm just a willing tart.' Bet doubts her judgment after spending the afternoon in Len Fairclough's bed.

Unfortunately he wasn't ready to give up crime and went on the run after mugging Bet's friend Lucille Hewitt of money she was banking that belonged to bookie Dave Smith. After Dave's heavies had caught up with him, Dave told Bet that Frank wasn't worth looking at any more.

When Bet became a barmaid at the Rovers, wowing the menfolk with her plunging neckline and short skirt, Hilda Ogden was amazed: 'Talkin' of Rovers, you ought to see the new barmaid, if you can call her that. The first time I saw her I thought it were a jukebox.' Annie Walker, though, had been quick to realize that Bet was an asset to the pub: the sight of her behind the bar encouraged men to spend more time – and money – there. However, she asked Bet to dress more conservatively and to limit the amount of time she stood chatting up the customers.

Bet loved the attention she attracted and lapped up all the admiring glances and lewd comments. She played up to the customers, letting them watch her legs, as she reached for glasses, and her cleavage as she stooped for bottles. It was during a typical session at the pub that Martin Downes, a nineteen-year-old soldier, came in seeking the mother who had given him up as a baby. The sight of Bet showing off her body to wolf-whistles appalled him, and he fled without speaking to her. Six months later Bet received a visit from his pal, to explain that Martin had been killed in a car crash.

The death of her son shattered Bet. 'He was the only thing I ever got from a feller. And the whole time he went from bein' a kick in the belly to a soldier, I went from nothin' to nothin'. Wasn't very easy, but then it wasn't very hard.' It was only the support of her friends that brought her through the darkest period of her life. Afterwards, she redoubled her efforts to find a husband. A brief affair with Len Fairclough resulted but as he was not interested in commitment Bet dumped him.

The main difference between Bet and Elsie Tanner was that Bet had no qualms about taking on a married man or breaking up a home. She figured that if a feller was interested enough to cheat on his wife then the marriage couldn't be that firm in the first place. In 1976 she moved into No. 5 Coronation Street with Mike Baldwin, knowing that he had a wife and children in London. Mike was just the sort of man who gave Bet butterflies inside – sexy, self-assured and rich.

Mike spent weekends in London with his family and the rest of the time at No. 5, looking after his business across the Street. When his wife, Anne, came up to inspect the factory Bet was indignant when Mike asked her to make herself scarce. Anne, however, was quick to match the long blonde hairs in the house to the blonde barmaid at the pub and, after checking that Bet used the same cheap scent that hung in the air of No. 5, confronted her. Bet was ready to fight her corner but was stunned when Anne told her that she herself was no more married to Mike than Bet was, and that he was not the father of her children.

Bet was horrified that Mike had lied to her to avoid commitment. He tried to make her believe that he was merely living up to her expectations: 'Your trouble, Bet, is that you like rats. I'll tell you what turned you on about me. I was a gamble. You don't know if I mean what I'm saying. But you're not bothered, cos you've got a bit of cash bein' spent on you and a flash bloke to go around with. That's all you want.' After slapping his face, Bet told Mike he was very, very wrong: 'What do you think keeps people like me going? Hope. You hope that one day there'll be someone who won't cheat or lie or pretend they care about you when all they really want is a willing tart. I've been kicked in the teeth often enough so it doesn't really come as a surprise. But it doesn't stop hurting.'

She moved back into the flat over the Corner Shop, but landlady Renee Bradshaw

> "Talkin' of Rovers, you ought to see the new barmaid, if you can call her that. The first time I saw her I thoght it were a jukebox."
>
> HILDA OGDEN

objected to the number of men she brought back from clubs to warm her bed, so, after stealing Dan Johnson from Elsie Tanner, Bet moved into a bedsit on Victoria Street with him. He walked out on her when she started making plans for the future. Bet couldn't understand what she was doing wrong.

The fact that she wore availability on her sleeve never entered her head, and she continued to attract men on the lookout for a pushover. Jack Duckworth was typical of the married men who pursued Bet until she gave them bed room. These liaisons always ended with her having a slagging match with the wife and the bloke returning home, repentant.

When her bedsit was demolished, Bet moved back to the Corner Shop flat, now owned by her old friend Alf Roberts, for whom she unwittingly caused trouble when she told a newspaper reporter that he allowed her to live rent-free over the shop. The result was a damaging front-page story, telling all

Weatherfield that Alf had given house-room to a busty blonde barmaid and implying that they were more than friends. Alf told her that in future she would have to pay rent. His life was further complicated when Bet took up with his fellow councillor, Des Foster, a married painter and decorator. Bet refused to agree with Alf that she should consider Mrs Foster's feelings, maintaining that as far as she was concerned it was a case of dog eat dog: 'The first wink came from him, Alf. Not from me. All right, so I winked back. But in my book that's Queensbury Rules. Married or not. And it will probably end in tears. But don't worry about it. It'll probably be me who'll be doing the crying. It usually is, love.' When Des told her he intended to leave his wife, Edith, she planned to move in with him. However, when Edith called at the shop she told Alf that Des was leaving her for a woman with two children. Bet was stunned to hear that he was keeping another woman as well as

Len Fairclough epitomized the sort of man the Walking Wounded were attracted to – here three of a type fight for his attention.

her and his wife and reluctantly put a stop to the relationship, feeling he would never be honest with her.

In 1984 the Walkers left the Rovers and, to her amazement, Bet became manageress. The job came with living quarters and she had to adapt overnight. She went on management courses and refined her appearance and manners to win the approval of the brewery bosses. No amount of expensive hairstyles or costume jewellery could really change her, though, and she continued her search for Mr Right. At the same time, she had become desperate to be her own boss, and borrowed money from theatrical agent Alec Gilroy to buy the Rovers' tenancy. She looked upon him as a business partner and shrugged off friends' warnings that he was using her to get his hands on the pub.

While Alec hung around the place keeping a beady eye on his investment, Bet began to feel trapped by all her responsibilities. She struggled to keep up the repayments on the loan but in the end, deciding she couldn't cope, jumped aboard a plane for Spain. For three months she worked in an English café, serving egg and chips to homesick tourists, but she longed to return to the Rovers: it was her home and the one place where she felt in control of her life. When Alec tracked her down, he told her that the brewery had given him the pub to run, but that there was a way she could take back the Rovers – if she agreed to marry him. Bet accepted her first proposal, and in September 1987 became Mrs Gilroy.

Friends and customers assumed that the marriage would be over within six months but Bet was determined to prove them wrong. To the outsider they looked a comical pair – the short, chubby man and the overdressed, busty wife, just like a seaside postcard – but Bet knew that she and Alec needed each other.

Alec was a shrewd businessman, keen on fiddling the taxman, and Bet let him look after the books while she managed the bar and the staff. There were moments of unhappiness for the couple, such as when Bet miscarried their baby, but the only tension came when Alec was involved with a foreign tour company as entertainments' manager. In 1989 he took a group out to the Middle East, leaving Bet twiddling her thumbs at the Rovers. However, when her friend Stella Rigby's husband Paul took her out one evening she kept him at arm's length. Paul became a regular visitor, though, and upon his return, Alec jumped to the wrong conclusion: he sued for divorce, citing Paul. Bet protested her innocence but Alec and Stella would not accept that she had refused a man's advances. Bet left home and threatened to move away, which brought Alec to his senses, and the pair were reconciled.

Bet's mothering instincts came out when Raquel Wolstenhulme moved in as resident barmaid and Alec's granddaughter, Vicky, was orphaned. Bet had two vulnerable young girls under her roof and did her best to build up their confidence, giving advice on how to deal with men. In 1992 the Gilroy marriage fell apart when Alec took a job in Southampton and Bet refused to leave the pub she adored.

Trucker Charlie Whelan was next to whisk Bet off her feet, and against her better nature, Bet fell in love with him. She considered making it legal by divorcing Alec, but Charlie proved just like all the others: he had an affair with barmaid Tanya Pooley.

Faced with the news that she needed to find £66,000 to buy the Rovers or lose her home Bet felt badly let down when Rita Sullivan and Vicky refused to lend her the money or go into partnership with her, telling her that she was a bad risk. Now she was alone but this time without the advantage of youth. Who would come to the rescue of a fifty-year-old blonde barmaid with no prospects and nothing to look forward to? The answer was no one. She packed a couple of bags and jumped into a taxi to head into the unknown.

"I've been kicked in the teeth often enough so it doesn't really come as a surprise. But it doesn't stop hurting."

ELSIE TANNER

Character Name:	RITA SULLIVAN
Date of Birth:	25 February 1932
Husband:	Len Fairclough (1977–83) Ted Sullivan (1992)
Parents:	Harold and Amy Littlewood

During the seventies and eighties Bet's best mate was redheaded Rita Littlewood Fairclough, one-time night-club singer. Like Bet, she was on the constant look out for a feller and wore her heart on her sleeve. Rita, too, had been pregnant at sixteen but her mother had forced her to have a back-street abortion, which had left her sterile. She was attracted to the same sort of man as Bet and longed for commitment and a secure future. Both women were fighters and sur-vivors, and understood each other's pain. In an unguarded moment with Rita in 1986, Bet let her mask slip: 'I've picked myself up and started over again too many times. I'm tired, Reet. I'm norra kid any more. It gets 'arder and 'arder to paste on the smile. 'Ow long can I go on doin' that? 'Ow do you go on, kid?' Rita gave her the fairest answer she could: 'With pain. Sometimes so frightened. Sometimes so alone you're too numb to cry. But, you go on. We both know about that, don't we Bet? You go on.'

Rita came to the Street as an exotic dancer, friendly with Dennis Tanner, then took up singing in clubs, where she became an instant hit: 'They named a sherry trifle after me at one Labour Club I played.' Her love for chil-dren was tested during the four years she lived with Harry Bates and looked after his son Terry and daughter Gail. Through Terry she met teacher Ken Barlow and dallied with the idea of an affair with him; however, he dropped her after his headmaster disap-proved. Instead she took up with Len

Fairclough in the hope that he could use his influence on the council to rehouse her family. Harry didn't like the idea of Rita using her charms to get them a new flat and threw her out, after giving her a 'good seeing to'.

With nowhere else to go Rita dumped her-self on Len's doorstep and asked for help. Having just bought a newsagent's shop, Len installed her as manageress and she moved into the flat above, keeping Len on tenter-hooks by refusing to give him a spare key. For four years Rita and Len's relationship went through troughs and peaks, during which time he dated Bet and Rita enjoyed making him jealous with conquests of her own, of whom one was estate agent Jimmy Graham.

Rita found his refined manners appealing, and he took her out to the best restaurants. She cooked the occasional late-night meal for him at her flat, making sure that Len knew when Jimmy stayed for breakfast. Yet despite his gentlemanly ways, Jimmy turned out to have a wife and children he refused to leave. Rita ended the affair: 'Truth is, love, I don't want to be patient. I'm fed up of being some-body's little bit of stuff. Somebody's spare wheel. I'll be honest with you. I want to get

Len's engagement ring was off and on Rita's finger so often that not even Hilda Ogden could keep up with events.

married. As much out of fear as anything.'

It was only when Len faced losing Rita to a singing contract in Tenerife that he proposed to her. She accepted, and they were married in April 1977. She felt a certain satisfaction in knowing that she had achieved what Bet and Elsie had not in becoming Mrs Leonard Fairclough.

Rita moved into Len's home, No. 9 Coronation Street, and set about installing feminine touches. A typical builder, Len had neglected his own home in favour of working for others and Rita was appalled by its dilapidated appearance. Len, though, saw nothing wrong with it and took no notice of Rita's complaints. The final straw was when he rushed round to mend Elsie's dripping tap when Rita had been asking him to put a new washer on their tap for weeks. She packed and moved out: 'I'm a woman, Len, a woman. Someone to be looked after, cared for and capable of giving a bit back in return. But you're too wrapped up in your own grotty little world that stretches no further than the bottom of a pint pot in the Rovers.'

At first Len thought he'd be better off without a nagging wife but he soon began to miss Rita and started to search for her. He found her working in a Blackpool launderette and begged her to come home, promising that he would change his ways. Rita agreed to return as she was touched that he'd needed her enough to look for her. True to his word, he decorated and modernized the house, even installing central heating.

Now that she had the house right, Rita turned her attention to the other disappointment in her life: her childlessness. Len was happy as they were but finally agreed to see an adoption agency where they were both upset to be turned down due to their age. The fostering people were more welcoming and, in due course, the Fairclughs fostered sixteen-year-old Sharon Gaskell.

In a matter of months, the secure family

life that Rita had longed for so passionately was turned upside down: Sharon took a job in Sheffield, and Len was killed in a car crash driving home from his mistress in Ashton. Rita was left a wealthy widow but all the money in the world couldn't compensate her for the loss of the man she loved.

Len's best friend, Alf Roberts, proposed to her but she wasn't ready for commitment, especially to a man she didn't find attractive. Instead she returned to fostering, taking in fourteen-year-old Jenny Bradley when her mother was killed.

Looking after Jenny was a challenge as Social Services asked Rita to try to reconcile the girl with the father she hadn't seen for eight years. Alan Bradley was an engineer living in Leeds and had no objection to taking on the responsibility of his daughter but Jenny was full of resentment towards him. By the time Rita had succeeded in making her see that Alan was not an ogre, she herself had fallen for him and was delighted when he decided to set up home in Weatherfield so as not to disrupt Jenny's schooling.

It seemed to Rita that God was smiling on her once again, having given her replacements for Len and Sharon. Alan seemed genuinely attracted to her, but she refused his proposals and insisted that she couldn't go through with another marriage for fear of losing him. Instead, she invited Alan and Jenny to live with her and for them to be a family in all but name.

For a while Rita was content and happy, running the Kabin newsagent's by day and curling up on the sofa with Alan of an evening – she even enjoyed being cheeked by Jenny. Unknown to Rita, though, Alan was annoyed that she wouldn't marry him and that she seemed to stop him getting too close to her. He started an affair and moved out, telling Rita that she had never shown him any affection and that he was tired of being held at arm's length.

> *"I'm fed up of being somebody's little bit of stuff. Somebody's spare wheel. I'll be honest with you. I want to get married. As much out of fear as anything."*
>
> RITA SULLIVAN

Rita was devastated and continued to throw herself at Alan, begging for a second chance as she saw the destruction of the family life she had begun to take for granted. She was thrilled when he returned, unaware that his only motive was to bleed her of money. Having assumed Len's name and stolen the deeds he mortgaged the house behind her back. He used the money to start up his own business, and Rita, innocent of the truth, was proud of the way he was proving himself. That was until his receptionist told her that Alan had tried to rape her and that he had received official letters at the office addressed to Len Fairclough.

Rita undertook her own investigation and uncovered the truth. She confronted Alan, telling him she was reporting him to the police, and was taken by surprise when he attacked her savagely. It was only Jenny's arrival that prevented him from suffocating her with a cushion. While Rita recovered in hospital Alan was tracked down by the police and imprisoned.

Rita had lived through one nightmare only for another to take its place. After serving time on remand Alan was released by the court and returned to haunt her. He took a job across the Street on a building site and kept breaking into the house to move furniture so that she knew he had been in. In desperation Rita started to drink more than usual and found no support from the police, who felt she was a lonely old lush. Even Jenny refused to believe that Alan meant her harm and moved out. Eventually Rita had a nervous breakdown: believing herself still to be Rita Littlewood, she took a singing job in Blackpool, where Alan tracked her down. His appearance forced her to remember what she had run away from and she tried to escape. Alan, following her across a busy road, was hit by a tram and killed instantly.

For a brief time Rita was reconciled with Jenny and worked hard to make the girl see

Rita was proved right to be suspicious of Alan Bradley.

that she loved her as if she were her own daughter and that they shouldn't allow Alan's death to affect that. However, as Jenny grew older, she made it clear that she was only interested in Rita because of her bank balance. Rita saw her off by writing her a cheque for £1,000 and told her that that was all she'd ever get from her.

Moving the Kabin from Rosamund Street to a new site on Coronation Street and setting up home in the flat above gave Rita plenty to occupy her and she put all thoughts of future romance out of her mind. She was unprepared when retiring toffee salesman Ted Sullivan asked her out to a dance. She went with him but was quick to tell Bet that Ted was far too much of a gentleman for her to be interested in him. Ted had other plans, though, and set about courting Rita in a whirlwind romance that culminated in a three-week holiday in Florida. On their return he broke the news that he had a brain tumour and begged her to make his last months happy ones. They were married and Rita tried hard to make the most of her time with Ted, but watched him deteriorate before her eyes. After just three months together he died in her arms. It had turned out a marriage of pure love, of two gentle, kind souls joining to give each other happiness.

After Ted's death any beauty there had been in the marriage was ripped apart by his grasping relatives, who dragged Rita through the courts to overturn his will, but judgment was passed in Rita's favour. The battle, though, left her shocked and battered.

Since Ted's death Rita has been wary of other relationships. She has moved gently into the role of Duchess of the Street, dishing out words of advice and wisdom with the dolly mixtures. It came as a big jolt when her assistant for twenty-five years, Mavis Wilton, retired and settled in the country. Rita toyed with the idea of joining her in Cartmel to run a B&B but just one day in the country was enough to make her see that her place was in Coronation Street with friends and memories.

Character Name:	DEIRDRE ANN RACHID
Date of Birth:	8 July 1955
Husbands:	Ray Langton (1975–79)
	Ken Barlow (1981–92)
	Samir Rachid (1994–95)
Children:	Tracy (1977)
Parents:	Donald and Blanche Hunt

One woman on the Street has suffered more than most, has been battered and flung around by her heart just as much as Elsie, Bet or Rita. The difference is that she has crammed as much into forty years as they did in fifty or sixty. For a long period she had the secure home and loving husband that the others dreamed of but, like them, she lost everything.

Deirdre Hunt first walked down the Street as an eighteen-year-old in knee-length boots and a short mini-skirt. Brought up in nearby Victoria Street by her blowzy mother Blanche, her father having died when she was just five, Deirdre concluded early in life that older men had far more to offer than lads. The attraction in Coronation Street was Alan Howard at No. 11, but he was frightened of her forthright nature and, anyway, his wife Elsie was ever-present. Instead she transferred her attention to Annie Walker's son Billy, Alan's partner at the Canal Garage, who was in his mid-thirties. When he took Deirdre out he had no qualms about spending money on her to ensure she had a good time. Deirdre was an independent girl, who supported herself by working as secretary in Len Fairclough and Ray Langton's building firm. Ray became jealous of her involvement with Billy, much to Deirdre's amusement: she felt that Ray had had his chance when she had been fancy free.

Blanche hoped that her daughter wouldn't settle down too early but Deirdre was keen to have a wedding ring. She encouraged Billy to stand up to his mother Annie, who despised Deirdre: 'You mark my words, Billy, that girl will grow up just like her mother, and Blanche Hunt puts me in mind of no one so much as Elsie Tanner!' The wedding date was set but with just a week to go Deirdre began to panic that if she married Billy she'd be pouring pints in the Rovers for the rest of her life. She voiced her fears in the hope that he would tell her she was being stupid but he admitted to feeling the same way and broke off the engagement.

Deirdre hit back by going out on the town with Ray. Just a week later she told a stunned Blanche that she was going to marry him. The ceremony was quick and simple: Len was best man and Rita was Deirdre's attendant.

The wedding had taken place with such haste that the couple had nowhere to live, so Blanche gave them a room. She struggled with the idea of Ray as a son-in-law – he was nearer her age than Deirdre's – but was pleased to see her daughter happy. Deirdre continued to work at the yard until she became pregnant and in 1977 gave birth to a daughter. She sent Ray off to register the birth, and was furious when he refused to give the baby the name his wife had chosen, Lynette, and named her Tracy.

Deirdre's world crumbled when Tracy was just six months old. As she was returning from a keep-fit class, late at night, a man tried to rape her. She managed to break free and fled home to Ray, but the incident preyed on her mind. She withdrew into a world of her own, neglecting Tracy and refusing to let Ray, or any other man, near her. One day, leaving Tracy crying in her cot, Deirdre walked out of the house and found her way to the motorway where she stood on a bridge, contemplating suicide. A passing lorry driver brought her out of her trance by asking for directions, and she returned home realizing that death was not the answer. Slowly, with Ray's help, Deirdre recovered from her ordeal and started to enjoy family life again. She was just beginning to relax into her marriage when she discovered that Ray had been having an affair with a local waitress. Her immediate reaction was to throw him out but he begged her to forgive him and swore that he would never be unfaithful again. Deirdre gave him a second chance but the rot had set in. She allowed him to take a job in Holland, leaving her and Tracy behind. She knew it was the end for them.

Ray's departure robbed Deirdre of financial and emotional stability, and Tracy's godmother, Emily Bishop, took the pair in at No. 3 Coronation Street. Shortly afterwards, Deirdre feared she had lost Tracy as well as Ray. A lorry driver suffered a fatal heart-attack while turning into the Street and collapsed at his wheel, his lorry overturned, throwing its cargo of timber through the Rovers' window. Deirdre clawed at the wood scattered outside the pub, screaming that she had left Tracy

there in her pushchair. However, the police found no trace of the child under the timber. In a bizarre twist of fate she had been kidnapped seconds before the crash by a disturbed girl. The police found them together in a park, and Tracy was rushed by Emily to the canal bank where Deirdre was threatening to throw herself into the water. The sight of her daughter forced her back to reality and the pair were united.

Billy Walker returned and offered her a new life in Jersey but his mother Annie used the knowledge that he needed £2,000 to blackmail him into abandoning Deirdre a second time. Bet Lynch's old flame, Mike Baldwin, was also an interested party but it was community worker Ken Barlow who persuaded Deirdre to marry him. Unlike Ray, Billy or Mike, Ken was a thinker who put principles before passion. However, he was solid and reliable, and offered the best future for Tracy, and respectability for Deirdre. They married in July 1981, two days before the Prince of Wales and Lady Diana Spencer, and Deirdre noted that the age difference between the royals was the same as that between the Barlows.

As Mrs Barlow, Deirdre inherited a terraced house filled with antiques, including Ken's first wife's uncle, Albert Tatlock, who occupied the front parlour. After a hard day working the bacon slicer at the Corner Shop, she would return home to look after a four-year-old, an eighty-six-year-old and a husband who, as soon as the honeymoon was over, seemed to take her for granted. With the marriage little more than a year old Deirdre fell into the arms of another man.

Mike Baldwin saw Deirdre as a desirable woman rather than the drudge into which she feared marriage was turning her. He was the same age as Ken, but acted much younger, and took Deirdre out to the best restaurants and clubs. They made plans to run off together with Tracy, but when it came to it Deirdre

"You can't resist them, can you Deirdre? You seem to pick the most unreliable boyfriends. It's your choice of slimy bed partners that get you into trouble!"

KEN BARLOW

couldn't face leaving Ken on his own. She confessed to the affair but when Ken ordered her out of the house she begged him to reconsider, frightened that if she crossed the threshold she would lose everything she had struggled to achieve. Ken took her back and set about rejuvenating himself and their marriage.

Soon after this Deirdre was amazed to find herself fighting Alf Roberts in the local elections. Ken set her up for it, hoping that Alf and Deirdre would split the Independent vote allowing Labour to win the seat, but Deirdre became the people's champion. She tackled issues such as child safety and housing and won the seat from Alf by just seven votes.

Being a councillor was hard work, but daily life became a minefield: Ken had become a newspaper editor and he questioned his wife on all aspects of council business. When he started to print information she had given him as a husband rather than as a journalist,

Deirdre keeps bouncing back to Ken, through marriages, affairs, and a prison sentence.

Deirdre objected – along with her fellow councillors, who accused her of leaking minutes of confidential meetings to Ken. Deirdre's name was cleared when she exposed town hall secretary Wendy Crozier as the mole and she hoped that this revelation would be an end to the matter. Unfortunately it wasn't. She discovered that as well as feeding Ken information, Wendy had taken him to her bed. After forcing a confession out of Ken, Deirdre refused to follow his example of forgive and forget and threw him out.

There followed a messy, bitter divorce, during which Deirdre lost her council seat and the respect of her daughter as she embarked on an affair with dodgy businessman Phil Jennings. She enjoyed the money and attention Phil lavished on her, then felt stupid when it turned out that he was married, and wanted by both the police and local gangsters. She wasn't helped by Ken's accusation that her lifestyle was having a bad effect on Tracy. He

continued to pester her, and attempted to see off any suitors. She accused him of harassment and eventually Ken realized she was no longer interested in him and started dating hairdresser Denise Osbourne.

While Ken's life seemed to be on the up – a new lady in his life and the prospect of a new baby – Deirdre faced a lonely future when Tracy declared she'd had enough of her warring parents and left home. To give herself a break Deirdre holidayed in Morocco, enjoying a fling with a twenty-one-year-old waiter, Samir Rachid. Back in Weatherfield, she was as stunned as her neighbours when Samir arrived with a suitcase, saying he loved her. The two embarked on a passionate, romantic affair, and in November 1994 they married, but almost immediately immigration officials jumped on them, making it obvious they regarded Deirdre as a sex-starved middle-aged housewife, who had been duped by a cunning younger man. In order to give their marriage a chance Deirdre emigrated to Morocco where Samir's family welcomed her.

Deirdre's third marriage was much shorter than her other two, and the three months she and Samir spent in Morocco were the happiest they had together. When Tracy overdosed on drugs they hurried back to England and searched for a kidney donor when it was discovered Tracy had a serious infection. By coincidence Samir was the perfect match and agreed to give up one of his kidneys. Unfortunately en route to hospital he mysteriously fell by the canal side and smashed his head. Deirdre was by his side when he died and gave permission for his kidney to be removed.

After Samir's death, Deirdre tried hard to set herself up with a new life. She took a job at Sunliners travel agent's and rented a flat over Skinner's Betting Shop on Rosamund Street. She was delighted when Tracy married a nice lad and settled in London, and her relationship with Ken tilted between lovers and best

---

THE WALKING WOUNDED CHART

In the ranks of boyfriends, husbands and one-night stands, Elsie Tanner currently tops the poll with twenty-one fellers. Here's how the other wounded souls compare:

Bet	**20**
Deirdre	**14**
Rita	**10**
Suzie	**6**
Irma	**4**

---

friends. When she met Jon Lindsay, though, she was wary of getting too involved – 'I'm fed up with this roller-coaster – I've been up and down it so many times.' – but the tall, handsome pilot pursued her. Deirdre was flattered, finding it hard to believe that he would be interested in someone as ordinary as her. They embarked on an affair, which was shaken by the revelation that he wasn't a pilot at all but managed a tie shop. Eventually Deirdre forgave him for lying to her and they made plans for the future. He gave her a credit card and bought a £100,000 detached home. Then the bubble burst: Deirdre discovered he had a wife and children, and when she attempted to use her credit card to withdraw her £5,000 savings, which she'd lent to Jon as a deposit on the house, she was arrested for fraud as the card and mortgage had been put in the name of one of Jon's friends.

A nightmare unfolded which saw Deirdre arrested and charged with fraud. After a harrowing court case, she ended up in prison, locked up and protesting her innocence. The judge had sentenced her to eighteen months but miraculously Jon's unlawful wife appeared on the scene proving that Jon was a bigamist, and Dierdre's name was cleared. After celebrating Deirdre found herself having to start her life over again from scratch.

BATTLEAXES

"I'm a professional busybody and proud of it!"

ENA SHARPLES

They sit bolt upright in corners, sipping drinks with ears cocked for tasty titbits, eyes riveted to the local scarlet woman or roughneck man. At work they cause trouble for the bosses and lead fellow workers in revolt. At home they nag their men into early graves and dominate their children, demanding complete obedience. Afraid neither of death nor age, they stand in judgement on others and face danger where others duck it. While making it their business to keep tabs on everyone's business, they guard their own privacy fiercely. Every street has one – the battleaxe who keeps her fingers on the pulse of the community.

Character Name:	ENA SHARPLES
Date of Birth:	14 November 1899
Husband:	Alfred Sharples (1920–37)
Children:	Madge (1921)
	Vera (1922)
	Ian (1924)
Parents:	Thomas and Mary Schofield

The queen of Coronation Street's battle-axes remains – even twenty years after her departure – Ena Sharples. The image of the hairnetted old woman in the mac with a heavy handbag swinging at her side has become a caricature and countless Enas have followed in other television series. But Ena was the original, and the best. When *Coronation Street* was first on the air she was in her early sixties, having served a lifetime in mills and munitions factories. Her hard-done-by husband Alfred had died of consumption during the Depression, marching for workers' rights, her only son had died of malnutrition and her daughters seldom came calling. She was a widow married to God, whom she served as caretaker at the Mission of Glad Tidings. When her neighbours stepped out of line Ena was quick to confront, condemn and offer advice back to the right path, but if any outsider dared to mess with one of her 'flock' she sprang to their defence: 'I won't see anyone on this Street made a fool of.'

Ena's long-time sparring partner was Elsie Tanner, the painted lady from No. 11, and it was only when Ena was feeling most vulnerable that she would admit that Elsie was one of her favourite people. She only got at her, she said, because she wanted her to get on in life. The whole Street turned out in the winter of 1961 to watch a show-down between the two women when Elsie accused Ena of writing her a vicious anonymous letter: 'I'd expect you to

know every lying bit of gossip that goes about. What you don't know you make up. We don't need sewers around 'ere, we've got Ena Sharples!' Ena pointed out that if she had written the letter she would have had the strength of her convictions to sign it.

Every ruler has a throne room and Ena was no exception. Where better to keep a finger on the pulse of the Street than in the Rovers Return? Ena occupied the snug, a small private area traditionally used by women customers only, and made certain that her two ground troops, Martha Longhurst and Minnie Caldwell, sat either side of her to alert her to any developments in the main area of the pub. Martha and Minnie had been Ena's closest friends since before the First World War. Like her, they had suffered during the lean years and were as much alone as she was. They joined her ranks fully aware that she would dominate and boss them around. However, having Ena fighting from your corner seemed to help you face life.

Ena delighted in taking on authority and made certain she won the fight, even if it meant playing dirty. She took on the Town Hall when it took forty minutes to boil a kettle on her gas ring, and wrote to Prince Philip for help when the council planned to rename Coronation Street 'Florida Street'. On both occasions she won her battle. However, in 1961, she came out the loser. She read a poster at the Town Hall advising residents on the demolition of selected houses. She rushed home with the news that Coronation Street was one of the doomed streets and the residents panicked. Finally an official was sent round: Ena had misread the poster and Coronation *Terrace* was to be flattened. The residents were furious and sent Ena to Coventry for a month, the committee at the Mission sacked her and so Ena became an outcast.

Relations between Ena and the committee, led by lay preacher Leonard 'he's a jumped-

"We don't need sewers around 'ere; we've got Ena Sharples!"

ELSIE TANNER

up bag of wind' Swindley, were never good. The committee did not approve of Ena's habit of drinking in the Rovers but Ena retorted that if the Good Lord had had the sense to turn water into wine he was hardly going to object to her little tipple of an evening.

Ena's relationship with the Almighty stemmed from her Sunday-School days. She had gone through full-body baptism and asked God's advice daily. She viewed herself as God's messenger on the Street and grew annoyed by the residents' lack of commitment to their faith: 'The only thing that would get this street out on a Sunday morning is two Tommies with flame-throwers.'

Ena often used her faith as an excuse to interfere in the lives of others, so much so that she was generally viewed as a hypocrite. As Elsie Tanner once commented: 'that woman's in league with the Devil.' But Ena clung to the Cross as her salvation, and tried hard to live as the Bible told her she should. On one occasion the Holy Book was the cause of distress in Ena's household. Her downtrodden daughter Vera Lomax was staying at the Mission after the break-up of her marriage and complained of headaches, which Ena dismissed as nonsense until the doctor told her Vera was dying of a brain tumour. Ena decided it was in Vera's best interests not to know the truth, but Vera grew suspicious of her mother's sudden concern and ordered her to swear on the Bible that nothing was seriously wrong with her. When Ena refused, Vera realized her days were numbered, and passed away the following morning.

Despite Ena's clashes with the committee and Swindley, she was reinstated at the Mission and hung on to her job until it was demolished in 1968. However, two years before that she lost her good name. After giving away all her savings, she found herself hard up and was caught shoplifting a tin of salmon from a local supermarket. The newspapers had a field day with their 'Mission Caretaker in the Dock' headlines, and Ena suffered the humiliation of a fine and notice that she would have to work with a social worker to 'keep an eye on her'.

She was furious when her home of thirty years, the Mission of Glad Tidings, fell to the demolition ball. She refused to tell the council's relocation officer where she was moving to and allowed his men to load her furniture into their van before admitting she was going across the Street to Minnie's at No. 5, where

'Sometimes we all tend to forget that Mrs Sharples is just an old woman.'
Annie Walker.

When not fighting to uphold morals, Ena was always ready to give advice – whether it was wanted or not.

she stayed until she was allocated one of the new maisonettes built on the site of the Mission. Once installed in her spacious new flat, Ena found herself in trouble with the council yet again when neighbours raised objections to her harmonium-playing in the evenings. She ignored an ultimatum not to play after 8 p.m. or on Sundays. Ena blew a raspberry in the face of officialdom and continued to play. The officials were ready to evict her when they were stopped by Val Barlow, who had put in the original complaint and was now withdrawing it.

In a lifetime of struggle and heartache, Ena grew into a good judge of character: she recognized early-warning signs in a man on the brink of an affair, in a neglected teenager planning to run away from home or in a suicidal housewife. She acted quickly: 'Only two

things worth rememberin' about dreams. One is they never taste as sweet as you think they will, even when they do work out for you. And two, thank God you have 'em. Because if you didn't you'd go out of your mind.' Experience taught many of the Street's residents that Ena's advice was sound and well-meant, but others told her to mind her own business then blamed her interference when their world caved in around them.

Ena returned to caretaking when the community centre was built in the early seventies, but her strength, both physical and emotional, flagged and she was forced to lean on neighbours for support. She always refused charity, though, and looked upon her job as a necessity: her wages were a pension supplement she had come to rely on. When a local councillor decided she was too old for the post he pressured her to resign, but Ena was petrified of entering a home and withering away like so many of her friends had. She pleaded with the council to let her keep the flat that went with the job, but in the end the neighbours saw off the councillor, threatening him with violence if he didn't leave *their* Ena alone.

In 1980 Ena walked down the Street for the last time. She still had old friends there – like Elsie Tanner, now heading towards sixty – but many new faces saw her as a daft old woman. She had no energy left for battles and moved to St Anne's to keep house for her old friend Henry Foster. She was sad to leave the Street but glad that the burden of being the local 'interfering busybody' had been lifted from her shoulders. While she had enjoyed some of her clashes, the task had been a heavy one: 'Do you ever believe I get tired of bein' blamed for everythin' that goes on in this street, from blocked sinks to wives leavin' home?'

Character Name:	IVY JOAN BRENNAN
Date of Birth:	8 April 1936
Husbands:	Bert Tilsley (1956–84)
	Don Brennan (1988–95)
Children:	Brian (1958)
Parents:	Jim and Alice Nelson
Date of Death:	23 August 1995

When Ena left the Street in 1980, Ivy Tilsley had been living at No. 5 for a year. She'd moved in from Inkerman Street with husband Bert and twenty-one-year-old son Brian, and the house was conveniently close to her job as a machinist at Baldwin's Casuals. Ivy was devoted to her family, although she'd have been the first to admit she pushed Bert around: he was too

easy-going and people took advantage of him. When they'd first married she'd had three miscarriages before Brian was conceived. Her only child, he had been pampered and petted by Ivy all his life and she was blind to his faults. When they moved to Coronation Street, Ivy believed her Brian was the best catch in town and was horrified when she discovered he was going out with Gail Potter from No.11: she wasn't a Catholic, had been named in a divorce case and was used goods. Ivy was all for forbidding Brian to see Gail, but Bert pointed out that their son was a man and could do as he wanted. He advised Ivy to accept Gail as she was a 'nice little lass' but Ivy couldn't bear the thought of losing control of her little lad and tried to poison him against Gail, telling him of the married man who had taken her virginity. But her bombshell backfired because Brian left home.

Despite all Ivy's efforts Brian and Gail married in November 1979 and almost overnight Ivy's attitude towards Gail changed: now she was part of the family she was taken under the mother's wing. However, Gail annoyed Ivy with her independence and the young couple left No. 5 to set up their own home. It was only two bus rides away, though, and Ivy made sure she visited at least three times a week, making sure Gail was feeding Brian the good food he was used to – 'plenty of mash on the cottage pie and he likes his boiled eggs a bit on the runny side'.

The only truly great thing Gail ever did, in Ivy's eyes, was to give birth to Nicholas Paul, who immediately became the apple of his grandmother's eye. She tried hard to keep Gail's mother, Audrey, in the background, and struggled to hide her contempt when flighty Elsie Tanner was asked to be godmother: 'Her renouncing the Devil, that I must see!' When Brian took work overseas, Ivy made it her job to look out for the welfare of his son, annoying Gail by calling unannounced and criticizing her if she spent any of the hard-earned money Brian sent home. When Gail returned to work, leaving Nicky with a child-minder, Ivy accused her of being a bad mother.

Although quick to condemn Gail for working, Ivy had not stayed at home with Brian when he was young. She had been brought up by a staunch Trade Unionist father and had followed him into factory work. Bert had worked in a foundry all his life and, together, they fought for the rights of the workers. Branded a troublemaker in more factories and plants than she cared to remember, Ivy enjoyed the taste of battle and was always on the lookout for hard-done-by co-workers. At Baldwins', she became shop steward and led the girls in revolt against Mike. The most violent clash came when she discovered that cleaner Hilda Ogden had been sacked for

Ivy and Gail lived through a thirteen-year period of mistrust and anger.

asking for a new broom. Mike justified himself by saying that Hilda had deliberately damaged the old one but Ivy accused him of victimization and called for a walk-out until her 'sister' was reinstated.

Stuck with an important order to get out, Mike brought in non-union workers to complete the denim outfits. Ivy was furious with the black-legs and led her girls in an attack on the factory, breaking windows and climbing over the gates. The police were called and Ivy was dragged away, hitting out at the bobby who held her. Peace was restored two weeks into the protest when Mike gave in and reinstated Hilda – who wasn't too happy as she'd found a better-paid job elsewhere.

Bert died in 1984 and Ivy lost the stabilizing influence in her life. She clung to Brian and Gail more than ever, desperate not to be

left alone in the world. She also turned to God for reassurance that she would be reunited with Bert in heaven. Brian encouraged her to widen her interests beyond work and the Church, but she combined the two by going out with George Wardle, the factory delivery-man who ran the Church youth football team. George was similar to Bert in that he was a down-to-earth working-class man who enjoyed the odd pint and game of darts. However, courtship had changed since the 1950s, and Ivy fought hard to keep George interested in her without having to go to bed with him. He seemed content with this but said they'd have to marry in a register office as he was divorced and not widowed. Ivy told him that in God's eyes he was still married and there was no way she could continue to see him. After the dust had settled, she realized she'd been a fool and sought him out, offering to forgo her princi-ples for love but he'd found another woman.

But everything seemed all right to Ivy so long as she had Brian to fuss about. She was happy to take him back at No. 5 when his mar-riage broke up due to Gail's infidelity and enjoyed casting Gail in the role of scarlet woman. Ivy had always known that Brian had strayed but he was a hot-blooded man. Gail had no excuse: she was married to the perfect husband. However, although Ivy was happy to take sides with her son she was worried that a divorce would offend God and, more impor-tantly, she would lose her grandson. She urged Brian to reconcile with his wife but was horri-fied when he said that Gail would have to abort the child she was carrying.

When Gail went into labour, Ivy took the opportunity to attack her nephew, Ian Latimer, the man Gail had slept with. He had a blood test, which proved Sarah Louise was Brian's daughter. Ivy was delighted to have a granddaughter and her happiness was cemented when the Tilsleys remarried. Shortly afterwards Ivy herself walked down the aisle when she married Don Brennan.

The darkest night of Ivy's life occurred in February 1989 when Don broke the news that Brian had been stabbed to death. In her grief, Ivy hit out at Gail, accusing her of being a bad wife, causing Brian to stray with other women. The final insult, to Ivy, was when Gail refused to bury Brian as a Catholic: 'When they low-ered my son into that grave this afternoon, he wasn't the only one who was dead. As far as I'm concerned, so is his wife.'

After Brian died, Ivy's own marriage suf-fered. She had met Don when he drove her home after a girls' night out. He had made her laugh and appeared keen on her. Like Bert, he was salt-of-the-earth *and* a good Catholic. It was only after the wedding that Ivy discovered Don's gambling habit but, she figured, if that was his only vice she could live with it. With Brian dead, though, Ivy became obsessed with the future of her grandchildren, pushing Don into the background. She was furious when Gail moved her toyboy Martin Platt into her home and had his baby. When Martin married Gail and attempted to adopt the children, Ivy called in Social Services to gain control of Nicky and Sarah Louise, say-ing that the Platts were unfit parents. Then she tried to turn Nicky against his mother by telling him that if he kept his name as Tilsley she would leave her house to him. Don was appalled at her interference – 'If my wife put her mind to it she could come up with reasons why Mary and Joseph were unfit parents!' – and Martin spoke his mind: 'You don't care how many lives you destroy, do you? But you've got it wrong this time. I'm here to tell you you won't ever see your grandchildren again. You get out of our lives!'

Once the adoption had gone through, Ivy was forced to back down for fear of losing the children for good. She made up her mind also to repair her failing marriage but Don had seen Ivy for the manipulator she was: 'You're twisted, Ivy. You're twisted and bitter. And I don't think I can put up with you any longer.

~

"When they lowered my son into that grave this afternoon, he wasn't the only one who was dead. As far as I'm concerned, so is his wife."

IVY TILSEY

~

35

You're more concerned with the dead than the living.' He took a mistress but, still deeply unhappy, tried to kill himself. The attempt failed and he was left with an amputated foot but he wanted no more to do with Ivy.

Manless and jobless, Ivy turned to the bottle for comfort. She let her appearance go and Gail refused to allow her anywhere near the children. Eventually Don returned, making Ivy swear that she would leave off the drink, but it was a hopeless, loveless union, and Ivy decided to move out. She went to a Catholic retreat where she dried out and found new joy in serving the nuns. She was bolted back to reality when Don wrote, seeking a divorce. The shock was too much for her: Ivy suffered a stroke and died shortly afterwards. She was buried after a full Catholic mass and laid to rest with her beloved Brian.

Character Name:	PHYLLIS PEARCE
Date of Birth:	7 February 1921
Husband:	Harold (1946–76)
Children:	Margaret (1948)
Parents:	Joshua and Violet Grimes

When Phyllis Pearce's stone face first peered into Coronation Street, in 1982, old soldier Albert Tatlock took one glance at her and scurried off home, muttering that Ena had been reincarnated with a blue rinse. Phyllis had come searching for Chalkie Whitely, who had bought No. 9 and moved in with his grandson Craig, who was also her grandson. Her daughter Margaret had married Chalkie's son, Bob. Bob worked on the oil rigs and Margaret had died, leaving Craig to be brought up by his grandfather. Phyllis, though, was determined to have her say in his upbringing.

Chalkie had always thought Phyllis an interfering old biddy, and did all he could to cut her out of his and Craig's lives. He had

pitied her husband Harold when he was alive for having to put up with the sound of Phyllis's dentures clacking day in and day out, and at his funeral had told the widow as much. He planned that Craig would grow up under his sole influence but Bob Whitely returned from overseas to announce that he was taking Craig to live in Australia. Phyllis, like Chalkie, was heartbroken at the news: she saw Craig as her last link to her dead daughter and feared that she would never see him again.

Phyllis was haunted by the death of Margaret, her only child, who had come to her with a lump in her breast, seeking advice, and Phyllis had told her not to do anything about it. Margaret had delayed seeing the doctor until it was too late for treatment.

With Craig on the other side of the world, Chalkie was forced to sell his house as Bob needed cash. Phyllis saw this as her big chance against a lonely future and offered Chalkie her spare room. He mistook her desperation for lust and told her that there was no way she was seeing him in his pyjamas. Instead his luck changed following a five-horse accumulator, which gave him enough money to follow Bob and he jetted off, leaving Phyllis well and truly alone.

When her home in Ondurman Street was demolished, Phyllis was moved into an old folks' bungalow at Mayfair Court in Gorton Close. She refused point-blank to vegetate there, so took a job washing up at Jim's Café and set about spicing up her life with a love interest. She settled on Percy Sugden, the caretaker at the community centre on Coronation Street, but was insulted when he overlooked her for Emily Bishop and moved in as Emily's lodger.

Although her pride was hurt Phyllis believed that Percy was her chap and decided to make him jealous. She achieved this by flirting with pensioner Sam Tindall – and so successfully that the pair brawled over her

during the over-sixties bowls trip to Southport. During the outing, Phyllis stole Percy's shoes and socks while he was paddling in the sea, causing them both to miss the coach back and forcing him to spend more time with her.

When she wasn't chasing Percy, Phyllis concerned herself with those she worked with – Gail and her marital problems at the café and later – as cleaner at No. 6 – Des Barnes. She looked upon Des as a grandson and tried to steer him away from the man-hunters with whom he shared his bed. Phyllis had only ever slept with one man, and she was upset that young women treated sex n the same way as eating or smoking. A man was different,

though, Phyllis thought, and he could sow wild oats for as long as he liked. Des might be 'a little bugger' sometimes but he just needed to find the right woman.

And Percy was the right man for Phyllis. It was her description of her love for him that won her a day out with him, courtesy of a national women's magazine. They were whisked off together to be wined and dined, and Phyllis told the readers why Percy was the man for her: 'Percy's one of the old school. He treats a woman as if she were a lady. He's very considerate. When he was in the Army he had men under him and he says he always made sure everybody else got their helping of pudding before he started enjoying his.'

What joy! Phyllis delights in the sight of two men doing battle for her hand.

37

Character Name:	MAUD GRIMES
Date of Birth:	1 April 1922
Husband:	Wilfred Grimes (1940–82)
Children:	Peggy (1942) Maureen (1945)
Parents:	Roderick and Beatrice Garson

"I also coped when a bull mastiff tried to mate with my left-side tyre. D'you have the same problem with that husband of yours?"

MAUD GRIMES TO DAUGHTER MAUREEN

The woman who succeeded where Phyllis failed was Maud Grimes who, in 1994, announced her engagement to Percy. Although his proposal stemmed from financial necessity and companionship, Maud enjoyed his company and was upset when he called off the engagement. During the Second World War, Maud had been working on munitions and looking after her daughter, Peggy. Her husband Wilf was serving as a bombardier and Maud was lonely until she met American serviceman Leonard 'Danny' Kennedy. When he was killed, on D-Day, Maud was carrying his child. After the war, Wilfred looked upon little Maureen as his own, but it wasn't until 1994 when visiting the war graves in France that Maud told her daughter who her real father was. When the news reached Percy, he said he could never marry a woman who had cheated on her husband while he was fighting for King and country.

Apart from the diversion with Percy, most of Maud's efforts went into controlling Maureen through a series of disastrous relationships. As a young woman she had fallen for Reg Holdsworth whose grammar-school education had left him with a vocabulary of long words and a pompous nature, which annoyed Maud. She did all she could to poison Maureen against him and eventually Reg gave up on her. When Wilf died, Maud moved to Preston where Maureen married electrician Frank Naylor who turned out to be violent. Maureen felt she couldn't break from him, fearing he would track her down and force

her back, but Maud reported him to the police and removed Maureen to Weatherfield where she got a divorce.

Maud lost the use of her legs after Wilf's death, and was often frustrated in her wheelchair. She took out her resentment on Maureen, ashamed that her daughter had to sacrifice her own independence to look after her. However, she did not give up on life, and although her legs didn't work her tongue did, and developed a razor-sharp edge. When Maureen nervously announced she had taken up with Reg, after twenty-five years apart, Maud was furious that the 'pillock' was back in her life. She pulled out all the stops to part Reg and Maureen, from falling out of her wheelchair to stop their love-making, to feigning illness, but while Maureen feared for her mother's health, Reg saw through her: 'If you carry on trying to turn your daughter against me I shall take her away from you and then you will have nobody to look after you. And I shan't have the slightest qualm because it will have been no one's fault but your own!' Maud realized that she'd be wise not to give Maureen cause to run off with Reg and, much as she hated the 'mountain of lard', she had to admit that he made her daughter happy and showed no signs of wanting to put Maud into a home. When the couple married in 1994 Maud gave them the run of her house, albeit with some misgivings: 'I have to take notice of his every word now, don't I?'

When Reg suggested they move to another house, Maud was horrified to learn she would be rehomed in a converted garage. To put a stop to the plans she sold her house to a finance company, on the understanding that she could live there until she died. Maureen accused her of robbing her of her inheritance, and moved into Reg's tiny flat. Maud hated being in the rambling house alone and staged a break-in to prick Maureen's conscience into returning. Maureen was genuinely torn between her mother and husband and Maud

relented. She ended her contract with the finance company and gave the house to Maureen on condition that she could live there as long as she wanted.

When Reg left Maureen and moved to Lowestoft Maud was delighted. She hoped that, with Reg out of the picture, she and Maureen could spend their days working side by side in the Corner Shop and their evenings playing cards and chatting. However, Maureen started going out with builder Bill Webster. Maud approved of Bill and was angry when Bill finished the relationship after Maureen slept with neighbour Curly Watts. Maureen was struck dumb when her mother attacked Curly in the Rovers shouting that no woman was safe with him around.

Maud continued to try to bring Maureen and Bill together. She was horrified when Maureen married butcher Fred Elliott, who resembled Reg in stature and pomposity. Fred moved Maureen into their own little home,

and Maud, taking charge of her own affairs before Fred could, sold her house and bought a flat in Mayfield Court. This infuriated Maureen: 'You selfish old woman! You're happy to go into a home now are you? Sort your life out now, will you? Well, why couldn't you have done that ten years ago? Why didn't you give me my freedom when it mattered?'

The day after moving Maud into her new home, Maureen fled Weatherfield with Bill for Germany, leaving Maud to deal with Fred. He was shattered by his wife's departure but took his revenge by forcing Maud to sell him the Corner Shop at way below its market value. In turn, Maud planted a piece of fish in one of his new display cases, which stank out the shop for days and cost him hundreds of pounds in wasted stock. Even though Fred owns the shop, Maud still works there, with his nephew Ashley Peacock, but it is an unholy alliance and Maud is ever watching and waiting to get the better of him – or anyone else who crosses her.

Maud lets Maureen and Fred know exactly what she thinks of the idea of them getting married.

MOTHERS

"The new pullover's turned out a treat. I'll never knit another one in that colour though. Navy blue plays the devil with my eyes."

IDA BARLOW

They scrimp and save and do without, not to buy themselves some little luxury but to make sure their children have the best food and clothing possible. They live for their families, idolizing their husbands yet alert to their weaknesses. They take pin-money jobs to support the male breadwinner and don't complain when another year goes by without a foreign holiday. They sacrifice their own dreams and aspirations and do all they can to help their men achieve their potential. When he comes home after work, he slumps into the easy chair and reaches for the paper – or nips off to the Rovers – while she, after a day of household chores and helping out behind the counter of the Corner Shop or at the Rovers, gets his tea on the table, keeping one ear open for a child waking up. They receive no reward other than watching their children mature into upright citizens.

<table>
<tbody>
<tr><td>**Character Name:**</td><td>IDA BARLOW</td></tr>
<tr><td>**Date of Birth:**</td><td>16 December 1916</td></tr>
<tr><td>**Husband:**</td><td>Frank Barlow
(1938–61)</td></tr>
<tr><td>**Children:**</td><td>Kenneth (1939)
David (1942)</td></tr>
<tr><td>**Parents:**</td><td>George and Nancy
Leathers</td></tr>
<tr><td>**Date of Death:**</td><td>11 September 1961</td></tr>
</tbody>
</table>

Shock in the Barlow household when Ida announces that from now on eggs will be scrambled and not boiled.

Ida Barlow was the original Street Struggling Mother. Unlike other local mothers, her world consisted of her family – Annie Walker was concerned with trade in the Rovers while Elsie Tanner was more interested in having a good time. Ida had lived at No. 3 since her marriage to postman Frank Barlow in 1938. The house had sheltered her during the Blitz of 1940 and it had been there that her sons Kenneth and David were born. Her happiest years were those immediately after the war when Frank had returned safe from Iraq.

All too quickly, though, the boys had grown up and began to fall out with each other and their father. Frank was a dogmatic stick-in-the-mud, who clung to traditional values and refused to acknowledge that he might be wrong, which often infuriated Ida. He believed strongly in the benefits of National Service and corporal punishment, and was infuriated by his son Kenneth's pacifism and disrespect for government and royalty. When the two argued over world issues Ida tried her best to shut them out and restore the peace: 'Now Frank, you know I think the world of you

and I wouldn't go against you for a minute if I thought you were right. I'm that mixed up I don't know who's to blame. Now sit down the pair of you and 'ave your eggs. And don't blame me if they've gone hard.'

Like most family-orientated women, Ida bowed to Frank's judgement in everything. When they had been offered the opportunity to buy the house for £200, Ida was disappointed when Frank refused, saying that the price was too high for a run-down terrace, but she accepted his decision. Once she went behind his back to buy loose covers on hire purchase, and he spent hours lecturing her on the sin of debt. However, when it came to the children, Frank humoured her attempts to keep them wrapped in cotton wool.

Ida was in her element surrounded by her family and encouraged the boys to bring home girlfriends. The only time Kenneth obliged Ida dug out the family album: 'There's you in your nappy and, let me tell you, you were a lot less bother then than you are now. And this one's 'im in 'is first long trousers at the Whit Week Walk.' At times like this, Kenneth was always at a loss as to how to deal with his embarrassment and indignation but David enjoyed teasing his mother. Whenever she moaned about him cluttering up the living room with his bits and pieces, he would say, 'You be quiet or I'll tek the clock apart again.' It was a loving family scene that visitors such as Esther Hayes or Christine Hardman longed for: Kenneth sitting at the table reading a book on social history, David tinkering with his crystal radio set, Frank puffing at his pipe and reading the paper, with Ida knitting contentedly.

But it couldn't last. The family home was ripped apart in September 1961 when Ida was knocked down and killed by a Corporation bus. At the funeral, David couldn't bring himself to join the others at the graveside and instead watched from the bushes. Afterwards he broke down and admitted to Kenneth that

he felt they'd all taken her for granted and he hoped so much she'd known she was loved. Another mourner at the funeral was Valerie Tatlock from No.1, a young hair stylist who had just started walking out with Kenneth. As she watched the outpouring of grief from the family she felt awkward, yet within a year she had become the next Mrs Barlow.

Character Name:	VALERIE BARLOW
Husband:	Ken Barlow (1962–71)
Children:	Susan (1965)
	Peter (1965)
Parents:	Alfred and Edith Tatlock
Date of Death:	27 January 1971

Pensioner Albert Tatlock was delighted when his niece Valerie moved into his Coronation Street home. She was a bright, cheerful, optimistic girl, full of life and fun. When she married Kenneth Barlow, though, she changed: she became weary, highly strung, and her optimism was clouded. Every now and again the sun broke through but, for the nine years of life left to her, Valerie felt trapped by marriage and circumstance. Things started to go wrong for her on the eve of her wedding when she overheard Ena Sharples airing her views in the Corner Shop: 'Valerie Tatlock must have mislaid her common sense the day she said yes to Kenneth Barlow. It sticks out a mile to anyone with 'alf an eye - it isn't a wife he's looking for, it's a mother.' What hurt Valerie most was the suspicion that Ena was right: Ken had never spoken of love or given any reason why he wanted to marry her, and he was a university graduate, handsome and smart with a wonderful future ahead of him, while she was just a normal girl from the back-streets struggling to run her own hair salon. Valerie thought she

While Ken looks to his creature comforts Valerie has her hands full with their twins and the cooking, washing, ironing, cleaning, scrubbing, shopping and mending.

would be happy to look after Ken and their home, but when she walked down the aisle at St Mary's on 4 August 1962 she was still uncertain that she was doing the right thing.

Two issues ran consistently through the Barlow marriage: Ken's roving eye and Val's inferiority complex. During their nine-year union, Ken had a secret affair with reporter Jackie Marsh and flirtations with, among others, an exotic dancer and a well-advanced schoolgirl. He took it in his stride that women found him attractive and refused to acknowledge that Val had any right to feel insecure. But when another man, such as builder Ray Langton, took an interest in her, Ken turned into a possessive, sullen, wounded child, which infuriated his wife: 'It's nothing, just a

look in the eye – nothing else. It doesn't mean I'm thinking of . . . Look, nothing has happened, nothing is going to happen. That's the plain unadulterated truth. Which is more than you could have said three years ago when you were carrying on with that reporter bitch. Isn't it?'

After their honeymoon, they moved into No. 9 Coronation Street and Val transferred her business from its Rosamund Street premises to her new front parlour. Ken worked as an English teacher at the local school, and life seemed to hum along nicely: they both had family living in the Street and knew all the neighbours. Yet at times Valerie felt put-upon: Ken, like his father before him, expected her to do all the household chores, and viewed her

hairdressing as part-time work to supplement his income, just as Ida's shifts in hotel kitchens had helped boost Frank's wages. Val's world consisted of the salon, the kitchen, the Corner Shop and the Rovers. Although she was happy for Ken to venture further afield, she felt uneasy when he spent time with his old university friends, having conversations she did not understand. During rows, which occurred regularly, she would tell him that he patronized and humiliated her: 'I'm surprised you were able to bring yourself to have kids with somebody as dense as you obviously think I am.' After one particularly messy row, when he'd thrown her across the room and told her he was sick of her acting like a door-mat and not caring about his failing career, Valerie packed her bags and left. However, she realized that she was a woman who needed to be a wife. As she felt Ken no longer wanted her she offered herself to his colleague Dave Robbins, but he was not prepared to steal his best friend's wife. When Ken followed Val, she returned home meekly with him.

A couple of years later, after the birth of her twins, Valerie decided to do something about her lack of education. She signed up for evening classes in sociology, which surprised Ken, who had assumed she'd be interested in dressmaking, cookery or millinery. However, she was quick to assure him that she didn't intend to change overnight: 'I'll never become one of those tweedy intellectual types, reading the *Financial Times* in bed, and writing stiff letters to the editors of women's maga-zines. I've got more important things to do, like looking after my husband, my children and the house.' Unfortunately she gave up her classes after only a week – she felt she couldn't leave the children. On the one night she attended, she had returned home to find the house filled with smoke after a coal had fallen out of the grate and set the rug on fire. The twins were asleep upstairs and Ken had nipped down to the Rovers for a pint.

After the birth of Peter and Susan, in 1965, Valerie had closed the salon and gave herself up to full-time mothering, and with twins it *was* full-time. Sleepless nights became the norm as she had struggled to keep the babies quiet enough not to disturb Ken, yet despite the continual tiredness and her frustration that the house was never tidy, Val was content. Ken was fine so long as he stuck to his work routine and didn't make too many demands on her, and she had even turned a blind eye when, with the twins only six months old, he had the affair with Jackie.

Val criticized Ken and his principles only when she feared for the stability of her home and the security of her children. She was furi-ous when he took part in a banned student demonstration against Vietnam. It was broken up by the police and Ken was brought before the magistrates. Ordered to pay a £5 fine, he refused and was sentenced to a week in prison. Val couldn't understand why he wouldn't pay the fine: 'Look, Ken, you've got two kids up those stairs. If there's any basic right going, it's their right to some sort of responsible carry-on from you. Your duty's to them, not to a bunch of larking students who've hardly got their nappies off!' But Ken fought back: 'Those two up there are the stu-dents of tomorrow. They've got to live in the world we make for them. Hell, do you think we'd have any kind of freedom at all if people always turned their backs on things the way you want me to do?'

'I'm not interested in great speeches, Ken,' Val retaliated. 'I'm interested in this family!'

To make life happier for Val, Ken agreed to sell the house and they moved into a new council maisonette directly opposite No. 9. It was spacious and light and, with the twins at school, Val made the most of her spare time to decorate it. She took a job helping out at Maggie Clegg's Corner Shop and the future looked rosy. Then the nightmare struck. A convicted rapist, Frank Riley, escaped from

> *"I'll never become one of those tweedy intellectual types...I've got more important things to do, like looking after my husband, my children and the house."*
>
> VALERIE BARLOW

Strangeways and broke into the maisonette. Alone, Val was petrified but her first concern was for the children asleep upstairs. Luckily she had arranged an alarm system for emergencies, whereby she would bang on the water pipes to alert Ena Sharples in the flat below. On the pretence of a water blockage she hit the pipes, which alerted Ena but also woke the children. When Riley grabbed a crowbar to quieten them down, Val offered herself to him, telling him he could do what he liked with her as long as he left the twins alone. But Ena had raised the alarm and the police crashed through the kitchen window and overpowered Riley before he could assault Val. As he was dragged out of the flat he shouted at her to tell them he hadn't touched her. Afterwards Val had a breakdown, not because of her ordeal but because Ken refused to believe she had not been raped. His angst came from a struggle with his own principles: as a pacifist what should his reaction to Riley be?

When Ken accepted a teaching post in Jamaica Val was desperately unhappy with the move: she had always enjoyed living as part of the tight community on the Street: 'I know what it's like out there. There's chip papers in the gutter an' pavin' stones all ends up but at least you can see it! An' as far as I'm concerned it's better than the woman in the next door semi peerin' through 'er net curtains an' wonderin' if you'd contaminate 'er if she spoke!' She had said goodbye to her family, packed and was getting ready for the residents' farewell party when she discovered the plug on her hairdryer was loose. She tried to repair it but gave up, and decided to hold it together as she dried her hair. The moment she plugged in the dryer electricity shot through her and she was killed instantly. As she fell she knocked over an electric fire and a blaze started, which gutted the flat and engulfed her body in flames. Like the first Mrs Barlow, the second had met a tragic end.

Character Name:	CONCEPTA REGAN
Date of Birth:	15 January 1926
Husbands:	Harry Hewitt (1961–67)
	Sean Regan (1972–)
Children:	Christopher (1962)
	Lucille (step)
Parents:	Sean and Shelagh Riley

On the day Valerie Tatlock married Kenneth Barlow her neighbour Concepta Hewitt went into labour. Two days later she gave birth to a 7lb 3oz son, Christopher. During the first few years of her married life Valerie had been grateful for the support and advice offered by Concepta who, although a few years older than Val, had married only the year before her.

Concepta Riley came to the Street in late 1960 to work as resident barmaid at the Rovers Return. She was an honest woman in her mid-thirties, homesick for her native Ireland and glad to be adopted as a family member by Jack and Annie Walker. Almost as soon as she set foot behind the Rovers' bar she fell for tall dark widower Harry Hewitt, a bus conductor struggling to look after a ten-year-old daughter, Lucille.

Like Valerie, Concepta had been brought up in a close-knit family and was devoted to her parents. She was considered a gem by Annie Walker, 'all right for a Paddy' by Ena Sharples and 'a right little belter' by Harry Hewitt. Over a year Harry's attraction to Concepta grew and during a Street outing to Blackpool he proposed. Concepta was delighted to accept and the Street looked forward to a big church wedding. However, that idea was a problem for Concepta: she was a good Catholic and Harry was Church of England. The priest agreed to marry the couple when Harry undertook to bring up any children as Catholics but Concepta was heart-broken when the Bishop refused to allow her organ music or flowers. A bigger blow was her father's reaction to the marriage: 'I'm afraid my father doesn't approve at all and my mother daren't disagree with him. My father's very strict and he thinks all Protestants are in league with the devil. The trouble with my father is that he hates the British. He's still fighting the war.' Despite that, Concepta married Harry and moved into his house, No. 7 Coronation Street. While Harry had worried about Lucille's reaction to having a stepmother Concepta was confident that she and the little girl would get on well. She set about transforming Harry's bachelor house into a smart, neat home, in which Lucille could learn how to be a lady.

In accordance with Harry's wishes, Concepta gave up work at the Rovers and settled down to keep house. She missed the lively atmosphere in the pub and found the small terrace constricting: She had grown up in the countryside, running free in fields and climbing trees for apples. Now the only garden she had was a dirty back-yard and the air was choked with smoke from factory chimneys. When she discovered she was pregnant, Concepta feared for her baby's health and longed to return to her idyllic home in Castle Blayney. When she brought the subject up, Harry refused to contemplate the idea: 'All me life, apart from the war, I've lived around 'ere. I can't go chasin' off now. I can't 'elp the way I'm made, love. I know it'd make you happier but this is my 'ome. You knew that when you married me.' Concepta was saddened but she knew she'd never be able to drag him from his roots.

There wasn't much joy for Concepta living in the Street. Like Valerie, she was stuck in the house with a baby while her husband worked

Mediating between husband and child was a task Concepta had not anticipated when she married into the Hewitt household.

47

and spent his evenings in the pub. Lucille was not much help either as she was given to sulking and never lifted a finger to help around the house. Concepta found herself blaming the child for anything that went wrong. Crisis point was reached when Lucille became jealous of all the attention shown to baby Christopher. She refused to look after him and whenever Concepta wasn't looking she pinched him to make him cry. To celebrate their wedding anniversary the Hewitts decided to throw a party and Lucille was sent out with Christopher to buy some ham. When she returned she was alone and hysterical: Christopher had been kidnapped from outside the shop. When the police could find no trace of the baby, Concepta lost control and ran through neighbouring streets screaming for her baby. She suffered torment for three days until Elsie Tanner located Christopher safe and well, and returned him. He had been snatched by a young woman whose own baby had died. Concepta attended the court proceedings against her and cheered when she was imprisoned.

In 1964 Concepta finally convinced Harry that they should leave for Ireland: Christopher suffered from bad chest infections and she was depressed by the bleak industrial north. Also, her father was ill and Harry would be able to take over his garage business. Three years of pent-up anger spilled out as she raged against Harry's stubbornness: 'You've never had a thought for me since the day we got married. Everything is self, self, self!' And while Harry tried to ignore his wife, Lucille fought her, refusing to leave her native town. In the end it was decided that Lucille would stay with the Walkers until she finished her education and the rest of the family would move to Ireland. Concepta knew there would continue to be struggles across the sea, but was confident that she'd be able to cope better where the air was purer and the nearest neighbours lived half a mile away.

Character Name:	GAIL PLATT
Date of Birth:	18 April 1958
Husbands:	Brian Tilsley
	(1979–87, 1988–89)
	Martin Platt (1991–)
Children:	Nick (1980)
	Sarah Louise (1987)
	David (1990)
Parents:	Audrey Potter
	(Father unknown)

In the history of the Street, two female characters have been allowed to grow from giddy teenagers, to young brides and mothers, to middle-aged women with growing children and broken marriages. Deirdre's troubled life has centred on her relationships with men, while Gail's has evolved around her extended family. Throughout the 1980s and early 1990s, Gail was a struggling mother with an independent business streak, which Valerie Barlow had always longed for.

Like Val, Gail had first come to the Street as a giggling teenager, living over the Corner Shop and fantasizing about Prince Charles and David Cassidy. It was the mid-seventies and she had a string of boyfriends, but she wasn't a completely modern girl: she hung on to her virginity against all odds. That was until 1976, when she fell under the spell of Roy Thornley, a sales rep in his late thirties, who worked alongside her at the lingerie shop, Sylvia's Separates. He seduced her in the stock room and let her fall in love with him, only for her to be cited as co-respondent in his divorce case. This episode changed Gail: the shy, naïve young airhead became wary and more astute. Nearly three years after the Thornley business, his name reared its head again during the early stages of her romance with Brian Tilsley. Brian was a twenty-year-old motor mechanic and Gail fell for his good looks and athletic body. The only cloud on the horizon was Brian's interfering mother, Ivy, who was against the match and told Brian about Gail's involvement with Thornley. Gail was heartbroken when Brian tackled her about it, fearing that he'd look upon her as damaged goods and finish with her. However, he saw her as Thornley's victim and turned against his mother for stirring up the past. On November 1979 the couple married in church after Gail had converted to Catholicism.

At the time of their marriage, both Gail and Brian were twenty-one. He had lived all his life with his parents and had been pampered by his indulgent mother. Gail, on the other hand, had left home at sixteen after falling out with her unmarried mother over her boyfriends. Well used to independence, Gail was looking forward to being Brian's wife and continuing with her job as a waitress. Things started to go wrong for the couple almost straight away when they returned from honeymooning in the Isle of Man and moved into the Tilsleys' back bedroom. Gail struggled to stamp her own personality as Brian's wife by arguing with his mother over who should cook his meals. She insisted that, while she was grateful for the roof over her head, she was going to look after *her* man. For once in her life Ivy backed down.

No. 5 Coronation Street offered hardly any privacy for the young couple and the situation became claustrophobic once Gail discovered she was pregnant. Brian didn't seem to see anything wrong with their circumstances and she had to threaten to leave him before he agreed to buy a one-bedroomed house just before Nicholas Paul was born and Gail gave up work to look after him. Unlike Valerie and Concepta, half of Gail's struggles in the home stemmed from financial problems. However, the other half mirrored those of the other local wives in as much as Brian had set ideas on roles within marriage: 'Brian, when is it going to dawn on you that you're a married man with a baby? It has to be share and share alike.'

Finance was a big concern to the newly-weds: they had taken on a big mortgage with only Brian's income as a garage mechanic. To help pay the bills he took a second job, working nights as a petrol-pump attendant, but this put a strain on the marriage. The couple hardly saw each other and Gail grew bored stuck at home with Nicky. The situation grew worse when Brian took a six-month contract working in Qatar and Gail felt imprisoned in the house. To alleviate the boredom, she returned to work as waitress at Jim's Café.

When Brian returned, the couple sold their home so that he could build up his own garage and they moved back to Ivy's house. Much to Gail's distress, Brian easily slipped into being pampered by his mother and the rows became more frequent and more bitter. When Nicky went down with chicken-pox Gail struggled to look after him and maintain her new job as manageress at the café, frustrated by Brian's belief that she should give up everything to nurse their son: 'I work damn hard all day. I have to. Let's face it, Gail, some things are a mother's job. And when Nicky needs looking after you should be there with him. At home.'

'At home?' retorted Gail. 'What home? This is your mother's home, Brian. I haven't got a home!'

Fed up with Brian's failure to find them a new home, Gail and Nicky moved into a bedsit. Brian took advantage of her absence, acting as if he were single, until Ivy threatened to throw him out if he didn't attempt a reconciliation. Eventually the couple moved into a council house, but the marriage was rocky and Gail felt she had the most to complain about. She yearned for something to break up the monotony of her routine and when it came along she grabbed it with both hands.

The something – or rather someone – was Brian's cousin, Ian Latimer, who visited the Tilsleys while on holiday from Australia. Brian encouraged Gail to spend time with Ian,

~

"I'm sick of being a drudge, which is what this marriage has made me. No one can live their life, year in year out, for other people."

GAIL TILSEY

~

49

unaware that she was deeply attracted to him. When Brian went away to Scotland on business, Gail declared her feelings to Ian and invited him to stay the night. For the first time in years she felt free and silly, able to laugh and lark about. Her mother's suspicions were aroused by the change in her personality, and she took no time in working out the cause and confronting Gail, who didn't try to dodge the issue, or deny her affair: 'I resent this, Mam, you interfering in my life. You've got no right to come poking your nose in, stirring up bad feelings. If I want to feel alive again, feel loved again, why shouldn't I? What about all Brian's "bits on the side"?' All Audrey could do was tell her daughter to come to her senses before it was too late but when Ian returned to Australia, Gail learned she was pregnant. Audrey advised her to let Brian think the baby was his but Gail felt he deserved the truth and admitted that she wasn't sure who the father was. She was amazed when Brian forgave her infidelity but horrified when he told her to

have an abortion. She refused and the couple went through a messy, bitter divorce in which Nicky was fought over and Gail's morals were dragged out for inspection.

Following the birth of Sarah Louise in 1987, Ian had a blood test which proved that Brian was her father. Slowly the Tilsleys drifted back together again. Brian proposed that they remarry and Gail, although not in love with him any more, agreed for the sake of the children. Less than a year later, the couple were leading separate lives, Gail concentrating on her café business and Brian having a good time with various girlfriends. He was furious when Gail asked for another divorce as he knew that, once again, he would be separated from his son: 'You're a hard selfish rotten little bitch, Gail. I just wish to God I'd never set eyes on you.'

Gail fought the urge to blame Brian for everything and attempted to show him that they'd come to the end of the road: 'I married too young. Grew up afterwards. Knowing

Nick introduces Gail to her new daughter-in-law. Ivy Tilsley had the same reaction when Gail married Brian.

there wasn't enough between us to spend the rest of our lives together. What was so wrong with me having an identity of my own? You couldn't cope with that. You're like summat from the Dark Ages. Women should stay in their place, they're all right in the kitchen, in the bedroom, and that's about it!' That night, after the biggest row of their marriage, Brian stormed out and was stabbed to death outside a nightclub.

It was just four months after Brian's death that Gail began to rely on the support of her assistant at the café, Martin Platt, ten years her junior. From time to time he took Nicky off her hands, giving him the masculine input he was missing. Gail found herself attracted to the chirpy youth and soon they were involved in an affair, which shocked Audrey and Ivy alike. Gail maintained she had no need to honour Brian's memory and was doing the best for herself and the children. Never for one minute did she think that the romance was anything more than a short-term affair and was as surprised as everyone else when Martin moved in with her and looked after the children while she worked. Then Gail found she was pregnant. She didn't want to be tied down to yet another child and felt that it wasn't fair to force Martin to be a father when he was still so young. Without telling him she planned an abortion. When Martin discovered the truth, he begged her to change her mind, saying he would support her and love her and the baby. Gail returned home, still pregnant, and David was born on Christmas Day in 1990.

After their relationship had lasted two years Martin suggested they got married and was upset when Gail refused. She had gone through too much anger and frustration as Brian's wife to risk ruining this love by making Martin feel he could never walk away from her and the children. But Martin wasn't Brian: he was a caring, sincere man who had no wish to walk away, and Gail changed her mind. She

JILTING SITUATIONS

Plenty of confetti has been thrown over the cobbles of Weatherfield in the last 38 years. Elsie Tanner, Gail Platt, Deirdre Rachid and Maureen Elliott have all said 'I do' three times and thirty-seven brides have been married in forty-five weddings. However, the path to the altar is never smooth as Fiona Middleton discovered in 1997. She wasn't the first bride to be jilted, in fact she was the seventh:

- **1964** - Emily Nugent decided at the last moment not to wed her boss, Leonard Swindley.
- **1969** - Pensioners Albert Tatlock and Alice Pickens decided to call it a day when the vicar's car broke down en route to the church.
- **1969** - Teenager Gordon Clegg told Lucille Hewitt he couldn't marry her. She was trying on her wedding dress at the time.
- **1984** - Mavis Riley decided she couldn't go through with marrying Derek Wilton, unaware that he too had bottled out.
- **1987** - Alan Bradley lured Rita Fairclough to the registry office before announcing it was her own wedding she was attending. She refused to go through with the farce and stormed off home.
- **1989** - Barmaid Tina Fowler's dreams of happiness were shattered when builder Eddie Ramsden jilted her during her hen party.

went down on one knee to propose and became Mrs Platt in the summer of 1991.

Martin trained to become a nurse and it was while he was on his course that he befriended Carmel Finnan and invited her to babysit for his family. The moment she saw him Carmel fell for Martin and convinced herself that he would love her if Gail was not on the scene. Slowly she infiltrated the family home at No. 8 Coronation Street and played the role of saintly nanny while plotting against Gail, who had no idea what was going on until Martin threw Carmel out of the house after she had made a pass at him. Before she left Carmel urged her to face the fact that she was too old for Martin and that she had trapped him into marriage. Gail refused to let Carmel undermine her: 'Listen, Carmel, you think you know me. You wheedled your way into my house and you think you know me, but you don't. I didn't get this family easily. And I won't let some twisted little girl like you take it away from me!' Finally Gail snapped when Carmel announced she was pregnant with Martin's baby and tried to kidnap David. She confronted the girl at her bedsit and struggled with her until Carmel fell downstairs. As she recovered in hospital, Carmel asked the police to charge Gail with assault, but it all ended with the arrival of her grandfather, who revealed that Carmel had undergone psychiatric treatment for obsessional behaviour and took her back to Ireland.

Marriage to Martin had not been easy for Gail. When he had a one-night stand she feared that she'd grown too old for him and he would leave her. It took him months to prove that he was desperately sorry for his drunken lapse.

More difficult, though, in the Platt household has been Martin and Nicky's stormy relationship. Like Ida Barlow, Gail has found herself caught continually in the middle of their battles. As Nicky became a teenager, he objected to Martin's role in his life as he was not his real father. Gail tried to prove to her son that Martin was a far better father than Brian had ever been, but Nicky had built Brian into a God-like figure beside whom Martin made poor comparison. At times Gail wondered if the rows would ever stop, but since Nicky came back from spending time with his uncle in Canada he and Martin have been able to build a solid relationship. Now Gail finds that it is she who is always in dispute with her eldest child. It was a nightmare for Gail to discover that Nick had married Leanne Battersby at seventeen and she saw him throwing his life away, just as she feared she had by marrying Brian at such a young age.

Character Name:	SALLY WEBSTER
Date of Birth:	11 July 1967
Husband:	Kevin Webster (1986–)
Children:	Rosie (1990) Sophie (1994)
Parents:	Eddie and Elsie Seddon

Another young bride was Gail's neighbour and friend Sally Webster. She'd been nineteen when, as Sally Seddon, she had fallen for mechanic Kevin Webster and married him in October 1986. A native of Weatherfield, Sally had had a terrible childhood, physically abused by her drunken father. She had grown up in fear, watching her mother struggle to keep a home together and feed her two daughters. As soon as Sally left school, Eddie Seddon had pushed her to sign on and had taken her dole cheque for himself, but when she married Kevin, she was devastated at her father's refusal to attend the ceremony in case he had to pay.

The young couple lodged with Hilda Ogden at No. 13 Coronation Street until Sally landed a job as assistant at Alf Roberts's Minimarket, with the flat above the shop thrown in. Marriage gave Sally the stability she needed and, for the first time in her life, she could relax and enjoy herself. She adored her sober, reliable husband: 'Life was a mess before I met Kevin.'

Sally was quick to show Kevin that while she was happy to look after him she was no doormat. When he decided to take up racing old bangers Sally wanted to be involved but he felt that it was a dangerous sport and girls should keep out of it. Sally demanded equal rights, and Kevin gave in and let her drive the car in time trials. He was confident that she would lag way behind him but when her time proved the best he was angry and refused to allow her near the banger again, adamant that

only men could handle the action. Sally hit back by sneaking the car into a race. Unfortunately it turned over and she broke her ankle but at least she had the satisfaction of knowing she had tried her best.

Sally's first daughter, Rosie, was born on Christmas Eve 1990. At the time Kevin was out at work with his breakdown truck, so Sally rode to hospital with Liz McDonald in Don Brennan's taxi. The baby started to come during the journey and Liz delivered her. Sally named her Rosie as she'd been born on Rosamund Street.

If marriage to Kevin had given her stability, their home, which they had bought from Hilda, had given her security. In motherhood Sally felt fulfilled, as if she had everything she could ever have dreamed of. Life was still full of problems, mainly financial, but at night,

curled up with Kevin while Rosie slept peacefully in her carry-cot, Sally felt whole.

She gave up working at the shop to become a registered child-minder and took in children including Gail's little David, and Jonathan, the son of tax-inspector Joe Broughton, whose wife had recently left him. Sally felt sorry for Joe and stuck with disruptive Jonathan until she had gained his trust and calmed him down. Joe was grateful, and Sally was pleased when he invited the Websters to share a holiday cottage with him at the Lakes. Sally had no idea of his true intentions until he declared his love for her and urged her to break free of her marriage, which he thought was turning her into a drab housewife. 'I know why you married him,' he told her. 'You got stuck in that Weatherfield whirlpool, that grow-up, get married, have

Sally tries to explain to Sophie why Daddy has gone to live with Natalie, or is she trying to explain her relationship with Chris Collins or Greg Kelly?

kids Weatherfield that never looks beyond the M62. I just don't think you're happy.' Sally was indignant: 'Well, that's where you're wrong, Mr Joe Broughton. I didn't get trapped, I picked that life because it's what I wanted. Kev's what I wanted.'

Yet no matter what she had said to Joe, Sally was aware that cracks were appearing in her marriage. Kevin worked long hours at the garage, and he was involved in a court case: he had allowed Steve McDonald to pose as him to avoid prosecution after a car accident and had been charged with perverting the course of justice. Sally feared that the bailiffs would be sent round as they couldn't afford Kevin's £800 fine. They bickered and rowed with each other, while Rosie and the other children tired Sally out. She began to feel sick of the inside of No. 13 and that Joe might have been right: she wasn't happy any more and she felt trapped, but she was still not going to be unfaithful. She stopped minding Jonathan, told Kevin what had happened and never saw Joe again – after Kevin had thumped him for good measure.

The Websters' second daughter, Sophie, was born in 1994 and, once again, Sally was happy. There was even financial security in the shape of a £5,000 cheque given by lonely newsagent Rita Sullivan.

Money aside, Sally's relationship with Kevin continued to be shaken by domestic issues and her post-natal depression. She felt again that she was condemned to a life of nappies and household chores while Kevin was free to enjoy himself. Starved of adult company, she found herself analysing every word Kevin said, challenging him constantly and flaring up at the slightest hint of criticism. 'I'm sick of it as well, Kevin. Sick o' your moaning, your whingeing. Think I want to live like this? My life's going nowhere. I'm a rubbing-rag. A doormat everyone walks on.'

As the girls grew older, the stresses lifted from Sally's shoulders, thanks to playgroups,

nurseries and then school, but she had had enough of Kevin's moans about working for other people and encouraged him to strike out on his own. They celebrated together when he went into partnership with Tony Horrocks and bought MVB Motors. But the celebrations turned sour just months later when Tony had a breakdown after killing Joyce Smedley, Judy Mallett's mother, in a road accident. He left the garage, handing over his interest in it to his mother Natalie.

At the same time, Sally's mother suffered a stroke and Sally rushed to Scarborough to nurse her back to health. She was gone for three months, during which time Kevin occasionally visited her at the weekend. When she returned to Coronation Street, she was relieved to be back in the security of her home with her husband and children. But that security had been violated by Natalie, who had seduced Kevin and had spent nights of passion in Sally's bed. When she discovered the affair, Sally flew into a frenzy of hatred – towards Natalie, towards Kevin for deceiving her and breaking his marriage vows and towards herself for not realizing what had been going on. She threw Kevin out and, with her daughters, faced an unreliable future.

After she had collected herself, Sally determined that the girls wouldn't suffer and made heavy financial demands upon Kevin, which he found unmanageable and which caused rows between him and Natalie. When Natalie tried to intervene, Sally punched her and pulled out hanks of her hair as they brawled on the cobbles of the Street. Then, in an act of what she conceded as petty revenge, she caused hundreds of pounds' worth of damage to Natalie's house by flooding it while she and Kevin were holidaying in the sun.

Despite all her defiance, Sally was desperately wounded by the break-up of her ten-year marriage. When alone, or with friends, she wept: 'Why did Kevin have to put me through this, Gail? I just lie there every night, crying me eyes out 'cause I can't understand what I've done to him to make him put me through anything as awful as this.' Encouraged by Gail, Sally found some solace in the arms of Chris Collins, Kevin's handsome assistant mechanic. However, when he talked of moving in and commitment, Sally ended the affair, fearful that he, too, would leave her one day and that the girls would have to go through turmoil once again.

Christmas brought Kevin back to Sally when he realized he couldn't cope without her and his children. Although she felt she couldn't trust him as she had before, Sally welcomed him with open arms. Life has settled down again for her: she had fought for and won her man, and now she is building secure walls around the girls again.

Character Name:	JANICE BATTERSBY
Date of Birth:	17 June 1965
Husband:	Les Battersby (1994–)
Children:	Toyah Leanne (step)
Parents:	Rod and Dottie Lee

Someone who has the makings of a classic struggling mother is Janice Battersby, even though she is the sort of neighbour who would have horrified Ida Barlow! Janice keeps the Battersby clan together, with her daughter Toyah, her step-daughter Leanne and husband Les. They've been together a long time and pull togther as a family unit, ranting against the world, the system and the neighbours. But behind closed doors at No. 5 Coronation Street Janice is the first to lash out at Les when there's a risk of the council moving them on – yet again: 'I'm sick of you. Sick of you rowing with the neighbours, sick of sticking up for you, sick of lying for you, sick of being moved out of one house after another. You get us chucked out of here, I'm telling you, the day we have to leave you'll be carried out!'

In her own way Janice is house-proud, even though the family home is stacked full of market rejects and bulk orders that Les is always attempting to offload on to some unsuspecting soul. She worries about Toyah's schooling (or, rather, lack of it) and hates the way her life is a continual round of work, work and work. Still, at least she has her home, even if it isn't the little palace she used to dream of: 'Y'know, as a kid I loved all them adverts of cooking mums. It were like another world. Baking these dream pies in these dream kitchens. I wanted to be like them when I grew up.'

No matter what exploits the family get up to, whatever offences Les commits and no matter how often Toyah is done for shoplifting, Janice will be there at the centre of things, giving out clouts around ears and worrying herself sick that, this time, the Battersbys have gone too far.

The female residents have difficulty in understanding Janice's attraction to Les.

> *"The hoi polloi don't mind being insulted you know, not by a social superior. At least I am talking to them."*
>
> ANNIE WALKER

In the terraced streets of the north there has always existed a slight 'attitude' between humble tenants and house-owners, and those who stand behind counters. Viewed as 'them' rather than 'us', shopkeepers and licensees seemed to hold power over their neighbours by keeping a stern eye on the credit book while swanning around town in fancy clothes bought out of the profits gleaned from honest workers' money. The Coronation Street community has had its fair share of 'thems', both male and female. They tend to lead separate lives from their customers, having one special friend rather than the group associated with their neighbours. They are looked upon as pillars of the local community and ideal for committee or council work. Leonard Swindley stood for the local council, Alf Roberts is a committee man through and through, as well as being an ex-Mayor of Weatherfield, and Fred Elliott is Grand Master of the Square Dealers. Their female equivalents can also hold high office and would agree with the gents that being a Leading Citizen is a thankless task.

Character Name:	ANNIE WALKER
Date of Birth:	11 August 1909
Husband:	Jack Walker (1937–70)
Children:	Billy (1938)
	Joan (1940)
Parents:	Edward and Florence Beaumont

Annie Walker was the Duchess of Weatherfield, lording it over the serfs who frequented her hostelry, the Rovers Return. Within the pub's walls she reigned supreme, just like her heroine Queen Elizabeth I. She served as Mayoress of Weatherfield and was a leading light in Licensed Victuallers' circles: 'The Ladies' Committee has a very responsible position in the community. Making decision, introducing motions. If the Ladies' Committee disagrees with the national policy they take firm action. We're watching NATO at the moment, very closely indeed.'

For more than forty years the Rovers was the centre of her life: 'I have been the hub of a community – you might even say I've had my own little kingdom.' Clitheroe, in Lancashire, was Annie's birthplace and she had been brought up in a humble home, constantly reminded by her mother that they were part of a noble family now down on their luck, and considered herself a cut above her schoolmates and neighbours. She came to the pub as a newly-wed, with husband Jack and baby son Billy. During the Second World War she stood alone at the beer pumps, seeing the residents through the darkest hours. Daughter Joan completed the Walker family, and it was during preparations for the young girl's wedding that we first met Annie in December 1960.

In her youth Anne Beaumont had involved herself in amateur operatics and dramatics – 'Mr Nuttall used to say I was the most promising soubrette he'd ever handled' – and brought her theatrical bearing into play behind the Rovers bar as she lectured her customers on their lifestyles, advised on matters she knew little about and always gave herself the best exit line.

Annie's undisguised snobbery often offended her patrons but Jack was always on hand to smooth things over. They were a solid couple, and to celebrate their silver wedding anniversary in 1962, Jack threw a party for all the regulars. While he manned the bar at lunch-time, Annie spent the day in the kitchen: as the guests arrived the couple were bickering and retired to early to bed.

Jack was a stabilizing influence in Annie's life, reining her in when she went too far in her bid to lift the Rovers from back-street alehouse to refined hostelry, but no matter what his personal feelings were, he never allowed the customers to abuse his wife verbally and, in public, always stood up for her. On one occasion, however, he turned a blind eye as the regulars rebelled against Annie's new ruling that gentleman would not be served unless they were wearing ties. Also, during a short holiday in Paris she had been impressed by the gallant Frenchmen: the customers were soon put off their beer by the sound of Marcosignori's 'Museta Waltz' bellowing from Annie's record player while the scent of *lapin roti* tickled their nostrils. Annie had anticipated trouble in implementing the new dress code but the residents refused point-blank to co-operate and hit back by ordering pints in wine-glasses, calculating that five were the equivalent to a pint. Annie admitted defeat.

After Joan and Billy left home their place was taken by teenager Lucille Hewitt, who became the Walkers' ward. She brought the pop culture of the sixties into the Rovers and into Annie's living room, which the landlady was not prepared to tolerate. She attempted to rub off some of Lucille's back-street edges, giving her elocution lessons and introducing her to Gilbert and Sullivan, but Lucille continued to mix with the wrong crowd, smoked and drank.

When she left to join a hippie commune, a distraught Annie pleaded, 'Come home, Lucille, come home where it's nice!' Annie and Lucille were united in their grief over Jack's sudden death. It was the summer of 1970 and the Walkers had been visiting Joan when Jack suffered a fatal heart-attack. After the funeral Annie took over the pub's licence and Billy moved back to Weatherfield. He encouraged his mother to take more of a back seat and, as the pub's hostess, she kept in the background, talking to her customers while barmaids Bet Lynch and Betty Turpin served.

Annie kept a close eye on Billy and the staff, insistent that they should keep to her own high standards: 'Billy, I wish you wouldn't embrace Bet Lynch behind the bar. It lowers the tone and it probably gives her ideas.'

When Alf Roberts was elected Mayor of Weatherfield Annie gladly stood by his side as Mayoress. She made Billy manager of the pub and even contemplated retiring from the licensed trade, but Lucille discovered her plans and warned the regulars. Ena Sharples led the fight to keep Annie's name over the door, reckoning that with her in charge the juke-boxes and brawlers wouldn't take over. Annie was touched by their concern and agreed to stay on, although she had to take a

Keeping the bar counter safely between her and the customers, Annie worries for the glasses as Ena and Elsie square up to each other.

Jack looks on with fear and trepidation as Annie announces a new scheme for the Rovers.

gold with her initials. Annie agreed to pay £5 a yard and threw a sherry evening for her friends to show it off. She was horrified when Bet Lynch broke the news that the 'exclusive' carpet was an off-cut left over from the local bingo hall, the Alhambra Weatherfield.

Many of the regulars were fond of Annie although sometimes annoyed by her patronising ways. They admired her strengths and knew her to be a basically kind person. However, there were occasions when her rank-pulling became vicious and she reduced someone to tears. In 1979, Alf Roberts spoke for many when he laid into his ex-Mayoress for belittling his wife, Renee: 'You've always been the same. Too good for people round 'ere. A cut above. Well, that's what *you* think. It's all put on. It's all swank. Because without them airs and graces you're nothing. You've picked on a lot of people round here in your time. Sneering at 'em, trying to make 'em feel common and stupid. Well, you're not picking on my wife!'

For many years Annie liked to believe that she did not fit into life on the Street, that she was biding time until that little pub in the Cheshire countryside beckoned. However, her aspirations were no comfort when she was faced with the knowledge that her daughter Joan looked down upon her because she ran a back-street pub. Billy had turned into a rogue, leaving broken hearts and gambling debts every time he flew into and out of her life. The Rovers became the only stability in a life which, Annie thought, had offered much more: 'I was always two people, really. The landlady of the Rovers Return and someone quite different. I've always been able to retreat into my dreams. The places I've travelled to inside my mind. The people I've met. Ambitions I've had.' When she retired in 1983 and moved into Joan's back bedroom, she left most of her belongings in the pub. But the memories she took with her could not have been contained in a thousand suitcases.

more active role after discovering Billy had been gambling with the pub's takings.

Annie tended to split her regulars into two groups. The first contained the small band she considered friends, such as school-teacher Kenneth Barlow and councillors Alf Roberts and Len Fairclough. The rest of the community fell into the wider second group of non-professionals and manual workers, who were tolerated as long as they spent money over the bar. Unemployed rogue Eddie Yeats fell firmly into the second category, with Annie standing guard beside the till every time he stepped over the threshold. Eddie used the pub as a marketplace to offload items he had acquired and once, only once, Annie was lured into making a purchase. Eddie approached her with an exclusive carpet for her living room. At first she tried hard to ignore him, but Eddie ensnared her by showing her that the carpet was monogrammed in

Character Name:	FLORENCE LENA LINDLEY
Date of Birth:	12 June 1922
Husband:	Norman Lindley (1949–)
Parents:	Arnold and Nellie Arkwright

When Florrie Lindley bought Coronation Street's Corner Shop in December 1960 it was as dream come true for the former barmaid. She'd saved for years to become her own boss and see her name over the door. The shop was a thriving business when she took over, but Florrie believed she could boost trade by offering new lines to her customers. She bought in exotic fare such as Danish pastries and pasta but these were left untouched on the shelves and Florrie fell into debt. If they had known of Florrie's problems some of the regular customers might have advised her to stick to sausages and beans, but Florrie believed she needed to keep herself aloof from them, which meant that she had no one to socialize with, as Annie Walker viewed Florrie as being beneath her social standing. In this way Florrie was caught between the established retail class and her neighbours.

It took pensioner Albert Tatlock to point out that Florrie wasn't doing herself any favours by treating customers with suspicion and disdain and she dropped her defences, let the regulars befriend her and, suddenly, life became easier.

Even with the customers on her side, Florrie struggled to make a success of the shop. She opened a sub-post-office in the hope of increased profits, and took on Irma Ogden as an assistant but it never got off the ground. Romance was also stagnant in Florrie's life: her husband Norman had deserted her to work overseas and Florrie

Florrie takes over the shop and is faced with her first customer – the formidable Ena Sharples.

looked upon herself as a divorcée. However, as divorce was still frowned upon then, she allowed everyone to assume she was a widow. She was interested in neighbour Harry Hewitt but he married someone else. Then she turned her attention to Frank Barlow but he offered only a platonic relationship. By 1964, she felt so alone and unloved that she had a breakdown.

Norman re-entered Florrie's life with an offer of reconciliation and a fresh start in Canada. Florrie put aside the fact that he had been sleeping with her neighbour, Elsie Tanner, and decided that he was the only way she could rid herself of the shop. She put it on the market and jumped on the next boat sailing from Liverpool docks.

Character Name:	MARGARET (MAGGIE) COOKE
Date of Birth:	12 June 1924
Husbands:	Les Clegg (1946–69)
	Ron Cooke (1974–)
Children:	Gordon (adopted 1948)
Parents:	Harold and Margaret Preston

Margaret Clegg was a quiet soul, who tried hard to keep herself to herself and went through life behind the counter of her shop with a pained expression. It was as if she carried all the troubles of the world on her shoulders. Before she took over the Corner Shop in 1968 she had had an unhappy life: unable to have children, she had adopted her sister Betty's son Gordon and he had been her only comfort when her husband Les had turned into a violent alcoholic. The family moved from street to street, with Maggie always hoping that no one would find out about Les's drinking. Then there would be an incident, the secret would be out and

they'd move on. Buying the Corner Shop on Coronation Street had been Les's last chance to prove to Maggie he could remain sober. But after another drinking binge Les hit her, and Gordon knocked him unconscious. The last Maggie saw of her husband, he was lying in a hospital bed reeking of whisky. He was admitted to a psychiatric hospital and Maggie filed for divorce. No one but Gordon knew what had happened and Maggie made preparations for yet another move. However, when her customers found out, they urged her to stay: no one could blame a wife for her husband's failings.

Maggie always tried to get on with her neighbours and customers, but made it clear that credit was only available to trusted regulars although she always lent a sympathetic ear to tales of woe. However, there was one woman in the Street who annoyed her, and that was Annie Walker. In the winter of 1968 Gordon fell in love with Annie's young ward, Lucille Hewitt, and although she disapproved of the match on grounds of age, Maggie decided not to interfere. She thought Gordon would tire of the girl. Annie, though, felt that a shopkeeper's son was an unsuitable partner for her ward. Both flew into a panic when the youngsters eloped. Annie blamed Maggie, accusing her of bringing up the boy badly and classing him as the son of a drunkard. Maggie tried hard to bite her tongue but in the end let rip: 'I'm only interested in my son! If your ward works in a shop that's your affair. You let her leave off school and waste her talents. I've seen her in those skinny dresses, showing herself off. She's obviously not controlled by you!'

Both Annie and Maggie were relieved when Gordon and Lucille returned home still single, and Maggie decided to respect Gordon's choice of bride. She helped them to prepare a wedding they would be proud to remember and was secretly delighted when, after months of planning, Gordon jilted Lucille. But the end of the wedding also

meant the end of having Gordon around the place: he was so upset at finishing with Lucille that he took a job in London. Maggie settled into a peaceful, if lonely, existence at the shop and tried to brighten herself up by going for the odd drink with divorcé Len Fairclough.

The quietness of No.15 Coronation Street was shattered eventually by the arrival of her sister, Betty, and her overbearing but jovial husband Cyril Turpin. They announced that Maggie needed looking after and within days of moving in had driven her to distraction. Before long Maggie lost her cool: 'Why are you making it so difficult? Do I have to say it? I don't want you in my shop. I know you don't mean it but you just take over. And this shop is mine. I'm not going to be organized by you or your Cyril. You've made my life your property between the two of you.' Shortly after that outburst the Turpins moved out.

Romance was never high on Maggie's agenda and she allowed Len to slip through her fingers after making it clear she was only interested in marriage. Another admirer was councillor Alf Roberts, who looked upon Maggie as an ideal wife – full of social graces as well as being kind-hearted and attractive. Unfortunately he did nothing for Maggie.

Ronald Cooke *did* set the embers glowing. He was a draughtsman whom Maggie met after her well-meaning assistant Norma Ford placed an ad in a lonely-hearts column on her behalf. At first Maggie was affronted by this intrusion into her privacy but after reading Ron's delightful introductory letter she allowed Norma to talk her into meeting him. She fell for Ron immediately but was appalled when he confessed to a drink problem. She wouldn't saddle herself with another Les so sadly stopped seeing him.

Two pillars of the community who constantly clashed. Whilst Annie put on airs and graces, she resented Maggie's natural poise and gentle nature.

"I don't dislike bein' on my own. It's just this feeling that you're not really there. Not in relation to the rest o' the world."

MAGGIE COOKE

Maggie continued to comfort deserted wives and lovelorn young girls. She made a point of remembering the names of her customers' children and grandchildren. The perfect shop-keeper and a loyal friend, she remained the loneliest woman on the Street: 'I don't dislike bein' on my own. It's just this feeling that you're not really there. Not in relation to the rest o' the world. I've started lying awake at night thinking of all the things I've never done, all the places I haven't been to.'

And then the impossible happened: after an absence of two years Ron returned and announced he had been dry since their last meeting. Furthermore, he was taking a job in Zaïre and wanted Maggie to go with him as his wife. Maggie grasped her chance with both hands and agreed. After their summer wedding the Cookes emigrated to Africa, with Maggie leaving the sale of the shop in Gordon's capable hands.

Character Name:	IRENE (RENEE) ROBERTS
Date of Birth:	3 March 1943
Husband:	Alf Roberts (1978–80)
Parents:	Harold and Daisy Bradshaw Joe Hibbert (step)
Date of Death:	30 July 1980

It took two years for Gordon to find a buyer, during which custom ran down and ex-supermarket assistant Renee Bradshaw was able to snap it up at a bargain price. As her name was painted on the shop sign, residents hoped she would turn out to be another Maggie but they were soon disappointed when confronted with fast-talking businesswoman Renee. Hilda Ogden was her first customer and was shocked when Renee refused her credit:

'I've made it clear, Mrs Ogden, and I've tried to be polite about it. I do not give credit. Go down Rosamund Street to the supermarket. See if they'll give you tick. And I'm open Sunday morning. I'm open all the hours God sends and all I ask is I'm paid cash.'

Renee bought the shop with her life savings, mainly in the hope that it would provide a stable home for her younger brother Terry, who had had itchy feet since leaving the Army. Since their father's death and their flighty mother's disastrous marriage to a no-hoper, she had looked after Terry's interests at the expense of building up a life for herself. Ungrateful Terry re-enlisted, though, telling Renee he had to escape her. With no one to care for, Renee turned her attention full time to the shop. She decided that profits would rise if she sold alcohol, so she applied for a licence – and sparked off the Third World War in Coronation Street.

Annie Walker was livid at the prospect of an off-licence at the end of *her* street, taking her profits. She opposed the application and the Street's residents were forced into two camps: while Annie brought in all the old favours she could muster, Renee set up a petition in favour of the idea for customers to sign. Eventually, it came to a show-down in court with both parties giving evidence. The judge was undecided over the merits of granting the licence until Rovers' barmaid Bet Lynch admitted that if a customer asked for a bottle of wine at the pub it was the practice to buy one in from an off-licence, so he decided the case in Renee's favour. Annie called Bet a traitor.

Bet became one of Renee's closest friends after she moved into the shop as a lodger, but she attracted the wrong sort of attention from men and the sensible, respectable Renee had to forbid her from walking through the shop for ciggies early in the morning dressed in her baby-doll nightie. Eager to find a fun-loving lady inside Renee, though, Bet set them up with a couple of lorry-drivers, who had chatted

her up in the Rovers. Renee was doubtful about the arrangement but set off with Bet for their date. They were stood up as the men raided the empty shop and made off with most of Renee's stock. After this Renee avoided Bet's men.

Alf Roberts was still on the scene, adamant that a woman with a grocer's shop was the ideal wife for him, and he turned his attention to Renee, who was thrilled when, after a night out together at a club, he proposed. The next morning, before she had a chance to accept, Renee was humiliated when Alf apologized, saying that the drink had got the better of him and, of course, he hadn't meant it. Within months he was back with another proposal, this time cast-iron. Renee wasn't certain that she should accept – she didn't want to give the impression of being too eager or available – but in the end she decided that as she intended to marry him at some stage there was no point in hanging about.

The wedding, at Weatherfield register office, was spoilt by Renee's loud-mouthed stepfather, Joe Hibbert, who told her that she was so ugly Alf must have married her for the shop. Alf tried to take her mind off the incident by taking her on a honeymoon to Capri, home of the woman she most admired in the world, Gracie Fields.

Once back in Weatherfield the honeymoon soon ended for Renee when she clashed with Alf. He objected to having Bet around the place and suggested that he give up his job at the GPO to run the shop with his wife. While admitting that Bet might have outstayed her welcome, Renee was aghast at the idea of Alf's portly frame standing behind her counter. The shop was her own little world, with everything placed exactly where she wanted it. She enjoyed having someone to chat with in the evenings and to warm her feet in bed at night, but had no intention of being with Alf twenty-four hours a day.

The friction at No.15 was resolved in a

dramatic and terrifying way. A lorry crashed into the Rovers and Alf, who was drinking with friends, was knocked unconscious. For three weeks Renee sat at his bedside until Alf came out of his coma. Renee realized how much he meant to her and told him that she wanted him to join her full-time at the shop. Serving alongside Renee seemed to help in his recovery, but Renee was alarmed by a strange new side to his personality: he became aggressive at any hint of criticism of himself or Renee. When Annie Walker complained that Renee didn't stock game soup, he shouted at her. Renee was so shocked and frightened by the new Alf that she begged him to seek psychiatric help, which slowly calmed him.

Poor Alf and Renee never had a chance to see how their marriage would have survived and grown over the years. They made the decision to sell up and move away to Grange to run a sub-post-office. Renee started taking driving lessons and enjoyed making Alf jealous by flirting with her instructor. Out

The marriage between Alf and Renee was viewed as natural and appropriate – he was a councillor, she was a shopkeeper. The two went hand in glove.

celebrating their move one afternoon Renee took the wheel on the way home. When she stalled the car down a quiet country lane, Alf was exasperated and got out to take over whereupon a lorry, speeding up the lane, smashed into the car and Renee was flung through the windscreen then back on to the seat. Her liver and spleen were pierced by flying glass and by the time the emergency services arrived Alf was a widower.

Character Name:	MAUREEN ELIZABETH ELLIOTT
Date of Birth:	13 January 1945
Husband:	Frank Naylor (1975–82)
	Reg Holdsworth (1994–96)
	Fred Elliott (1997–)
Parents:	Maud Grimes and Leonard (Danny) Kennedy

The move to Grange had been partly down to Renee's desire to revive her sagging marriage. Another female shopkeeper with a similar idea was Maureen Elliott, who deserted her husband of nine days and ran off with another man after realizing that she had married a man she didn't love. Not that that was new for Maureen: she had married her first husband Frank Naylor on the rebound from her real passion, Reg Holdsworth. They had lived in a lovely house in Preston, had membership to the golf club and gave swish dinner parties, but Frank hated Maureen for not loving him and took to verbal abuse, which soon became physical. Maureen fled and set up home with her mother in Weatherfield. As she needed to support them both, she took a job in a local supermarket, Bettabuy, and discovered that

her old flame Reg was the manager. Love rekindled over the cream crackers. Reg was eager to consummate his love for Maureen, but her mind was never far from her mother and the worry that she might not be coping without her. When Reg finally succeeded in getting her into his waterbed, it burst, drenching and humiliating her.

Maureen became Mrs Holdsworth in January 1994 and, after a very short honeymoon, took control of the Corner Shop – now a mini-market – with her husband. Reg had bought the shop when Alf Roberts retired and had plans to turn it into an emporium of unusual foodstuffs. Maureen, however, was more sensible and saw the shop as providing essential items for the local community. She had a ramp built behind the counter to ensure that Maud could reach the till, and developed a sharp head for business. This was just as well as Reg was soon bored with the smallness of his new arena. He took a job managing a frozen-food store, leaving the shop in Maureen's capable hands.

Maureen was nothing like Florrie, Renee, or even Maggie Clegg: she could be tough and career-minded but most of the time she breezed through her days with her mind on Reg. She was a hopeless romantic, deeply in love with her Prince Charming. But a brutal awakening was just round the corner, when Reg took promotion in Lowestoft and allowed his libido to lead him astray. He ran off with one of his workers, a younger woman who made his dreams come true by becoming pregnant. Suddenly Maureen found herself fighting for her rights in a divorce case that ended in her keeping the shop and losing her pride.

Being stuck in the shop all hours with Maud was not Maureen's idea of fun and she had a breakdown. It was quite a shock when her friend Bill Webster admitted he found her attractive. He was a quiet sort, a man's man, not at all the romantic, dashing blade that

Reg and Frank had been, and Maureen wasn't sure that she wanted to get involved with a man who didn't fill her with passion. Still, he got on well with Maud and made no attempt to interfere in Maureen's life or the running of the shop, so she drifted into a relationship with him.

Curly Watts had been Reg's assistant and best friend until one night, in a drunken and emotional haze, Maureen had slept with him. Now, when Bill deserted her to spend Christmas with his ex-wife and son, Maureen found herself in the same situation: she reached out and again found Curly available. However, this time there was no Reg to forgive her and pledge not to neglect her in the future: Bill thumped Curly and finished with Maureen.

A night out with the girls ended with Maureen being given a lift home by master butcher Fred Elliott, a man as full of himself and lard as Reg had been. To the surprise of her friends, and the dismay of her mother, Maureen started to see him regularly and, after his third proposal, decided that as she had had no better offers she would say yes. She went into the marriage knowing that although she didn't love Fred he offered financial security and devotion. Maureen reckoned that marriages had been built on a lot less. However, as soon as the confetti settled she knew she had made the biggest mistake of her life. Bill threw a life-line: he announced that he was going to live in Germany and invited her to join him. With Maud's blessing, Maureen grabbed her passport and jumped into Bill's taxi determined that this time *she* would live her life – not Maud, Frank, Reg or Fred, but her, by herself and for herself!

The Elliott marriage lasted less than a fortnight, with Maureen wondering how on earth she could have ever said 'I do'.

67

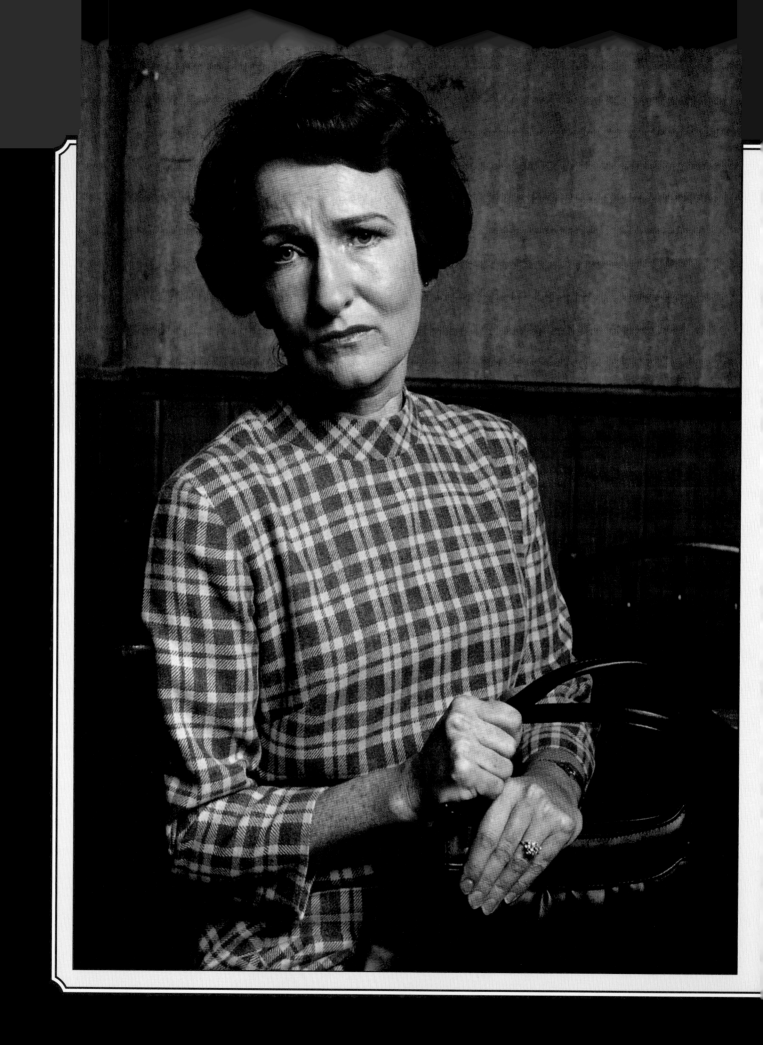

> *"I've always wanted to be stormy, passionate and tempestuous. But you can't be. Not when you're born with a tidy mind."*
>
> EMILY BISHOP

At local dances they were referred to as 'wallflowers', in different ages as 'old maids' or 'spinsters'. They were often dominated by an overbearing parent, sacrificing their youth to look after siblings and other family members. In the Street they have often been flustered, easily embarrassed by innuendo, and taken advantage of by unscrupulous gents. Esther Hayes was the original stay-at-home, appearing regularly from 1960 to 1963. Miss Nugent first appeared in episode fifteen and was quickly established as the frightened mouse, living in the shadow of the overbearing, pompous Mr Swindley. As Emily Bishop, though, she blossomed, and a new mouse was introduced in Mavis Riley. All three ladies were hindered by elderly relatives – Esther by her bedridden mother, Emily by her invalid father and later her aunt, and Mavis by *her* bedridden aunt. None of them had children but all would have made caring, guiding mothers. Emily and Mavis both married men who were ridiculed by the other menfolk and were both left widowed in tragic circumstances.

Character Name:	ESTHER HAYES
Date of Birth:	10 May 1924
Parents:	Sid and Alice Hayes

Esther gives Elsie a surprise by springing to Christine Appleby's defence and giving Elsie a piece of her mind.

Esther Hayes had been born in the Street and brought up in a close-knit family and community. Her father, Sidney, was a lay preacher at the Mission of Glad Tidings while her mother, Alice, kept the house clean and warm. Like her elder sister Ada, Esther was fascinated by literature, and while other girls of her age ran riot in the Street, Esther spent her evenings curled up with a book. But her safe world was shattered when Sid was killed during the Blitz on Manchester, Ada married, and Alice took to her bed. Esther was left alone with her mother and, over the years that followed, slotted easily into the role of faithful daughter and carer, avoiding promotion at work that might take her away from Weatherfield, ignoring romance and channelling any spare energy into helping her neighbours. As Christine Hardman at No.13 once said: 'For as long as I can remember it's been the fashion in Coronation Street – if you've got a problem tek it to Esther Hayes.'

When Alice died Esther was ashamed that she felt glad to be free to lead her own life at last. Shame was no stranger to Esther. She also worried (had she given Elsie Tanner the right advice on challenging a bailiff's order?), felt guilty (had she been right to splash out ten bob on that new hanky rather than darning her old one?) and concerned (she'd better

make an extra pie and give it to pensioner Albert Tatlock). She never entered the Rovers and always paid cash at the Corner Shop. This wasn't to say that she didn't enjoy herself: she was often out at the pictures or having a frothy coffee at Snapes Café on Rosamund Street. She had a wonderful dry sense of humour and those who took the trouble to get to know her – like Christine, or Kenneth Barlow – were seldom off her doorstep. But at night Esther was at her most vulnerable and lonely. Once, her wayward brother challenged her over why she stayed in the Street when she could so easily take a better job and climb the social ladder. Esther tried to make him understand that there was something worse than loneliness: 'Do you think I'm happy to be happy ever after in Coronation Street? Well, I'm not but I can't leave as I've left it too late. When I come back home, I come back to people I can talk to, people who'll ask me in. I'm lonely sometimes, but never desperately lonely – there's always someone. If I went away from here, there might be no one at all. As it is, I might not be content but I'm never completely alone.'

Overlooked by many local men as being 'too homely' or plain, Esther was engaged during the war but her fiancé was shot down coming home for the wedding. In the 1960s she harboured romantic ideas about her boss, Brian Foley, but they came to nothing.

Esther did move from the Street, in 1962, when she decided she deserved a few home comforts like an inside toilet. She rented a flat in nearby Moor Lane, taking Christine with her as a lodger, but often popped back to the Street. Her last appearance was at Emily Nugent's wedding, and it was there that she met another wedding guest, Mavis Riley. Emily and Mavis had met at the Mark Britain Mail Order Warehouse where they both worked as clerks. However, both Emily and Mavis were better known for serving the community behind shop counters.

Character Name:	EMILY BISHOP
Date of Birth:	18 October 1929
Husbands:	Ernest Bishop (1972–78)
	Arnold Swain (1980)
Parents:	James and Margaret Nugent

When we first met Emily Nugent, she spent her days running her own shop on Rosamund Street, selling baby linen, and her evenings and Sundays helping out at the Mission of Glad Tidings. The secretary of the Mission board was Leonard Swindley, a draper, who struggled to keep a firm hand on cantankerous caretaker Ena Sharples. By the end of 1961 Emily and Swindley had merged their shops and had been taken over then by the chain-store Gamma Garments, owned by Greek Niklos Papagopolous. Emily's working life was important to her and while others, such as Elsie Tanner or Christine Hardman, might take days off or be disrespectful to their bosses, Emily was a conscientious worker, taking on all chores with a willing spirit and believing that the customer was always right. Not that this won her any favours or approval from Swindley, who took her for granted. Emily stuck to her counter and to her job because she believed against all the odds that Swindley would one day ask for her hand in marriage.

Of course, he never did, so in the spring of 1964, a Leap Year, Emily fed her ideal man on Parma ham, veal escalopes with broccoli spears, and proposed: 'I suppose it's a fact of womankind . . . I look for permanence . . . We have each other but will we always? We share so much, I wonder that we don't share it all. Share our lives. Why don't we join our interests in nuptial agreement?'

After Swindley had had a chance to weigh up the pros and cons he decided that Emily would make a sound wife: 'Her loyalty and consistency have always been a mainstay of her character. I wonder if I have the right to spurn, the right to withhold what is within my power to give.'

No one was particularly surprised when, as they waited at the Mission hall to witness the union, Emily calmly told Jack Walker that she couldn't go through with it: 'I always wanted Mr Swindley. I used to look at him in the shop and imagine doing things for him . . . laughing at who should have the broken egg at breakfast and shouting at him – only joking sort of – for forgetting to take his library books back. Things like that. He doesn't want to get married, Mr Walker. Not to me. Not to *anybody*. It was just me. He probably wouldn't admit it, but we both know. There's got to be affection, you see. If there isn't . . . I'm right aren't I, Mr Walker?' It was a dignified non-wedding, with no passionate outbursts. Swindley went on the honeymoon weekend alone, telling Emily that he'd see her in the shop on Monday, business as usual.

James Nugent was a man not unlike Swindley in character – bossy, stubborn and self-opinionated. When his wife had died in childbirth, his elder daughter, Emily, had taken on running the home and looking after her siblings. She had stayed until the others had married and left home, which was when she then left Harrogate and moved to Weatherfield. Some years later, when James had a stroke Emily was faced with a dilemma: a holiday friend had offered her a job running his souvenir shop in Majorca and she had been packed and ready to go when she received the news of her father's illness. The residents urged Emily to leave James in the care of her sisters and to go and enjoy herself in the sun. They threw her a farewell party, presented her with a parasol and waved her on her way to the station and caught the Harrogate train but she knew she would follow her duty rather than her heart.

With Swindley gone and her father well again, Emily took over Gamma and reopened it as a trendy store selling finger-on-the-pulse clothes and accessories. To go with the new look, she underwent a change of image herself, swapping her smart woollen suit for flowery frocks. Inside, however, she remained true to herself. Returning from a shopping trip for a new outfit, she admitted to a crime that had hung over her for years: 'I'm passionate about coat hangers. I once even stole one from a hotel in Brittany. When I left I gave the maid a big tip and all the French postage stamps I had left over. It's something that's often risen up to trouble me since.'

With the new look came a new man, Hungarian demolition expert Miklos Zadic. The residents had grown used to seeing Emily romantically involved with sombre, trilby-hatted short, balding types and were stunned by tall, burly, handsome Miklos. Emily couldn't believe he was truly interested in her until he explained that he recognized in her a suppressed passion and rebellious spirit he had not seen since before the uprising in his beloved country. Miklos taught Emily to dance barefoot, to feel the rhythm of music inside her heart and not to constrict her long hair by always wearing it pinned up in a bun. When he offered a weekend of romance and passion in Newcastle Emily decided the time had come to shake off her shackles: 'Always responsible, always guaranteed to do the right thing. Good old Nugent, everybody's muggins. We can rely on her. Oh, they all did it. Mr Swindley, Mr Papagopolous. Father. I tell you, I'm sick of it. Sick to death of being a blasted human crutch.'

Ernest Gordon Bishop entered Emily's life in 1969 at his mother's funeral. Like Swindley before him, he was a lay preacher who owned his own shop, a photographic supplier's. But unlike Swindley he was a gentle, caring man, whom Emily recognized straight away as a kindred spirit. Like her, he railed against

"I'm passionate about coat hangers. I once even stole one from a hotel in Brittany."

EMILY BISHOP

injustice in society and, also like her, he was often knocked back by the world. Emily took a job as assistant in his shop and slowly, cautiously, the pair embarked on a courtship that led to an engagement, which thrilled Emily: 'I'm just very glad I'm marrying somebody who checks three times if they've locked up at night.' This time there were no second thoughts and Emily married her Mr Right. They bought No. 3 Coronation Street, and settled down to married life.

Like many couples marrying in middle age, the Bishops missed out on the binding experience of having children. They settled quickly into routine and familiarity: working and living together, they were in each other's pockets twenty-four hours a day. Emily was happy to cook and care for her husband but was annoyed when he objected to sharing the household chores – after all, she worked the same hours he did. When the business went into liquidation, Emily became the bread-

winner after taking a job as a hospital porter. There was a job available for Ernie at the hospital, too, but he turned it down. Instead he became the first house-husband in the Street, which led the female neighbours to offer Emily their congratulations.

Where Ernie was concerned Emily was highly jealous of other women. When singer Rita Littlewood employed him to accompany her on the piano, Emily feared their professional relationship would lead to an emotional entanglement – and she was furious when she discovered a stripper practising her act in the living room while Ernie played along on the piano for extra cash. The only time Emily had to fight for her man, though, was when Ernie took a job as wages clerk at Baldwin's Casuals and one of the machinists, Thelma James, sent him a Valentine. While Ernie worried about his admirer being a lonely woman in need of companionship, Emily cornered Thelma in the street: 'He sees you as the shy,

Emily looks daggers at Ernest as he complains she hasn't cut his toast into soldiers.

Fighting for the survival of the Red Rec. Spending the night up a tree gave Emily a new breath of life.

retiring, wallflower type. Whereas I see you as you really are. More of a Venus fly trap. Ernest happens to be the sort of person who'll go to nearly any lengths to avoid hurting somebody's feelings. I'm not. Not any more. So could I make it quite clear, once and for all, Miss James, that if this nonsense doesn't stop forthwith, our next conversation won't be half so polite?'

On the morning of 11 January 1978, two gunmen burst into Ernie's office at Baldwin's and demanded the wages. As he handed over the money their shotgun went off and Ernie was hit in the chest. He was rushed to hospital but died in the operating theatre. After only

five years of marriage, Emily was a widow but her life was far from empty. She continued with the hospital and other good causes, and eventually opened up a secretarial bureau with Deirdre Langton.

One of her first clients was pet-shop owner Arnold Swain. He was so taken with her accounting skills that he proposed to her, but Emily turned him down, much to Mavis's horror: 'Do you know how lucky you are, Emily Bishop? How fortunate? Well, obviously not!' Emily was bemused by her friend's reaction: 'Well, obviously it's nice to be asked.' At which point Mavis, full of woe that no one had ever asked for her hand, exploded, 'Nice? It's a miracle!' So jealous was she that when Emily changed her mind and agreed to become Mrs Swain, Mavis went on holiday rather than be a bridesmaid. However, three months later, she was present when Emily made the horrifying discovery that Arnold was a bigamist. He explained that his wife had left him and, out of shame, he had told everyone she'd died. Emily forced Arnold out of the house and out of her life. Having to explain to the police that she had married a bigamist was the most humiliating experience of her life.

After everything that had happened to Emily over the years, her closest friends were not surprised when she had a nervous breakdown. It came on slowly and only her lodger, Percy Sugden, saw her real pain and anguish. As she became forgetful and had mood swings he tried to alert her friends but they thought he was meddling in Emily's life. It was only after she was found wandering the streets in her slippers that she was admitted to hospital for treatment. Months later, with hindsight, Emily was able to talk about the experience with Mavis's husband Derek Wilton: 'You mustn't worry about me. I know I must seem rather confused and introverted just now. I just don't feel wonderfully spirited. Foolishly I'd invented a rosy future for myself but I was just setting myself up for the inevitable let-down. I don't mean to be self-pitying but in my experience the let-down is inevitable.'

Over the years Emily has shrugged off her naïvety and shyness. She's capable of standing up for herself and others, taking on issues such as wheel-clamping and the fight to save the trees on the Red Rec. She has even been known to hurl a brick through a window when her passions are aroused. When her nephew Geoffrey called her a 'protest virgin' early in 1997, Emily chose not to disillusion him. As she told Ken Barlow, 'He thinks I'm just his dotty aunt Em.'

Character Name:	MAVIS WILTON
Date of Birth:	7 April 1938
Husband:	Derek Wilton (1988–97)
Parents:	Tom and Margaret Riley

Like Emily before her, Mavis worked behind a shop counter too, as Rita Littlewood's assistant at the Kabin, a newspaper shop with a tiny café at the rear. Despite being the best of friends, Rita and Mavis were totally different in temperament: Rita was loud, gregarious and sexually confident while Mavis stood in her shadow, afraid of life and envious of Rita's ability to carry on even when life kicked her in the teeth: 'I like having Emily around as she's sensible, but you're fun. No matter how big a problem is, you can always see some laughter in it somewhere. It's a gift is that.' Their partnership at the shop lasted twenty-five years, longer than most Street marriages, and was built on a carefully structured foundation of respect and affection, which started the day Mavis was interviewed for the job. She felt that she had blown her chances by hiccuping throughout Rita's questioning but Rita instinctively knew that she was right.

Mavis was born in Weatherfield but brought up in Grange, where her teetotal parents ran an off-licence. She returned to her home town in 1969 to live with her auntie Edith and took secretarial and clerking jobs. It was while working at the mail-order warehouse that she met Emily, who had attended the same school. The two became friends and it was as such that Mavis was introduced to the Street's residents. She hit it off immediately with Jerry Booth, who shared her hesitant nature and could never bring himself to declare his feelings for her.

Mavis's aunt was a cantankerous old woman, who became bedridden after a stroke and a burden to Mavis, refusing to co-operate with the Social Services' home help. Mavis's cousin, Ethel, refused to take her turn in looking after their aunt, pointing out that as Mavis lived with her rent-free she had an obligation to look after her. Mavis agreed that it was her duty, but felt it unfair that she had to spend her evenings clearing up, fetching and carrying after long hours at the Kabin while Ethel, who didn't work, never lifted a finger. All Ethel did was sit with the old lady and join her in pointing out Mavis's shortcomings. Rita urged Mavis to stand up for her rights and made a point of keeping her late at work, to annoy Edith and Ethel. One evening, after being forced into some stock-taking, Mavis returned home to find that Edith had died of a heart-attack. Ethel accused Mavis of killing their aunt through neglect, and was horrified when the will was read and the house went to Mavis for 'her kindness and devoted care'. Mavis was thrilled until she learned that the property had been mortgaged years before and wasn't hers at all. It was at times like this that she was glad to be able to lean on her man, Derek Wilton.

For twelve years before he married her, Derek had been the man in Mavis's life. During their long courtship, they allowed misunderstanding to keep coming between them. They first met in 1976 when furniture salesman Derek called in at the Kabin for a cup of coffee (milk, one sugar). He was so taken by Mavis's service that he invited her out for a drink, and romance blossomed. Things were looking good for Mavis until the fateful day he took her for tea with his mother. Mrs Wilton took one look at her son's new 'friend' and made up her mind to split the pair up: 'I know she's nice. She's nice to the point of being a walking ice-cream sundae. She's also you in a tweed skirt. You're alike as two robins. Neither of you could decide what time of day it was in a roomful of clocks. You need somebody with a bit of spirit behind you. Not somebody to confuse you even more.' Derek protested that he had strong feelings for Mavis but the romance fizzled out. Other men were interested in Mavis, all of a similar type, passionate about their own interests in art and seeing the artist within Mavis, which they wanted to release. Victor Pendlebury, a potter, offered her a trial marriage in remote Saddleworth and Mavis was tempted but, as she told Emily: 'He's very Bohemian, the trouble is I'm not. It is an opportunity and I don't get many. It's the first time any man's actually asked me to live with him and he might be the last one who does!' In the end Mavis refused to share Victor's bed without a wedding ring.

Instead, she settled down to life with Harry, a budgie rescued from within her chimney-breast. She doted on the bird and was stunned when 'he' laid an egg. She quickly renamed her Harriet and carried the egg around with her in her bra in an attempt to incubate it until she discovered that the egg wouldn't hatch as it hadn't been fertilized.

After his mother's death Derek proposed to Mavis, and they planned to marry in September 1984. Mavis bought a new lilac two-piece suit with lace gloves, but on the morning of the wedding, as the guests gathered at the church, she broke down and told Rita she couldn't marry Derek. She had only

agreed to the proposal as she hadn't wanted to hurt him. She was sad to put him through the humiliation of being jilted, but her concern turned to outrage when she learned that he had not turned up either. It took another four years for Mavis and Derek to tie the knot, but during that time he married a domineering career-woman to gain promotion at work.

Like the Bishops before them, the Wiltons were middle-aged newly-weds with no hope of children. They were both used to their own company and had developed peculiar habits that annoyed the other. They had shared interests – gardening, nature, the Lakes, literature (*Wuthering Heights* was *their* book) and music. Both were delighted when a fox, which they named Freddie, took to appearing in their back garden. When the other residents planned a fox hunt, both Wiltons acted as decoys to save their friend. They also enjoyed sharing a routine: 'I love this time of day. When I'm sitting here in my own little home, with my own wonderful little hubby, and we talk about the issues of the day and discuss world affairs and generally just snuggle.' It didn't seem to matter that the neighbours thought them a bit of a joke: they were a strong unit. A couple of times, though, the good ship *Wilton* went through stormy waters, and Mavis once left Derek after he had accused her of infidelity with a fellow night-school art student, but they rode the storm. On one occasion, a little drunk, Derek issued Mavis with a warning on the signals she gave out to other members of the opposite sex: 'You know, I really think we ought to wrap you in pink cotton wool. You're too delicate, too innocent a creature to be allowed to roam at will in this nasty, brutish world. You have a lot in common with Marilyn Monroe – you're not aware of the power of your sexuality . . . a smile, a twinkle in your blue eyes, and passions are aroused, Mavis.' Mavis secretly loved the thought of herself as a Jezebel, captivating men's hearts, like a character from a Bette

~

"I know she's nice. She's nice to the point of being a walking ice-cream sundae. She's also you in a tweed skirt."

DEREK WILTON'S
MOTHER ON
MEETING MAVIS
FOR THE
FIRST TIME

~

Davis film. When Derek died suddenly, in his car of a heart-attack, Mavis realized, perhaps for the first time, just how much she and Derek had loved and complemented each other. At his funeral, she turned on the mourners: 'Perhaps you thought us figures of fun. Well, it doesn't matter to me. Not a bit. Because I loved him. And I know he loved me.'

Over the years Mavis became quite shrewish, eager for a gossip with Rita and unwittingly putting others down, including Emily. Her mouth tightened and she lost the generosity in her nature. 'Not many people have been let down in life as much as I have' seems to sum Mavis up: she was continually let down by men, friends and herself.

A romantic soul, she dabbled with the arts, writing a novel *Song of a Scarlet Summer* (which was rejected by the publishers) and winning a radio competition with her short story 'A Night To Forget'. When it was read over the radio Mavis glowed with pride and ignored Albert Tatlock's remark, 'It's a load of tripe.' Decorator Maurice Dodds saw in Mavis a fellow artist and begged her to allow him to paint her in the nude. Rita was struck dumb with surprise when Mavis agreed, explaining that this was art, not pornography, but at the last moment she lost her nerve.

It is in the nature of the stay-at-home to put others' feelings before their own, and Mavis was no exception. In 1980 she suffered disturbing phone calls from a mystery man, who frightened her by explaining what he wanted to do with her and begged her to meet him. She called in the police, who encouraged her to agree to meet the caller under police surveillance. The idea of espionage appealed to her but she feared setting up the meeting as she worried about what would happen to the man when he was caught.

Having been persuaded that it was her duty to help catch the foul-mouthed beast, Mavis arranged to meet him at the shopping precinct and waited at the given time, watched by a number of policemen. When Eddie Yeats saw Mavis and stopped for a chat, he was stunned to be jumped by six coppers who dragged him, protesting, into a police van while Mavis tried in vain to make them release him. The caller must have been watching the scene because he never called again – much to Mavis's disappointment. She admitted to Rita that she'd actually quite liked his voice. Rita couldn't believe her ears: 'You're not safe to be out on the streets, you. Take my advice and stay at home!'

There has to be more to life than this. For a woman who always fantasized about adventure and romance marriage to Derek had little high points.

INDEPENDENTS

"I know men think that women were created to cook for 'em and clear up after 'em and darn their socks but I'm not one of them women, mate."

ANGIE FREEMAN

They strike out on their own, centre their energies and often run their own businesses. When the Street was built in 1902 they were unheard of in a street where the main breadwinner was male and his wife and daughters bowed to him in all things. Two world wars changed all that for the Weatherfield women and, since the early sixties, we have seen many independent, clear-minded women taking charge of their own destinies with only romantic waves causing their boats to rock. These women have a huge support system and often appear hard-faced, especially when dealing in business circles. They are often heard to say they can cope without men, but when involved in relationships they become passionate and behave like the frivolous girls they once were. They tend to have strained relationships with their mothers, who normally long for their daughters to settle down with Mr Right. Relations with fathers tend to be closer, with the daughter aspiring to make him proud and being frustrated when he fails to recognize success.

Character Name:	CHRISTINE APPLEBY
Date of Birth:	19 April 1939
Husband:	Colin Appleby (1962–)
Parents:	George and May Hardman

Christine was the first Street girl to strike out on her own and demand more than her mother's lot.

Christine Hardman's father died when she was in her late teens, in 1956. He had run a grocery business and it was only after his death that Christine and her mother, May, discovered he had left behind a tangled mess of debt. May was heartbroken when Christine forced her to sell the business and her detached home to return to renting No.13 Coronation Street, a house they had left in 1950. Christine slipped back easily into life on the Street and took an undemanding job as a machinist at the raincoat factory. May, however, could not adjust so easily and had a breakdown. She underwent psychological treatment after being found screaming on the cobbles at night and returned home only to die of a brain tumour. Christine felt guilty about her mother's death, because she had never believed in her mother's headaches.

Beautiful Christine led the life of a drudge and often felt like the Cinderella of the Street. At the time of her mother's death she was twenty-one and the world was open before her. She could go anywhere, do anything, be anyone she wanted, but she felt trapped in the Street and the factory, whose walls towered over her house. It was a miserable existence but Christine remained chirpy and cheerful, drinking in the Rovers with pals, laughing with Elsie Tanner over the back-yard wall and attracting the attention of young men. While other girls might have moved in with older relatives, Christine clung to her independence, enjoying her own company. Men came and went, and some, such as local plumber Joe Makinson, wanted to marry her. Christine realized though, that marriage to the likes of Joe would take her no further than her front doorstep: 'I was born round 'ere, I live round 'ere, but I ain't gonna die round 'ere.' Joe couldn't understand her attitude: he was hard-working, would some day earn enough to buy a little house; she'd be able to give up working and look after their children. But domesticity held no allure for Christine and she finished with Joe – and every other lad who offered the same stability.

Eventually Christine herself had a breakdown. She climbed on to the factory roof and looked over Weatherfield, to the cemetery where her parents shared a grave, to Bessie Street Infant's where she'd had her first kiss, and down to the rooftops of Coronation

Street. It was her old schoolfriend Kenneth Barlow who talked her down, making her see that death wasn't the answer and that she had friends. Most of them, however, didn't know how to cope with her and she was regarded as a loose cannon by the factory girls because she wasn't interested in going down the Palais, or gossiping about lads or even the latest tunes. They were stunned when, just after her rooftop exploits, Christine eloped to London with sales rep Colin Appleby, whom she'd known only for a week, leaving the Street without a backward glance.

Four months later she returned. Colin had been killed in a car crash and Christine came back to her roots, like a wounded animal. She moved into No.11 as Elsie Tanner's lodger, and took a job alongside Elsie at the Slightly Better Dress Department in the department store Miami Modes. The neighbours were sympathetic, but Christine felt cornered by their concern: most had known her since birth and she felt as if her identity as a wife had been snatched from her.

Then Frank Barlow, Kenneth's father, from No. 3 started taking her out for drinks and on visits to the cinema. He fell for her in a big way, and although the attraction wasn't mutual, Christine had nothing else to occupy herself with so she did not discourage him. It wasn't long before he produced an engagement ring and booked the church for a May wedding. Christine allowed herself to be carried along with his plans: Frank had become a father figure to her. Eventually, with just two weeks left before the planned wedding, she told him she couldn't marry him, or anyone else: she would never marry again as no one would be able to cope with her: 'I trap myself. I run into traps. I should stand still. But I run on roofs, away from men, towards men. Away from myself, mainly. Why do people never hit me for what I do to 'em? They should hit me more.'

While Frank retired to lick his wounds,

Christine moved out of Coronation Street and into Esther Hayes's nearby flat. She was promoted at work to supervisor and was moved to the Southampton branch, after attempting to get her old friend Elsie the sack for bad time-keeping. She had no regrets about leaving Weatherfield and decided to concentrate on her career rather than affairs of the heart.

Character Name:	STEPHANIE LAURA BARNES
Date of Birth:	11 June 1965 (1990–93)
Husband:	Des Barnes
Children:	Matthew (1995)
Parents:	Maurice and Carrie Jones

There was a gap of nearly thirty years before another truly independent woman lived on the Street, in the shape of Stephanie Barnes. Throughout the 1990s more Street women have striven to be independent in relationships and business than at any other time. Of course, like their sixties, seventies and eighties sisters, they have entered love affairs – which have often ended in heartache and tears – but have struggled to show that a woman is equal to a man in both workplace and home.

We first met Steph on her wedding day, when she arrived with her groom, Des, after their reception, at their new home. Steph was close to her father, Maurice Jones, the property developer who had built the new houses on the even-numbered side of the Street. He gave the couple No. 6 at cost price as a wedding present. Steph certainly started married life as she meant to continue. As Des attempted to carry her over the threshold he bashed her head on the door post: she cursed him loudly and locked him out of their new home.

Steph was a fun-loving young woman, who

"I was born round 'ere, I live round 'ere, but I ain't gonna die round 'ere."

CHRISTINE APPLEBY

Steph Barnes was a woman of aspirations. Here she outlines her plans for the garden to bemused husband Des.

enjoyed flirting and using her sexuality to cause trouble for others. In a bet with Des she caused trouble between the Websters by making a play for Kevin, getting him drunk and shaving off his moustache. She thought the escapade a laugh, but she did not appreciate it when the tables were turned on her, and Kevin's wife, Sally, told her that Des had made a pass at her. Furious, Steph refused to believe Des's pleas of innocence and threw him out.

During the day Steph worked behind a perfume counter at a department store in town but at night she joined a promotion company, helping to sell 'Pomme Delight' a new brand of cider. Des didn't like Steph spending her evenings in crowded pubs being leered at by other men as she wandered around in a skintight costume inviting customers to taste her wares, but Steph refused to be dictated to: 'For the last time, I won't be told what I should and shouldn't do. When we got married you agreed that we were both entitled to have fun. I'm a fully grown woman. I can handle half-cut louts in pubs. That's how we met, remember?' During a promotion at the Rovers she started a striptease in front of all the regulars when Des ordered her to get out of the costume and give up her job.

The Barnes' relationship often seemed like a merry-go-round, made up of violent rows and passionate reconciliations. Steph often led the marriage as Des pampered the child in him and never seemed to grow up. The rowing hurt Steph more than she cared to show but Des shrugged off confrontational situations. Unlike meeker female residents, Steph demanded equality in her home and refused to do all the housework. When Des refused point-blank to wash up Steph broke every plate in the house, and was even angrier when Des's solution was to buy throwaway paper plates and plastic cups. She refused to back off from the conflict even though she was aware that the rows were driving them further apart: 'What else can I do with a fella like Des. Stubborn, stupid, self-centred. If I buckled now, do you think he'd ever let me forget it? Never. And I'd hate myself for the rest of my life.' Eventually the rows ended when they employed Phyllis Pearce as their housekeeper, but Steph was determined to have the last say: 'I still think you've been behaving like an overgrown schoolkid. And whatever daft scheme you come up with next to try to assert your masculine superiority, I promise you I'll top it. With knobs on.'

One thing that scared Steph was Des's assertion that a baby would help him to grow up and end all their problems. She knew she wasn't ready for motherhood and resented the way Des took it for granted that every woman yearned for a child. Instead, she encouraged him to spend his time repairing and working on an old boat he had bought and stuck in the back garden. Des threw himself into it and Steph found herself neglected. Rather than join him in it or enjoy his contentment, she allowed herself to fall into an affair with architect Simon Beatty. Des didn't seem to notice that she was spending more evenings out with friends than usual and for two months the affair dominated Steph's life. By the time Des found out, Steph had decided to leave him. At this point Des sprang to life, pleading with her to stay. When she refused, he blew up the boat, allowing her – just for a few seconds – to believe he had killed himself. After he'd slashed her suitcases, Steph announced she couldn't take any more and went.

Life with Simon wasn't a bed of roses and Steph drifted around Manchester, changing jobs and bed partners as she embarked on a downwards spiral. It was while she was at her lowest – living in a grotty bedsit and working at a burger bar – that Des entered her life again. She was pregnant, but she had finished with the baby's father. Des took pity on her and gave her the deposit for a better flat and Steph remembered why she'd fallen for him in the first place. Hopes stirred that he would take her back but Des read her mind and told her he wouldn't be able to love her child and he believed that a baby needed two loving parents. He hasn't heard from her since.

Character Name:	ANGELA FREEMAN
Date of Birth:	20 June 1967
Parents:	Geoffrey and Ann Freeman

Angie Freeman dumped herself at No.7 Coronation Street in 1990. She was a northerner who had been brought up in Canterbury, returning to Manchester as a fashion student at the Poly. She moved in to lodge at No. 7, paying rent to Rita Fairclough, and shared the house with Curly Watts, feeling that he was a man she could trust not to make advances towards her. Curly came fresh from lodging with the Duckworths at No. 9, and Vera was affronted that he should leave her comfy home to live with Angie: 'Who's going to do your cooking? 'Cause she won't. You only have to look at her to know she's never peeled a spud in her life!'

For a short while Angie and Curly rattled along nicely at No.7 until the fateful day when, after discovering someone had stolen all her designs, she drank too much red wine and fell into bed with him. Curly was keen to develop a relationship but the thought horri-

> *"For the last time, I won't be told what I should and shouldn't do. When we got married you agreed that we were both entitled to have fun. I'm a fully grown woman. I can handle half-cut louts in pubs. That's how we met, remember?"*
>
> STEPH BARNES

Curly Watts remained the one stable man in Angie's chaotic and jet-setting life. Unfortunately she could never return his love.

because this isn't my house. This house is now owned by a man. A weak, pathetic man. And like most weak, pathetic men, he quite likes having a bimbo around the place. Now have you got that? 'Cause I'll write it down for you if you like.'

After she graduated, Angie took a job at Onyx, Hanif Rupparell's fashion house and embarked on a love affair with builder Neil Mitchell. Neil made her laugh, satisfied her passions and produced great lasagne, but he was obsessed with his ex-wife Denise Osbourne. He took to following her around and pestering her and her boyfriend, which complicated matters for Angie as Denise was dating Hanif. To escape clinging Curly, and to give her relationship with Neil a chance, Angie rented the flat over Jim's Café but soon realized that Neil was not as committed as she had hoped. At her flat-warming party he attacked Hanif over Denise, and Angie decided she'd had enough. She threw his belongings into his concrete mixer and shut herself away so no one would see her heartbreak.

Fed up with Weatherfield, Angie set off for pastures new in Mexico, where she hoped to research native designs. For four years she travelled the world, taking up short-term work contracts and drifting into and out of relationships, fearful of another big split.

In 1997 she returned to Coronation Street and rented Des's house where she allowed mechanic Chris Collins into her bed while insisting he maintained his own bedroom at the back of the house. The ten-year age gap between herself and Chris bothered Angie but she told herself it wasn't a meaningful relationship leading to marriage and babies, just sex and laughs over a chicken tikka take-away.

Using her new designs for underwear, she started up a business with Mike Baldwin called Underworld, but her hopes of designing sensual undies for sophisticated people were put on hold when the business's biggest order came from the Dutch army. Then Chris

fied Angie, who viewed Curly as a good mate but a no-go area on the sex front. When he persisted she embarked on a passionate affair with Des Barnes to prove to Curly that he wasn't her type of man. She started work behind the bar of the Rovers but lost her job when she poured a pint over Des and threw her shoes across the bar at Raquel Wolstenhulme whom she discovered had replaced her in Des's bed. After Curly bought No.7 from Rita, Angie was horrified when he invited homeless Raquel to move in with them. In the confrontation that followed, Raquel was left in no doubt about Angie's feelings towards her: 'I wish you weren't here, Raquel, but I can't do anything about it admitted that he did not take her career seriously and Angie felt that, like Mike, he was belittling her talents. She finished with him and was annoyed when he didn't seem to take the rejection too badly.

Partnership with Michael Vernon Baldwin was a venture for a woman of spirit and ambition: he is patronizing and chauvinistic, and encourages business ties with like-minded souls. When buyer George Dixon threatened to withhold an order unless Angie prostituted herself, Mike was amazed that she could refuse and had even told George where to stick his order. Angie fought all the time to remind Mike that she was his partner and not an employee.

After less than a year Angie had enough of Mike's business practises and left to join a London firm.

Character Name:	DENISE OSBOURNE
Date of Birth:	1 December 1955
Husbands:	Frank Knight (1984–89)
	Neil Mitchell (1990–94)
Children:	Daniel (1995)
Parents:	Roy and Irene Osbourne

Around the time Angie left for Mexico, Neil Mitchell left Weatherfield for Australia, and his ex-wife Denise Osbourne heaved a huge sigh of relief. She had moved to Coronation Street after separating from him in 1992. He had been her second husband and their brief marriage had been based mainly on sex and the fact that he had rescued her from her first disastrous union with an older man. The split with Neil was amicable – he even lent her £3,000 to start up her own hair salon at No. 2 Coronation Street.

As soon as she'd landed in the Street,

Denise attracted the attentions of the local menfolk and, on discovering that three had bet on who could bed her first, she invited them all, separately, to her flat. When each arrived, they were stunned to find not only the others present but also their womenfolk.

Through Angie, whom she recognized as a kindred spirit, Denise met Hanif Rupparell and fell for his Asian good looks. She enjoyed weekends away in his sports car and loved being wined and dined in exclusive restaurants. She had promised herself not to get involved with another man so soon after Neil but the warning signs came too late: 'I don't trust myself to make decisions any more. I've lost faith in myself. I've had two unhappy marriages. And now I'm happier than I've ever been. I like my independence but I know I love him.'

Denise was stunned when Hanif's mother confronted her and informed her bitterly that her son's arranged marriage had had to be cancelled. Denise was thrilled by this but her delight turned to dismay when Hanif admitted he'd used her as an excuse to get out of his marriage and did not love her.

During her affair with Hanif, Neil made a complete nuisance of himself, trailing them, shouting abuse at them and pleading with Denise to give their marriage a second chance. Denise was adamant that Neil was in the past but when he finally accepted this he demanded back his loan. Desperate to pay him off, Denise asked Hanif for the money but he refused: she was a dangerous investment as her temperament was too volatile. Denise threw a glass of wine over his expensive jacket.

Financial help came in the unexpected shape of cabbie Don Brennan, who gave her the money to repay Neil. Denise was grateful to him and set up monthly repayments. She had no idea that Don had fallen obsessively in love with her. Over two months she was subjected to a series of phone calls in which the caller never spoke. At first she shrugged it off but after a while she felt she was being watched and that the caller meant her harm. She turned to Hanif for help, and he used his contacts to supply her with a list showing all the telephone numbers that had dialled hers. She recognized one number over and over again: the Brennans'. At once she confronted Don's wife, Ivy, accusing her of being warped with jealousy but Don admitted that it had been he who had made the calls: he had done it so that she would reach out to him, her friend, for comfort; to be with her and near her was all he lived for as he loved her so much. Denise was sickened by this and threatened Don with the police if he came near her again.

The allure of the Independent woman. The menfolk were attracted to Denise like iron filings when she moved into the Street.

For a while she stayed clear of men, devoting herself to building up her business, and repaying Don's money so that he would no longer have any hold over her. She took on more staff – Fiona Middleton and Jon Welch – and, for a short while, lived peacefully. Her determination to avoid relationships backfired when she became too close to Jon and he reacted violently when she refused to go to bed with him. 'I've watched you doing this and I still leave myself wide open. Leading yourself on, all your usual bag of tricks. Then when the poor sucker bites, wham, it's stick-the-knife-in time. You're right, you are sick.'

Her next romance started by trying to guess a client's age, finished with heartbreak and left her with a son. Denise was forced to

admit that Ken Barlow looked very good for fifty-five. He was unlike the sort of men she usually found herself attracted to: he wasn't passionate or sexy, he was respectable and a gentleman. Rather than wining, dining and discoing, Ken's courtship tactics included long walks in the country, open fires and poetry. Despite herself, Denise fell for his olde-worlde charm and decided it was perhaps time she settled for the faithful, caring sort. The discovery that she was pregnant caused her to reassess her life. Of course, Ken offered marriage, a home and a future together, but deep down Denise knew that she could never be happy as Mrs Barlow, that part of her would always yearn for freedom and independence: 'I was lonely. Felt a total failure relationship-wise. I wanted something more. Passion and cuddles. A man who was a friend and a lover. But that soulmate isn't Ken. Sometimes when I'm with him I'm a helluva lot lonelier than I ever was on my own.'

Ken wasn't pleased with Denise's unconventional attitude towards the future of their child and grew angry when she told him that she was preparing to bring the baby up without his input or influence. When he made too many demands, she left to stay with her sister Alison in Macclesfield. Ken might have been out of the picture but Alison's husband, Brian Dunkley, wasn't. Before he'd married Alison, he had had a minor flirtation with Denise, which had resulted in a one-night stand that they both agreed was best forgotten. But, with mother-to-be glowing Denise in his house, Brian was drawn to her again and Denise was still attracted to him. Petrified of the repercussions of an affair, she returned to Weatherfield for the birth of her son, Daniel Albert, at which Ken was present.

After Daniel's birth Denise realized he needed a stable environment in which to grow up and took steps towards a reconciliation with Ken. 'I took a long hard look at Denise Osbourne, career woman. And I saw a terri-

fied single mum on the edge of middle-age. No-one to give a damn and it terrified me.'

The 'family' moved into No.1 Coronation Street, where Denise made her mark by rag painting the living-room walls. Outwardly all was stable and happy, but Denise had a secret: Brian had pursued her and they had become lovers. She had kept on her old flat over the salon, where Brian, an accountant, would meet her to 'go over the books'. Guilt made her try to break it off but Brian announced that he was falling in love with her. Then Denise ended the affair, saying that she had no intention of taking him from her sister. To prove to Brian that she was sincere, she proposed to Ken. But Brian shattered everything by telling Ken that he was Denise's lover. Ken reacted violently: he hit Brian and threw out Denise, telling her she wasn't fit to be near his son. Brian left the distraught Alison and offered Denise a new life with him. She knew that Ken was right, that she had nothing to offer Daniel, so she left to live with her brother-in-law.

Months later, after Ken had built a secure life around Daniel, Denise swooped in to snatch him back. She knew that as she and Ken were not married she had absolute rights over the baby but even so she had to lie during the custody battle that followed, telling the judge that she'd always told Ken she'd be back for the child.

Denise sold the salon to Fiona and took Daniel to live with Brian in Scotland, telling Ken she wanted no maintenance payments from him but offering him reasonable access to his son. It wasn't long before Ken tired of making the long journey north to see him. Daniel grew to see his father as a stranger and Brian as his daddy. Denise knew she had broken the rules, had lied, cheated and hurt those close to her, but she also felt she had done what she'd had to do to keep her sanity and to provide her child with the best chance he could have in life.

> *"I took a long hard look at Denise Osbourne, career woman. And I saw a terrified single mum on the edge of middle-age. No one to give a damn and it terrified me."*
>
> DENISE OSBOURNE

Character Name:	FIONA JOY MIDDLETON
Date of Birth:	2 December 1975
Children:	Morgan (1998)
Parents:	Clive and Pam Middleton

When Denise left Weatherfield for a new life, her assistant, twenty-year-old Fiona Middleton, borrowed money from her brother Lee to buy the salon from her. She had arrived in the Street a month after Denise had opened it and assisted her while working for her stylist's diploma.

As soon as Fiona saw Steve McDonald she was attracted to him and the stories of his bad ways made him all the more appealing. It wasn't that she was attracted to low-life, but she agreed with Denise that a man of adventure and spark was better for a girl than a devoted puppy. To her amazement, Steve asked her out and, before long, they were considered an item. However, Fiona refused to allow him to take her for granted and was annoyed when he insisted on following her to Tenerife where she was holidaying with schoolfriends. Sick of trying to explain that she had no intention of flinging herself headlong into a holiday romance, she poured a pint of beer over him.

After her holiday, Fiona moved into Steve's plush quayside flat, but in spite of the dishwasher, the stereo system and the low lighting, she found it uncomfortable and was happier when they moved into the tiny flat over Jim's Café: Steve's gambling debts had mounted up and they needed somewhere cheaper to live. The new flat heralded a new start for the couple and Fiona was happy to treat it as their first home, cooking cheap meals to help Steve economize. What she didn't know until later was that Steve was continuing to run up debts across Weatherfield as his gambling addiction worsened.

Fiona was aware of Steve's previous involvement with 'Miss Money Knickers' – Vicky Arden, an orphan due to come into a fortune when she reached eighteen. Vicky was also attracted to Steve and they had once been lovers, which caused Fiona much anxiety when Vicky started to show an interest in Steve's T-shirt business. Shortly after Vicky's eighteenth birthday, when Steve admitted to Fiona that he'd gone into partnership with his ex-girlfriend, Fiona hit the roof. Steve swore that his interest in Vicky was purely professional but Fiona knew that Vicky spent more time with Steve than she did – and that hurt. What also hurt was the heavy who came round to the flat and threatened to beat her up if Steve didn't pay his debts. Stunned by the way Steve shrugged off the threat then went to borrow more money from Vicky, Fiona threw him out of their flat, telling him they were finished.

Having rid herself of Steve, Fiona concentrated on working at the salon, where Denise had made her manageress. They took on her old schoolfriend Maxine Heavey as an assistant, and Fiona attempted to introduce some light-hearted fun into her life, sharing the flat with Maxine and going out clubbing. But the irresponsible young thing she had been at sixteen had gone for good: while Maxine came home with the milk Fiona always got her full eight hours. Hard work and her talent with scissors gave Fiona the courage to buy the salon and she threw a grand opening in the hope that her train-driving father, Clive, would show the approval she had always longed for but had never received. In the event he came late and ignored his daughter's achievements.

Local theatrical agent Alec Gilroy caused Fiona some amusement when he announced that she had a great singing voice and offered to turn her into the next Shirley Bassey, but she went along with the pipe-dream and found herself belting out numbers in a succession of working men's clubs. The

enterprise wasn't a huge success but it did one thing for Fiona: it introduced her to Alan McKenna.

Alan was a tall, good-looking policeman, who drew attention to himself by dealing with some drunks who heckled Fiona's performance. He invited her out for a drink and, cautiously, Fiona lowered her defences and allowed Alan into her life. He was charming, good company, had a wicked sense of humour and was a great lover, but he was also a possessive bully. Fiona was troubled by his jealousy of Steve – even though Steve was now serving a prison sentence in Strangeways – and that she always had to be at Alan's beck and call but was not allowed to make any demands on his time: his work was always far more important than hers.

Shortly after Alan had moved into Fiona's flat, Steve finished his sentence and returned to the Street. Fiona soon found that if she stopped to pass the time of day with Steve Alan saw this as a betrayal. Eventually she challenged Alan when Steve told her how Alan had threatened to have him arrested if he pestered her in the future. But Alan's jealousy ate away at him to such an extent that Fiona decided she couldn't carry on with the relationship. He moved out and, while Steve celebrated, Fiona reached out blindly for comfort. Unfortunately, Steve's father Jim was at hand and responded by taking her to bed. The next day, deeply ashamed, Fiona made it clear to Jim that she regretted the encounter and was horrified when he insisted that he was falling in love with her.

Alan reacted badly to the news that Fiona had slept with the father of her ex-boyfriend, although she was quick to assure him he was definitely the father of her unborn baby.

Reconciliation and eventual engagement with Alan saw Jim off but relief turned to despair when Fiona discovered she was pregnant and couldn't be sure who the father was. She begged Jim to reassure her that his vasectomy had worked, and continued to plan her wedding to Alan. Jim told her that regrettably the baby couldn't be his, and Fiona was relieved that one nightmare was over. The other was that Alan might find out about her night with Jim.

In the event it was Jim who broke the news to him. Fiona and Alan were in church at the time – at their wedding, surrounded by all their family and friends. Jim burst in as they were making their vows and pleaded drunkenly with Fiona not to go through with 'the charade'. The priest ushered the couple into the vestry, and it was there that Fiona told Alan everything that had happened. He cancelled the wedding and accused her of being a whore.

Weeks later, looking back, Fiona admitted that Jim had done her a favour in getting her out of marrying Alan: she would have been frightened of him all her life. However, at the time, it felt as if her whole life had been turned upside down, especially when Jim's wife Liz informed the whole Street why Alan had jilted her.

Alone in the flat over the salon, Fiona felt well rid of Alan, Jim and Steve but when the baby started to arrive, five weeks prematurely, it was Steve she clung to as he drove her to the hospital and waited in the 'expectant father's' room while she gave birth to her son, Morgan. Alan refused to see his child and Fiona had been surprised by the realization that it was Steve with whom she wanted to share her life. Steve moved into the salon flat and tried hard to be a good father to Morgan, but Fiona continued to feel uncomfortable living across the street from Jim, knowing that his feelings for her remained the same, even though she was living with his son.

"I'm not staying here! It's all so ugly. It smells of beer and cigarette smoke."

VICKY AT THE THOUGHT OF MOVING TO THE ROVERS RETURN

Character Name:	VICTORIA FRANCES MCDONALD
Date of Birth:	25 November 1976
Husband:	Steve McDonald (1995–96)
Parents:	Tim and Sandra Arden

One lady who would warn Fiona against any further involvement with Steve McDonald is his wife, Vicky, now living in Switzerland where she is studying hotel management. Although their marriage broke up when she was just nineteen, Steve had put her through enough heartache to last a lifetime. Their relationship began when Vicky came to live with her grandfather, Alec Gilroy, at the Rovers Return. Vicky had grown up in a luxurious home in an affluent Cheshire town. Her father, Tim, was a successful solicitor and her mother, Sandra, a keen society hostess. Vicky had a horse, and a secure childhood, which was blown apart when her parents were killed in a car crash, leaving her an orphan at fourteen. Alec was her only relative, but Vicky was horrified at the thought of swapping her lovely home for the dingy back-street pub and demanded to live with friends: 'I'm not staying here! It's all so ugly. It smells of beer and cigarette smoke. Mummy wouldn't allow anyone to smoke in the house.' Her pleas were ignored and she lived at the Rovers during her holidays.

As far as Victoria was concerned, the Street's only salvation was Steve McDonald at No.11. She fell for him straight away, using her wealthy allowance as a bait to interest him. Right from the start, she knew money was important to him but kidded herself that he also liked her too. On her sixteenth birthday she skipped school to spend the night with him in a hotel, lost her virginity and decided that he was the man for her.

Alec was horrified by Vicky's romance with Steve, seeing him as a gold-digger and a rogue. He tried hard to show her that Steve was seeing other girls behind her back, but Vicky accused him of interfering and told him to stay out of her love-life.

When Steve moved in with Fiona Middleton, Vicky was indignant and tried to hit back by bringing a boyfriend to stay at the Rovers. She was too young to see that Steve's indifference wasn't masking deep longings. When she left school without any qualifications – pointing out to Alec's wife Bet that an expensive education couldn't help you if you weren't clever – she relaxed into her £240,000 inheritance.

As soon as she had the money in the bank, Steve was trying to interest her in investing in his print business. Vicky agreed to put up the cash he needed but on the condition that she became a partner in the business. Steve was forced to accept, and from then on it was only a matter of time before Fiona threw him out, upset that he was living on Vicky's fortune.

Vicky helped Steve celebrate his twenty-first birthday by seducing him and proposing to him. He accepted, but Alec was deeply alarmed and tried to buy him off. Steve, of course, wasn't going to take £5,000 when a quarter of a million was at stake. The couple eloped and married in St Lucia.

Back in Weatherfield Vicky watched as her fortune dwindled – a quayside flat, clothes for Steve, a car for Steve, with gym membership for them both and expensive meals out – but she didn't mind because she was in love. It wasn't long, though, before Steve started to show his true colours: he had been involved in passing on stolen whisky and used Vicky to bribe his supplier, Malcolm Fox, into keeping him out of a court case. Fox kept the money and cleared Steve, but Fox's estranged wife reported them all to the police. This time it wasn't just Steve who was arrested but Vicky too.

Vicky discovered just how much she meant to husband Steve when he asked her to take the blame for a crime he'd committed.

Alec made Vicky see that she was married to a scoundrel, and in their court case she gave evidence that cleared her name and sent Steve to prison for two years. Gathering what funds she had left, Vicky fled England for Switzerland and a new life.

Character Name:	SAMANTHA FAILSWORTH
Date of Birth:	5 March 1976
Husband:	Richie Fitzgerald (1996–)
Parents:	Clive and Marjorie Failsworth

From the moment that Samantha Failsworth appeared behind the Rovers bar the residents fell into two camps: the men lusted after her and the women tried to figure out why she hid behind a hard, cool shell. What no one knew until she had been around for over a year was that Samantha was busy re-creating herself. She had been born

A happy picture before Samantha started to scheme and lie to Des.

into a wealthy family in leafy Cheshire and her life had been full of privilege, which she had taken for granted, until at the age of sixteen, she was raped by her tennis coach, a family friend. After that she became withdrawn, and escaped home after A Levels to study in Manchester where she fell for barman Richie Fitzgerald. After knowing him only a few weeks, she married him. It was a disaster: she couldn't bring herself to sleep with him and ran away after two days. She arrived in Weatherfield, took bar work and hoped that no one from the past would track her down.

She moved into No.7 Coronation Street, renting from Curly Watts, spent her spare time tinkering with her motor-bike and became attracted to bookie Sean Skinner, but laid down her own rules of courtship: no kissing, no fondling, just walks in the country and plenty of 'friendship'. Sean was willing enough to go along with this, believing he could melt the ice maiden, and Samantha tried hard to give herself to him: she even attempted to drink herself into sleeping with him but Sean was insulted. Eventually he had had enough and finished with her, telling her she was a frigid tease.

Samantha worried about the way men leered at her and assumed that she must be encouraging them. Des Barnes was one of many, and his reputation as a womanizer was famous. Samantha was attracted to him, though, and when he offered a no-strings relationship she agreed. Shortly afterwards she heard neighbour Leanne Battersby screaming as two lads tried to rape her. Samantha sprang to her aid with a length of lead piping but the incident brought back the past in vivid detail. Samantha broke down and told Des everything. It was the first time ever that she had spoken of the rape and Des was so supportive that she was able to face her parents and tell them about it.

Slowly Samantha and Des moved into a sexual relationship, but Richie tracked her down and pleaded with her to give their marriage a chance. Samantha was tempted as she felt guilty about him, but in her heart she knew Des was the one for her. She moved in with Des and looked forward to a happy future with him. All that was spoilt when he started talking about marriage and gave her an engagement ring. Samantha accepted it but she felt unprepared for marriage to Des, or anyone else. Overnight Samantha turned into a scheming monster by dragging Richie into the situation by begging him to block their divorce. When that plan backfired she began an affair with mechanic Chris Collins but was devastated when he cast her over and Des washed his hands of her when he found out about the affair. When Des started seeing her friend Natalie Horrocks Samantha did all she could to break them up by announcing she was pregnant with Des's baby and threatening an abortion if he didn't take her back. He was happy to go along with her plans but then she told him she wasn't pregnant, while telling everyone else she'd miscarried. Samantha was eventually run out of town but not before telling Des she was pregnant and that he'd never know what would happen to his child.

Character Name:	JUDY MALLETT
Date of Birth:	14 August 1971
Husband:	Gary Mallett (1993–)
Mother:	Joyce Smedley

When Samantha first moved into the Street she made an instant enemy of Judy Mallett, who assumed she was interested in her husband Gary. Since then they have become firm friends, working together in the Rovers, and Samantha stood as godmother when little Katie Joyce Mallett was christened. The christening was one of the happiest days of Judy's life, but it ended in misery.

Unlike other independent types, Judy Mallett has always had to be a fighter, growing up in back-streets, blacking eyes in the school-yard, and she has hidden her feelings from the outside world since the day her father walked out on her. She was only thirteen and her mother, Joyce, had put up with years of violence. There followed a messy divorce and Joyce reverted to her maiden name, Smedley. From then on Judy searched for love from the lads who hung around their street and Joyce turned a blind eye as she blossomed into womanhood. She was on hand, though, when the girl found herself pregnant at sixteen. Joyce decided it would be best all round if the 'little problem' was dealt with. It was only after the operation that Judy realized she'd lost something she'd wanted so much it hurt.

A few years later, after a series of dead-end jobs and fellers, she met Gary Mallett at the dog stadium and fell in love for the first time in her life. The couple married and found themselves living in Joyce's back bedroom while they saved up for a place of their own. That place was No. 9 Coronation Street and Judy wanted it as soon as she saw its stone cladding and cocktail bar. Determined not to repeat Joyce's mistakes, she worked hard to ensure her marriage was a partnership, but

took no nonsense from Gary: 'I want you to keep your nose out of my business – you're not my guardian angel.'

Women like Samantha, full of bounce and beauty, worried Judy – she could never understand why Gary had chosen her: she'd never been clever, wasn't beautiful, she thought, and always opened her mouth without thinking. It took years before he convinced her that in his eyes she was the most wonderful woman in the world. Likewise, Judy couldn't see the point in looking at other men as none could ever compare with her Gary.

There was only one problem: both badly wanted children. It wasn't until after Joyce's death in a road accident that Judy decided the time had come to make a family. However, she didn't become pregnant and she had to face

NOT A SUITABLE JOB FOR A LADY

When the Street started, back in 1960, the female characters that earn a crust tended to do so from behind a shop counter or sewing machine. The nineties have seen Angie Freeman and Co. running their own businesses and beating men at their own game. The years leading to this have thrown up the occasional strange job to baffle and bewitch the local lasses.

- **Suzie Birchall** became a model in 1979 but her only assignment was demonstrating German sausages in a supermarket.
- **Elsie Tanner** took an evening job as a model for a life-drawing class in 1964. Her posed beauty drove art teacher David Graham to distraction. He became besotted with her and threatened to shoot her when she attempted to end their liaisons.
- **Lucille Hewitt** shocked the neighbours by taking a job as a go-go dancer, strutting her stuff on various Weatherfield bar tops, including the Rovers.
- Teenager **Audrey Fleming** was well paid for wearing a tight-fitting uniform and filling up businessmen's cars with petrol.
- **Phyllis Pearce** spent one December dressed in a red gown as Mother Christmas, inviting children (and their fathers) to sit on her knee at Bettabuy Supermarket.

Happy days, before little Katie tragically died of meningitis and Gary discovered Judy had had sex with her boss.

of reservations – what they planned was illegal – but Judy pointed out that without their care the baby would be handed over to Social Services.

Judy was furious when Zoe continued to drink and smoke throughout her pregnancy but she panicked when Zoe went into premature labour and was rushed into an emergency Caesarian. Gary was at the birth and broke the news to Judy that they had a baby girl. Immediately Judy took over: she named the baby Katie, and pushed Zoe into the background. To make her claim on Katie more valid, she ordered Gary to put his name as father on the birth certificate.

It was only after she had sent Zoe away with the £2,000 that Judy began to relax and enjoy motherhood. The authorities accepted that Katie should stay at No. 9, as Gary was her father, and for a while the little family were left alone. Then the nightmare struck.

Leanne Battersby, Zoe's friend, resented the way that the Malletts pushed Zoe away and when Judy spread rumours that Zoe had stolen the money from them and run away, she called her a liar. Judy lost her head and slapped Leanne's face, which made Leanne decide to bring Zoe back to the Street to tell her side of the story.

Judy insisted to Gary that they leave the area and they decided to go to his brother in Newcastle. However, before they could escape Zoe snatched Katie and, taking up residence at No. 4 with do-gooder Ashley Peacock, refused to hand her back.

Out of desperation, and believing Zoe just wanted more cash, Judy had sex with her old boss, arcade owner Paul Fisher, in return for a £2,000 advance on her wages. However, Zoe refused the money and worse was to come when the baby died of meningitis. Judy supported Zoe at the funeral, both of them grieving for a shared daughter, while Judy struggled with the knowledge that, by some miracle, she was pregnant herself.

the reality she had always dreaded: an infection after the abortion had left her sterile. When the doctor confirmed her suspicions, Judy told Gary the whole story, ending bitterly: 'Oh, easy for men, isn't it? Got all the names to call. Slut, tart, scrubber. But a randy young feller's just a bit of a lad.' She expected Gary to leave her – he wanted a baby so much – but Gary assured her they could adopt.

Then fate took a hand and threw into their path sixteen-year-old Zoe Tattersall, a kid on the run from council care, with a druggie boyfriend and a baby on the way. Judy knew instinctively that she and Zoe had been meant to meet and help each other. She ignored Gary's protests and brought the girl into their home. Then she suggested that when the baby was born they should buy it. Zoe was happy to go along with this, which would leave her £2,000 better off, and succumbed to being pampered by Judy whose main concern was the welfare of the unborn child. Gary was full

"If anything's sad and soggy in the middle, it's you, Minnie Caldwell."

MARTHA LONGHURST

In times of trouble, there's nothing so comforting as a mother figure to cluck around, put the kettle on and say, 'Eeeh, love.' Many Street women are primed to offer shoulders, tissues, and measures of often uninvited advice. Elsie, Rita and Bet have all been comforters – many a time Bet has crept out unnoticed from behind the bar to interrupt some private moment of self-pity or attempted suicide. She has tended to show the victim that what they are going through is not unique: 'We've all been down that road, chuck.'

Character Name:	MINNIE CALDWELL
Date of Birth:	26 September 1900
Husband:	Armistead Caldwell (1925–35)
Parents:	Bob and Amy Carlton

O thers dish out comfort as if it were nourishing soup – women like Minnie Caldwell and Betty Williams, who put others at ease straight away with their cosy, familiar ways. They put forward no solutions, which allows the victims to find their own.

Minnie is fondly remembered as the batty, soft-in-the-head member of the snug bar trio, Ena, Minnie and Martha. She always sat in the left-hand seat, furthest away from the door, wearing her beret and clutching a milk stout as she waited to be drawn into the conversation by one of the others. They were all pensioners, had known each other since they were children working in the mills, but Minnie was different: she hadn't any children and now that she was a pensioner she lived on the state rather than charring like the others. It wasn't that she was lazy: she just felt that she'd done her bit and all she wanted was to sit in front of the fire with her cat, Bobby. And if she couldn't afford the coal she and Bobby would move upstairs and snuggle down in bed.

Minnie had been married, to a railway shunter Armistead Caldwell, for ten years. Shortly after her honeymoon, when a doctor told her she'd never be able to have children, Minnie ran away rather than tell her husband, but Armistead borrowed a horse and cart to bring her home, assured her that he still loved her and it didn't matter. Left a widow during the Depression, she moved in with her mother, Amy Carlton, and spent her days working at Palmerston mill on a loom. There was no question of her marrying again – Armistead

had been her man. For the next twenty-seven years Minnie lived with her domineering mother, who took to her bed whenever she was faced with a crisis. When the old lady died, in 1962, Minnie took over the tenancy of No. 5 Coronation Street.

Minnie's life rotated around her friends and neighbours. At home she fussed over the row of cocoa tins on the mantelpiece: 'I'm trying to work out me money for the extra rent. You see, that tin's for food, light, gas, coal, the rent and Bobby's fish. Everything's going up and you know, sometimes Mr Caldwell only used to bring home half of what I get in me pension. But I always managed, we had meat nearly every Sunday.' During the winter months it seemed cheaper to buy a milk stout at the Rovers (in the snug where drinks were a ha'penny cheaper) than to buy coal to heat the house. She enjoyed listening to gossip, although hated hearing anything detrimental of others or that involved cruelty to animals.

In the spring of 1968, when Bobby went missing Minnie spent nights wandering the streets, clattering a fork against his bowl, but the cat never materialized. Then, by chance, she spotted him on top of the viaduct at the end of the Street. Window-cleaner Stan Ogden took pity on her and climbed his ladder to rescue the cat. After a chase along railway lines and through fields, he brought it back to Minnie, but as soon as she saw it she knew it wasn't Bobby. Her friends persuaded her to keep it, though, and she named it Sunny Jim, although she always called it Bobby. It must have enjoyed her care for it stayed with her until she moved away in 1976.

Minnie's mothering instincts were brought out by all the strays she took in. Jed was her first lodger, a chirpy Liverpool lad, known to the local police as a petty villain. He used Minnie's house as a warehouse to store all the 'merchandise' he acquired, and despite Ena's view that he was in league with the devil, Minnie enjoyed the little luxuries he brought

"Ena, if you're going to make jokes at my expense I think I'll wait outside. I'm not you're straight man, you know."

MINNIE CALDWELL

her. He explained the principles of hire purchase to her, and Minnie gleefully took possession of a television and a vacuum cleaner. He also employed her as a plant when he operated a market stall. While he tried, in vain, to move oversized jumpers and love potions, Minnie praised them and ordered in bulk. She tended to spoil the act by asking her lodger what he wanted for his tea.

Jed called Minnie Ma, and wouldn't include her in anything too illegal. In 1966, when he discovered the police were after him for handling stolen blankets, he didn't run away until he'd helped Minnie celebrate her birthday. When a detective caught him, Jed pretended he was an old mate and that they were going to visit another. Minnie wasn't fooled, though, and after Jed had been led away she broke down.

When she didn't have the back room filled with a surrogate son Minnie fell into a decline. She became easily confused and vulnerable. She never liked to ask for help or advice, and when her life savings matured she wondered how to spend the £75 and stored it in an old tin. When a couple of con artists heard of it they convinced her that her roof needed repairing and Minnie handed over the cash, whereupon the men disappeared. Hire purchase caused problems too, because without Jed to remind her about repayments Minnie fell quickly into debt. At such times Ena Sharples would appear to sort out the mess, see off oppressors and dig in her purse for a few coins to buy Bobby's food. Most of the time Minnie remained quiet while Ena meddled in her life but occasionally she stood up for herself: 'Ena, if you're going to make jokes at my expense I think I'll wait outside. I'm not your straight man, you know.'

Apart from cats, Minnie's passion was gambling. A keen follower of form, she was known by all the local book-makers who were amused by her love of horse-racing. She followed her own guidelines and was sensible

enough to realize she mustn't spend too much on bets but after a series of bad ones she found, in the winter of 1969, that she owed Dave Smith £10. Dave had a soft spot for her and was happy to give her time to repay him, until Ena remonstrated with him for taking a poor pensioner's money. He demanded full payment of the debt and Minnie panicked. She left a note urging Ena to feed Bobby and disappeared. Concern for her welfare united the Street and the residents turned against Dave as they searched through the snow for Minnie. As Dave's girlfriend Elsie Tanner put it: 'You look after yer own, Dave. One of our own needs us.' Eventually Minnie was found, having spent three nights sleeping on a park bench. She was rushed to hospital and slowly recovered while Dave wrote off the debt and gave her a gambling limit.

When she was seventy-three, Minnie was startled to receive a proposal of marriage from her neighbour, seventy-eight-year-old Albert Tatlock. He hastened to tell her that it had nothing to do with love and everything to do with practicality: it would be cheaper to run one house and they'd be better off on a

Bobby Caldwell was Minnie's child substitute.

joint pension. Minnie saw the sense in this and accepted him, but during the six-month engagement period she realized that living with Albert wouldn't be easy. For a start, he drank his tea out of a saucer and he disliked Bobby. She broke it off, telling him that they would be incompatible.

Minnie's old friend Handel Gartside had left England after the Depression and had made his fortune in Australia. He returned and settled in Whaley Bridge and, in 1976, after deciding she'd had enough of robbing Peter to feed Paul, Minnie went to stay with him for a relaxing holiday. She never returned, and six months after her departure Handel travelled to Weatherfield to empty No. 5 of Minnie's belongings. He explained to Ena that the countryside suited her and she had her own room, overlooking a farmyard where a family of cats played in the hay.

Character Name:	ELIZABETH (BETTY) WILLIAMS
Date of Birth:	4 February 1920
Husbands:	Cyril Turpin (1949–74)
	Billy Williams (1995–97)
Children:	Gordon Clegg (1948)
Parents:	Harold and Margaret Preston

In many ways Betty Williams is another Minnie: warm and comforting, she loves cats and has had her share of lodgers. But while Minnie wandered through life in a haze, Betty is sharp-witted, blessed with insight and wisdom. She hasn't always been the incarnation of lovable joviality: when she arrived in the Street, in 1969, she was loud, brash and a vicious-tongued gossip.

Following the break-up of her younger sister Maggie's marriage, Betty moved herself and husband Cyril into Maggie's shop on Coronation Street. She found a job as barmaid at the Rovers, but at first landlady Annie Walker fought hard to sack her as she feared her husband Jack would find Betty attractive.

After the war Betty had married Cyril Turpin but they had had no children. Before her marriage, though, Betty had given birth to a son, Gordon, who had been adopted by Maggie and her husband Les. Gordon's father had been a serviceman called Ted Farrell who had had an affair with Betty before returning to his family.

Betty had two great passions: darts and food. Cyril always objected when she dieted as he liked her plump, saying she looked homely and comfortable, so she stopped trying to lose weight: 'I had to choose between losing a few pounds or losing my marital partner. If my Cyril had wanted to marry a skinny rabbit he'd have married one.' Darts bought out the competitor in Betty and she delighted in beating the male customers. When not in the Rovers, Betty was happy to be at home, cooking and keeping house. Cyril was a policeman and had a keen sense of order, which fitted nicely into Betty's way of thinking.

Cyril's job caused Betty a problem when an ex-convict, Lucas, started to stalk her. He terrorized her over a couple of weeks but she didn't want to tell Cyril as she feared he would end up in trouble. When Cyril found out what was going on he attacked Lucas with a length of lead piping and had to leave the force.

After Cyril died of a heart-attack, Betty had a breakdown. She was so ill that the funeral was arranged without her, and it was only at the last minute that Maggie decided she was well enough to attend. Cyril had been the stabilizing influence in Betty's life, and without him she relied heavily on her job and friends at the Rovers – she couldn't face life alone at home. Like Minnie, Betty busied herself by taking in lodgers and for extra companionship she took in a ginger cat named Marmaduke.

Betty spent a lot of time and effort in looking after her workmate Bet Lynch, and from time to time Bet sought refuge in Betty's spare room, but spurned her advice on how to run her life: 'Betty, love, don't tell me you know about lonely fellers, tell me about lonely women. After all, you are one yerself.' On occasion Bet used Betty as a chaperone to ward off randy suitors, and it was as such that Betty picnicked with her and Fred Gee in Tatton Park. She made certain that the pair weren't left alone for a minute and when they got back into the car afterwards, she was pleased to have carried out her mission. Unfortunately when Fred slammed the boot shut, the car rolled forward with Bet and Betty inside it. It finally came to rest in the middle of a lake and Betty had to be carried to safety on Fred's back.

In 1982 Betty was savagely beaten up when muggers tried to grab her handbag as she walked home from work, leaving her with a broken arm and cuts to her face. She was shocked that one of her attackers had been a teenage girl. Yet having been married to a bobby all those years Betty was used to tales of conflict and aggression. She has a finely tuned sense of right and wrong and has never been afraid to stand up for her beliefs. Upset by the sight of her neighbours' children playing out all day until nightfall, she befriended them and was horrified to learn that their mother forced them out while she entertained her boyfriend. Betty gave the children sweets and drinks and reported the mother to the NSPCC. Although she was glad to have done her duty, she was relieved to have her other neighbours' support when the boyfriend threatened to harm her.

Betty had always maintained that Cyril would be the only man in her life but in 1995, on the fiftieth anniversary of VE Day she chanced upon the very man with whom she had celebrated the end of the war and to whom she had lost her virginity. Billy Williams was a widower and insisted that fate had brought them back together. They married just months after meeting again and, despite his occasional lapse into drinking, were happy until he died of a heart-attack in 1997.

Although way past retirement age, Betty soldiers on at the Rovers. She only works lunch-times but her hot-pot is the talk of Weatherfield. The Street's residents are her family and she doesn't like to be far from them. When she's finally had enough of standing behind the bar, she'll probably go to live in Wimbledon where Gordon and his family have a home – but, even then, her heart will remain in Coronation Street.

Now Billy is dead, Betty spends more time than ever serving in the Rovers while Marmaduke provides comfort at home.

GAD-ABOUTS

"It's not easy being a gad-about you know, late nights, tight dresses, high heels. You're always fighting your body. But what's a girl to do? You don't get gold bracelets by sitting at home pickling onions, do you?"

AUDREY ROBERTS

They sit in the booths at the Rovers, sipping gin and tonic, long slender legs crossed as they swap gossip with girlfriends while keeping an eye on the beefy builder drinking at the bar. They know all the words to 'Another Suitcase In Another Hall', and get weepy when drunk. The typical gad-about differs only slightly from the walking wounded ('we've all been down that road, darling') but tends to have spent longer married to the same man. When married they remain faithful, although they enjoy a good flirt, but any children they have despair of them as mothers. Renowned for enjoying a Good Time, they are easy prey for men looking for diversion, but above all, they enjoy being in the midst of drama, and love giving advice to other women, even if they don't heed it themselves. As Audrey Roberts admitted once to barmaid Gloria Todd: 'First rule is always to let him think you're independent. Even if you're actually not. Even if your heart does a pole vault every time you see him. I know it's not easy, love. Sew your knickers to your vest, that's what my mother used to say. And drink a lot of cold water. It's very good advice. Not that I've always taken it, mind.'

Character Name:	AUDREY ROBERTS
Date of Birth:	23 July 1940
Husband:	Alf Roberts (1985–)
Children:	Gail (1958)
	Stephen (1956)
Parents:	Robert and Nancy Potter

~

"She's very vulnerable is Audrey. It comes to us all in the end. We've all got to stop gadding about some time. Even Audrey."

ALF ROBERTS

~

Audrey Potter Roberts is the ultimate gad-about: high-pitched laugh, legs up to her armpits, full of the glad eye and a murky past. As Ivy Tilsley put it, 'She's no better than she should be.' The classic Audrey moment has to have been Christmas Eve 1993 when, during a party at the Rovers, she embarrassed her husband Alf by chatting up a burly bloke. Alf went off in search of something to eat and eventually returned to find Audrey flat out on the Rovers' floor, comatose after too many G and Ts.

Life started off hard for Audrey Potter. She had her first child, Stephen, at sixteen and had him adopted. Gail followed two years later and Audrey fought to keep her. The children had different fathers but Audrey has always withheld their identities. She brought Gail up with the help of her mother and a boyfriend, whom she allowed Gail to believe was her real father. When the truth broke, Gail left home, and for five years had no contact with her mother. That changed in 1979 when Audrey first appeared on the Street to celebrate her daughter's engagement to Brian Tilsley. She had humiliated Gail during the celebrations by attracting the attention of three men and causing a fight.

For the next couple of years Audrey dropped in and out of Gail's life, usually on the arm of her latest fancy man. The men never lasted and a mascara-stained Audrey would dump herself on her daughter. Gail tried hard to be sympathetic but often blew up: 'You never think about real life, do you? All you think about is yourself. Goin' out with your fancy fellers and gettin' kicked out an' comin' here an' ruinin' our lives!' Further upset was caused when Gail learned that Audrey had advised Brian to persuade her to abort the baby she was expecting just months after their wedding. Audrey worried that her daughter would get trapped into early motherhood and sacrifice her youth, but her way of dealing with the situation caused more harm than good.

In the autumn of 1981, after her latest feller had turfed her out of his flat, Audrey lodged with Elsie Tanner at No.11. She took a job serving behind the counter of the Corner Shop and opened a hair salon in the back room, ignoring the shop customers to build her own profits. Shop-owner Alf Roberts didn't seem to mind and even suggested the arrangement could be permanent if Audrey married him. He confided in his friend Len Fairclough that she was the ideal woman for him: 'I know she gives the impression half the time that she doesn't give a damn for anything but that's all a big act. All top show. She's very vulnerable is Audrey. It comes to us all in the end. We've all got to stop gadding about some time. Even Audrey.' Horrified at the idea of marriage to a man she didn't find attractive, Audrey bolted, but four years later she became Mrs Alfred Roberts. Her attitude towards Alf changed when she realized she was getting too old to cart her suitcase in and out of flats and bedsits. Also, the men she found attractive now looked upon *her* as a sad older woman while the men who found her attractive seemed seedy in the morning. However, she had to lure Alf into proposing a second time: she smashed his car on purpose then burst into tears of remorse so that he could comfort her and offer to look after her.

For Alf, the main attraction in marrying Audrey was that he would have a woman on his arm whom other men found desirable. He was big in the council and often attended functions at which Audrey became part of his attire. Not that she minded: marriage to Alf made her financially secure at last and she was soon exploiting Alf's love with his credit card. Hitherto shopping had been a treat; now it became a way of life – as did winding Alf around her little finger.

She didn't get her own way in everything, though: at the time of their marriage, Audrey was homeless and Alf was lodging in the flat over his shop. Straight away she convinced him that he needed a house to suit his official image and arranged for them to view a detached house overlooking the park. She was horrified when Alf saved himself £30,000 by purchasing No.11 Coronation Street.

In an attempt to stop Audrey spending her days denting his bank balance, Alf gave her the front room at No.11 as a hair salon. She had it fitted out (and enjoyed a good flirt with the fitter) and set up her business. The venture lasted only a few months: Audrey's heart wasn't in it, and then she left dye too long on Hilda Ogden's hair, turning it bright orange.

Audrey found it hysterically funny but Hilda demanded compensation and Alf closed the salon.

Audrey's past has always been a sore point with Alf and it wasn't until two years into the marriage that he discovered she had an illegitimate son as well as Gail. The news came out when Stephen was involved in a car crash and Audrey rushed to Canada to be with him. After he had recovered, Stephen's foster-father Malcolm Reid travelled to England to visit the Robertses. Alf took an instant dislike to him and suspected him of ulterior motives. He was right for as soon as his back was turned Malcolm declared his love to Audrey and begged her to return with him to Canada. Audrey kept him on tenterhooks for two weeks, but in the end she decided to value what she had in Alf.

Audrey was surprised by the depth of her emotions when Alf had a heart-attack and she feared he might not pull through. However, she searched his wardrobe until she found his saving books under his Hank Marvin record

When Alf retired from the council in 1998 Audrey fought for his memory and had herself elected councillor with her agenda for shopping bringing in the votes.

collection. What she saw convinced her that, whatever happened, she would be comfortably off for the rest of her life so long as she continued as Mrs Alfred Roberts.

In 1990, however, she came close to losing him. Ever since Gail had married Brian, Audrey had been at loggerheads with his mother Ivy, who disapproved of her love-life: 'She's had more fellers than Elsie Tanner. And she set a world record.'

Audrey couldn't abide Ivy, the martyr and fun-hating Catholic: 'That woman should be in perpetual black – like one of them old Greek women, little tufts of hair sprouting out of her chin, and her head cast down. Picture of flamin' misery.'

Alf was well aware of the friction between the two but kept Ivy as his assistant. When Audrey decided she'd had enough, she asked him to sack Ivy. He refused, so Audrey walked out and booked into a hotel. When she would not come home, Alf cancelled her credit cards and the hotel asked her to leave. After a raid on the house, in which she emptied Alf's safe, Audrey booked into a bed and breakfast and faced up to a bleak future as a middle-aged divorcée. It was when Alf had collapsed with a second heart-attack that they were reconciled.

Afterwards, Audrey convinced Alf to sell up and retire. To her delight he agreed to buy a bungalow in Lytham and put the shop on the market. However, Alf's idea of retirement was nothing like the life of ease and luxury Audrey had planned. As a first step he cut up the credit cards, explaining they'd have to watch their pennies, then dragged her round a golf course to introduce her to the over-sixties wives. Alf thought he'd found grocer heaven but Audrey backtracked and talked him into hanging on to the shop.

Audrey's finest moment came when Alf was elected Mayor and she became Weatherfield's First Lady, complete with a wardrobe of frocks and handbags. Alf grew annoyed by the way Audrey picked and chose their engagements:

a fashion show was fine but anything involving the elderly or the sick was another matter. The final straw came when Alf received complaints from the council that Audrey used the official car as a personal taxi. He announced they would use public transport in the future. Audrey was furious: 'Perhaps you'd like to travel the length and breadth of the borough with him in the back of a cab? Only get all your breathing done before you get in because there won't be room inside. And remember that the cab will more or less turn over on its side every time you come to a corner because all the weight is on his side. Don't even contemplate wearing your best tights and be prepared for a 10p by 10p running commentary on the meter. And make sure you get there early because when you arrive, you have to unload him in instalments!' She withdrew her services as Mayoress and Alf asked Betty Turpin to take over. Audrey was content to see her judging bouncing-baby contests but when she heard of a Royal Do, she demanded to come as Alf's wife. Betty took a dim view of this and was caught in the middle. He suggested the ladies went together as 'Mayoress and Friend'. Worse came, though, when Alf was awarded the OBE by the Queen. Audrey was late for the investiture and was horrified to discover Betty had gone into the Palace in her place to watch Alf's finest hour.

The one anchor in Audrey's life as a gad-about has been her daughter Gail, now a mother herself. Showing rare wisdom, Audrey has been sparing with her advice on childcare, but on the odd occasions has felt the need to interfere. She has always enjoyed using Alf's money to spoil the children, which has annoyed Gail.

Although never keen to be acknowledged as the grandmother of a seventeen-year-old, and terrified of the day he makes her a great-grandmother, Audrey enjoys keeping her finger on the pulse via Nick's language and attitude: 'Oh, chill out, Alfie!'

> *"She's had more fellers than Elsie Tanner. And she set a world record."*
>
> IVY TILSEY

Character Name:	ALMA MARIE BALDWIN
Date of Birth:	18 October 1946
Husbands:	Jim Sedgewick (1976–88)
	Mike Baldwin (1992–)
Parents:	George and Florrie Halliwell

Shopping till they drop – Audrey and Alma give the plastic a bashing.

Audrey's best friend since the late eighties has been Alma Baldwin to whom she took an instant liking: 'Her sort don't like work. They like to find a man who'll do it all for them. I should know!' Over the years they have spent afternoons shopping in Southport and Wilmslow and evenings in wine bars being chatted up by bored businessmen. Although Alma is more reserved than Audrey, she shares her friend's love of high jinks and adventure. She may protest when Audrey informs a handsome man that Alma was once a fashion model but she doesn't contradict her. It's true, but that was back in the sixties, before she married Jim Sedgewick and discovered she could never have children.

The marriage was a disaster from the outset but they stayed together, each tolerating the other's extramarital activities. For a time Alma lived in Spain with a body-building pools winner, but when she finally divorced Jim she settled in Weatherfield, taking his café as settlement. Washer-upper Phyllis Pearce took against the new boss: 'She chats a lot with customers. Specially if they're wearing pants and look as if they wash their necks regular.'

One clean customer was Mike Baldwin, whom Alma met in 1989. They seemed ideally suited – good-looking, with adventurous, murky pasts, interested in the same music, food and sex. Alma surprised Mike by taking control of the relationship early on – after beating him at golf, she won the privilege of selecting the restaurant of her choice, but Mike was pleasantly surprised when she announced they would be dining in her flat and taking dessert in her bed. When she heard of the manoeuvre, Audrey turned against her friend: 'She's a cheeky article. Dead common. I mean, it's one thing knowing how to set your stall out for a feller. It's different to shouting, "Roll up, roll up, everything's going cheap!"'

Mike and Alma's courtship was long and full of emotional upheaval. He had an affair with his boss, Jackie Ingham, and left Alma to marry her, while Alma romanced Mike's enemy Ken Barlow and became his lover. Mike's marriage lasted only two weeks as Jackie discovered he'd used her money to buy the lease on Alma's café, thus saving her from having to sell up. When Jackie threw him out,

Mike started to pester Alma again, but she was determined not to give in to him. Until Christmas Day 1991.

Mike had contrived for Ken to spend the day with his ex-wife Deirdre by suggesting to their teenage daughter Tracy that her parents might be reconciled if she brought them together on Christmas Day. Knowing that Ken had had to cancel his holiday with Alma and that she would be alone in her flat, Mike called with an expensive present. He declared his love for her; Alma, feeling vulnerable and alone, allowed him to carry her into bed. After they had made love, Mike cockily congratulated himself on using Tracy to get Ken out of the way which infuriated Alma, who vowed to have nothing more to do with him. Then she confessed all to Ken, who finished with her, saying he could never forgive her. That was on New Year's Eve, and six months later she said, 'I will,' to Mike. However, before they left the register office, she warned him: 'I've married you because I've got the measure of you now. I'm not scared of you any more, because you don't fool me any more. You'll never be able to lie to me again, Mike, because I'll know.'

Marriage to Mike and running the café with Gail Platt filled Alma's hours and she started to relax into a routine. Mike continued to surprise her with expensive gifts and weekends away while Audrey was always on hand to provide diversions. When Mike started to take her for granted, Alma formed her own company, Alma Baldwin Catering, and organized buffets and advised on menus. On the surface life seemed full but there remained a hole inside Alma, which refused to close with age. After they had married, the discovery that Mike had an illegitimate son caused her to break down, fearing that young Mark's mother would always be a pull for Mike: 'Why do I have to live like this? Why does every woman I know have some sort of marriage? I can't even trust I'm going to have a husband much longer because you're a father. You've got a son. And I can't have a son, or a daughter, because I'm too old!'

Throughout her marriage to Mike, Alma has suspected her husband of infidelity with persons known and unknown. In 1996 she put his feelings to the test when she fell for Stephen Reid, Audrey's son over in England from Canada on business. Even though he was her best friend's son, and the brother of her business partner, Alma allowed herself to mistake his polite interest in his mother's friend for attraction. She made a pass at him and declared her feelings for him. He did his best to let her down lightly but Alma realized that he felt nothing for her but friendship.

Ever the gentleman, Stephen put the incident out of his mind but Alma told Mike what had happened. He seemed amused by the idea and tried to use her infatuation to boost his business deals with Stephen. Alma's romantic ideas died when she learned Stephen was ruining Mike's business and she found herself fighting with Mike against Audrey's children. She slapped Stephen's face when he offered to end her frustration by bedding her, and she finished her partnership with Gail by selling her share of the café.

Although her marriage had been strengthened by the Stephen Reid incident, Alma was shaken by how cut-throat Mike's business world was. She became a victim of it herself after she spurned the advances of cabbie Don Brennan. He blamed Mike for his failing garage business, which had left him bankrupt. In revenge he burned Mike's factory to the ground and kidnapped Alma, telling her he was going to hurt Mike by ruining all he held dear. At first Alma feared Don would rape her but instead he drove his cab, with her inside it, off the quays and into the river Irwell. As the car sank Alma freed herself and dragged the unconscious Don to the surface. For a girl more used to the cocktail bar at the Midland Hotel, a dunking in Manchester's river was an experience never to be repeated.

Character Name:	ELIZABETH JAYNE (LIZ) MCDONALD
Date of Birth:	4 November 1957
Husband:	Jim McDonald (1974–95)
Children:	Steve (1974) Andy (1974) Katherine (1992)
Parents:	Arthur and Nancy Greenwood

Another Street woman who has had many never-to-be-repeated experiences is Liz McDonald. When she first arrived at No.11 Coronation Street in 1989 she looked a hard-working, struggling mother. Indeed, she had kept her family together while husband Jim had toured the world with the army and her twin sons, Steve and Andy, had grown up in army camps. Moving to the Street was meant to be a new start for them all after Jim's discharge, but it brought to the surface all the resentment that had laid dormant in the McDonalds' sixteen-year-marriage.

Liz took a job behind the Rovers' bar, investing in the plunging necklines and short skirts that became her trademark. Big, burly Jim was a good customer in the pub and spent most evenings at the bar making sure no man got too friendly with his wife. Liz enjoyed the work as it gave her plenty of opportunity to indulge in a favoured pastime: flirting. She gave it up when she discovered she was pregnant. At first she planned an abortion, feeling that with two sixteen-year-old boys a baby would be an unwelcome addition. However, Jim convinced her that it would bring them together and that he wanted an active role in its upbringing. Liz settled down to enjoy her pregnancy but her luck ran out in the seventh month when anxiety over Steve led to premature labour. Baby Katherine died just twelve hours after her birth.

After a prolonged period of grieving, Liz decided to step out from behind the kitchen sink and looked for a more fulfilling career. She attracted the attention of Richard Willmore, a brewery boss, who installed her as manageress of the Queen's, a posh city-centre pub. Although Liz's name was over the door she went into the venture with Jim as her partner, but he became jealous of the glances Liz attracted from the male customers. Just days into the new venture he accused her of getting the pub by sleeping with Willmore. She told him he was jealous of her success and refused to jeopardize it just to please him.

The couple split up and Liz hung on to the Queen's. She also moved barman Colin Barnes into her bed – if Jim thought of her as a whore she might as well act like one. The necklines became lower, the skirts higher and Liz started to enjoy her independence. Colin was younger and energetic, and a great support as she started divorce proceedings against Jim. However, the fancy new lifestyle and her freedom wasn't what Liz really wanted and she missed Jim. She finished with Colin and set about reconciling with her husband, giving up the pub to prove she wanted to put him first in future.

The McDonald marriage revived for a short time but the excitement died down and Liz was back where she had started from, disenchanted. She took a job as clerk at the local bookies, fighting off the attention of the boss Sean Skinner only to find herself falling for his assistant, Des Barnes, Colin's brother. Petrified of losing everything again, she resigned, telling Des they could never have a sexual relationship. However, Jim's suspicions had been alerted and he started to follow her.

After a particularly strained night out at an Army reunion Liz snapped and admitted that, years before, she had had an affair with his best friend. Jim saw red, hit her and drove off, leaving her alone at a petrol station. She managed to get to her friend Deirdre Rachid's for help, and immediately re-started divorce proceedings, taking out an injunction against Jim who, she feared, was going to kill her. This time the divorce went through and, after lengthy battles over money and property, Liz was able to take stock of her life: a single woman approaching forty with a job serving in a wine bar and living in a crummy bedsit.

One man attracted to the image – 'It's a classy dress but I like your other stuff better – shorter, tighter, less of it' – was convict Frazer Henderson, who noticed her when she visited Steve in Strangeways. At first she was startled by his style: he bought her expensive jewellery and his henchmen kept other men away from her. Then she began to find him appealing and was flattered by the attention of Weatherfield's gangland chief. Jim and Andy

Jim hit Liz and then abandoned her after she confessed to sleeping with his best friend.

were appalled that Liz had become a moll, but Steve basked in new-found security under Frazer's caring eye.

When Frazer was released he bought the wine bar where Liz worked and she moved into his flat to enjoy the high life. That all ended when a warehouse robbery went wrong and Frazer's right-hand man Gerry decided that Liz was a police informer. He pursued her through the streets of the city until she sought refuge at No.11, pleading with Jim to protect her. Gerry broke in and held the couple, along with Andy, at gun-point. Before he had a chance to fire, ex-army Jim jumped him, grabbed the gun and Liz knocked Gerry unconscious with the heel of her shoe. Frazer fled to Spain.

Liz took another crummy bar job and celebrated her fortieth birthday feeling washed up and bitter. She still clings to what little dignity she has left, but has become a figure of ridicule and abuse, attracting the attention of men out for a laugh.

She is now reduced to operating a sewing machine in Mike Baldwin's sweatshop. She drinks at the Rovers, bitterly watching the young barmaids who have replaced her. She knows, though, that Jim's shoulder is still available to cry on. They rekindled their sexual relationship, briefly, and she hoped for a complete reconciliation, until he confessed his love for Steve's ex-girlfriend Fiona.

Over the last ten years Liz has watched her secure family environment break down, until she had lost everything. Her husband and sons blamed her for everything that went wrong, but she hit back: 'I've stood a lot of abuse from you lot in my time. For one thing and another. Mostly because I don't sit at home knitting or doing a jigsaw every night, but I go out, and sometimes I actually speak to men. I make some mistakes. I do stupid things but if I make a complete mess of my life it will only be my fault and you won't find me blaming anyone else!'

HOME WRECKERS

"I didn't set out to be a man-grabbing bitch . . . it just happened that way."

NATALIE HORROCKS

The majority of straying husbands in the Street's history have tended to have affairs with lonely attractive women, who have sympathized with the my-wife-doesn't-understand-me routine. The liaisons have been brief and have often ended in reconciliation with the spouse.

There is, however, a small band of women who have wittingly dragged loving hubbies away from the slippers at the fireside to embark in mad, passionate and fulfilling sex. Janet Reid was a classic example, followed more recently by Natalie Horrocks. It is immediately apparent to other characters that once the home wrecker has her sights on a victim he is doomed. When the tears come, it's normally behind closed doors.

Character Name:	JANET FELICITY BARLOW
Date of Birth:	28 November 1942
Husband:	Ken Barlow (1973–77)
Parents:	Charles and Jacqueline Reid
Date of Death:	21 February 1977

"Everybody's got their nice snug little homes and their cosy little marriages and it's 'hands off', 'keep out', 'no admittance' and it's hard cheese for the Janets of this world."

JANET REID

Janet Reid was an intelligent and well-educated Town Hall clerk, who confided in Elsie Tanner that she feared Len Fairclough was about to propose to her, and went on: 'He's kind, he's generous, I can't stop him spending money on me. He fusses over me, holds me coat, he's everything I've ever wanted in a man. But I don't love him . . . I've never been as frightened by anything else before. How do you tell a man you don't love him? But I know that if he asks me to marry him I'll say yes and I'll regret it as long as I live.' She took Elsie's advice and finished the relationship the next day, but Len slapped Elsie's face and accused her of seeing Janet off.

For two years, until the summer of 1971, Janet stayed away from the Street. When she returned it was to help out Maggie Clegg at the Corner Shop. While taking a box of assorted fancies to the Canal Garage, Janet met its boss Alan Howard and was instantly attracted to him. The fact that he was married to her one-time confidante Elsie didn't put her off at all, and within a week they were clinching in the garage office, which put poor Maggie Clegg in a dilemma: Elsie was one of her best friends. She decided against telling Elsie, but had not counted on the wronged wife suspecting that if Alan was spending more time than usual in the shop he must be interested in Maggie.

When Alan went away on business to Leeds, Janet followed and they spent the night together in his hotel room. The affair built up momentum until two weeks later when Maggie's sister Betty Turpin told Elsie exactly what Janet was up to. Elsie knew that a public confrontation would do her no favours: her emotions might get the better of her. Elsie went to the shop, put the sign to 'closed' and bolted the door: 'Hotel bedrooms might be all right for one thing, but that's only one thing. It might be all you're good for but that's only the start, you dirty little bitch. One thing you don't understand is that fellers are a full-time job and I'm not doing your day shift.'

Janet didn't take Elsie's snarls on the chin: 'It's all or nothing, is it? Well, I know all about having nothing. What do you know about it? You're the one that's been wronged, because you've got everything and someone came along and took a small part of it. Spit on me. Scratch me eyes out, if you like, no one would blame you. I'm just the other woman. I'm just nobody.' Then she tried to explain why she'd thrown herself at Alan: 'You've been married three times. I haven't, not even once . . . All the fellers are married to other women, it's "the whole world and his wife", isn't it? And there's no place in it for people like me. Everybody's got their nice snug little homes and their cosy little marriages and it's "hands off", "keep out", "no admittance" and it's hard cheese for the Janets of this world.'

Elsie recognized a genuinely bleeding heart but she had to make Janet see that stealing her husband wasn't the answer: 'Once you meet a feller who only cares about you, you'll want him so he only cares about you and nobody else. That's the way it is, love, we're all that selfish.'

Two hours later, Elsie knew the battle was won but also that, as the affair had been public knowledge, the other residents had to be shown it was over. She forced Janet into the Rovers, bought her a gin and asked everyone to wish Janet all the best as she was leaving the street – for good.

Or at least for two years. In October 1973

Elsie Howard made a point of being the first to wish Janet much happiness when she married Ken Barlow. But the marriage was doomed from the start: Ken had married to provide a mother for his twins while Janet was after a large detached home in the suburbs and holidays in the sun. Just a month into the marriage, Janet gave vent to her feelings when Ken failed to secure a deposit on a house she wanted: 'Look at you, scared sick of responsibility all your life, no ambition, no initiative - you're useless, spineless, inadequate, weak.'

Although both knew that the marriage had been a mistake Janet tried hard to make the most of it, while Ken was content if his tea was ready for him when he came home. However, they were soon living separate lives, which hurt Janet: 'We can't talk, can we? We can swap words, but I'm beginning to think that's all we've ever done. We've never really exchanged anything, not ideas, opinions, certainly not love.'

The marriage fell apart when Janet admitted to Ken that the last thing she wanted to be was mother to his eight-year-old twins. Ken was shattered as the children had been living with his ex-mother-in-law in Scotland and he desperately wanted them with him. Janet disliked children and suggested that they went to boarding school. From that moment, the couple gave up on their marriage and Janet moved out.

For the next four years Janet came and went from Ken's life but never divorced him. Finally, in early 1977, she returned in

Janet made a big play for Alan Howard, fooling herself that he'd be man enough to leave his wife for her.

desperate need of love, or at least affection, but Ken wasn't interested so she took a fatal overdose. Janet had gone from relationship to relationship but had never found what she'd been looking for. She had realized early on that deceit was sometimes the only option left to her.

Character Name:	NATALIE HORROCKS
Date of Birth:	12 October 1957
Husband:	Nick Horrocks (1974–)
Children:	Tony (1975)
Parents:	Colin and Valerie Baines

Natalie pours a couple of wines and decides to turn her son's best mate into her newest bed partner.

We haven't known Natalie Horrocks long enough to figure out if she is a habitual deceiver yet, but she does seem to have the makings of one: she manipulates, uses emotional blackmail, lies and needs to have the upper hand, as Judy Mallett recognized: 'I'm not being bitchy but you do call the shots. If you want something, or someone, you go for it.'

A vicar's daughter, Natalie came to Coronation Street in early 1997 after her son Tony gave up his share of MVB Motors. The money he had used to buy the garage with partner Kevin Webster had been Natalie's and after the break-up of her twenty-three-year marriage she threw herself into working there. It had come as no surprise to her when husband Nick walked out to shack up with his young girlfriend: they'd been unfaithful to each other since Tony's birth. What hurt was the thought that she could be washed up and have no one to care for her again. The garage provided a distraction in the form of its accounts and her business partner, Kevin. His wife, Sally, was nursing her sick mother and Natalie made it clear to Kevin that she was available for some fun. She assured him that

she didn't want commitment and was only interested if he felt he could handle it: 'Guilt is dangerous. Guilt's what makes people want to confess. Even when they don't have to, even when it's all over.'

At first the affair was based on sex and, as such, was more than fulfilling. When Sally returned home, though, Natalie fully expected Kevin to drop her but he swore he wanted to carry on seeing her and Natalie, who felt more for him now than lust, agreed. The relationship became more intense and the pair started to take risks. The upshot was a messy scene when Sally confronted them at Natalie's love nest. While Kevin panicked Natalie realized that if she kept her head Sally would throw Kevin into her arms. This is exactly what happened, and Sally told him that he had wrecked their marriage and it couldn't be repaired.

When Kevin moved in Natalie struggled to hide her relief: now she would no longer be alone at night, there would be no more snatched moments in the garage, no more single dinners on a tray. For a short time it was blissful. Then financial demands from Sally took hold and Natalie, whose family had rejected her for living with her toy-boy, saw that she didn't have to fight just Sally for Kevin, but also his two daughters. She didn't stand a chance. In a moment of unguarded honesty, she broke down and told mechanic Chris Collins: 'I never wanted to threaten their marriage. I swear it. I was attracted to him. We were attracted to each other, but I was under no illusion about what would happen when Sally came back. I never asked for any commitment from Kevin. Quite the reverse, I never wanted any. I didn't know I'd fall in love with him. I've betrayed him by falling in love.'

The pull of the children at Christmas time was too much for Kevin and Natalie was devastated when Kevin explained he was returning to Sally. What hurt most was that he said he'd

ON THE ROCKS

Natalie and Janet aren't the only vamps to have fluttered their eyelashes and ruined marriages over the past thirty-eight years. A number of Street Sirens have lured innocent husbands to their doom:

- **Rita Littlewood** hoped Jimmy Graham would leave his wife and two children for her.
- **Annie Walker** found herself cited in a divorce case when she became the object of Arthur Harvey's desire and he left wife Nellie for her.
- **Dulcie Froggatt,** despite being married herself, took on Jack and Terry Duckworth at the same time and then accused Vera of sapping both her men of spirit!
- **Bet Lynch** was happy having Des Foster in her bed until she discovered she wasn't his only mistress.
- **Mavis Riley** was cited as 'the other woman' in Derek and Angela Wilton's divorce case.
- **Elsie Tanner** lost boss Mike Baldwin a huge order when her boyfriend's wife, Dot Stockwell, reported their affair to his boss.
- **Jenny Bradley** ran off with a dentist, knowing he was abandoning his wife and children for her.

never really loved her: 'You built me up, you made me feel fantastic, but that's you, Natalie. It's not really me. I was never really worth you.'

Shortly afterwards Natalie started work behind the bar at the Rovers pulling pints. She painted on the smile and, as Vera Duckworth put it, started looking out for her next victim.

He turned out to be bookie Des Barnes. For months Natalie struggled to fight her attraction to him as Des was living with her friend Samantha Failsworth. Natalie couldn't bring herself to steal a mate's man but when the couple eventually broke up she was quick to offer Des comfort and support. and it wasn't long before they were lovers.

"It isn't my fault if I can't spell. It's the government. I've never been taught properly. And everybody thinks I'm common and horrible as well. 'Cos I am. 'Cos I've been dragged up by that pair, and that's not my fault either."

TOYAH BATTERSBY

Childhood is never an easy time, especially for those growing up on the Street surrounded by drama, family break-ups and broken hearts. Only a handful of girls have survived the strain of teenage years on Coronation Street. Some, such as Deirdre Hunt and Gail Potter, found a place there as young women and, later, mothers of their own teenagers. Many, such as Debbie Webster, the Clayton sisters and Becky Palmer, fell by the wayside, tied to parents who moved away. The Street's teenage girls are occupied by the same issues as girls all over the country: makeup, music, fashion and boys.

Character Name:	LUCILLE HEWITT
Date of Birth:	4 May 1949
Parents:	Harry and Elizabeth Hewitt
	Concepta Hewitt (step)

The original teenager was Lucille Hunt, who started out as a pre-teen and left when she was twenty-four. In 1960, following her mother's death, she was living in an orphanage but kept running away to be with her father Harry at No.7 Coronation Street. Lucille was a bright child, full of energy and imagination, and felt quite old enough to look after herself and her father. Harry solved his problems by marrying barmaid Concepta Riley – after Lucille gave her consent. Finally she had a real home life and plastered her bedroom wall with pictures of Elvis and James Dean. After passing her eleven-plus she enrolled at the grammar school and became Harry's pride and joy as she learned about subjects he had never heard of.

As Lucille hit her teens she had to adjust to sharing Harry's love when Concepta gave birth to a son, Christopher. Lucille was quite fond of her little brother but resented the way he dominated her parents' time and concentration so she packed her satchel and ran away from home. She didn't get far: it started to rain so she sheltered under the viaduct at the end of the Street, where she was found by pensioner Ena Sharples, who told her to go home and give her parents time to get used to the baby.

Lucille heeded Auntie Ena and tried harder with Christopher, although she didn't like him crying all the time and being reprimanded for disturbing him: 'I don't see why I can't play me records. It doesn't matter about no one else 'avin' any sleep, does it? 'E meks more row than 'undred record players.

Bloomin' fog 'orn. An' they wouldn't mek records if you weren't supposed to play 'em, would they?' When the baby was kidnapped in his pram, the police suspected Lucille of being involved as she was the last person to see him and her jealousy was well known. It was only when he was found safe and sound that her name was cleared.

The creation of Liverpool singing sensation Brett Falcon rocketed Lucille to fame in the world of teenyboppers as president of his fan club. Lucille had known Brett because he'd lived in Coronation Street and, as Walter Potts, had cleaned windows for a living. He'd been turned into a pop star and renamed by Dennis Tanner and, right from the start, Lucille had declared him fab. When his debut single zoomed into the charts Lucille had to fight through hordes of screaming girls just to get to her own front door.

When Concepta's father became ill, the family moved to Ireland, leaving Lucille at the Rovers with Jack and Annie Walker. The original plan was for her to remain in Weatherfield until after her exams, but then she took a job in the lab of a local cotton mill.

Living with the Walkers was very different from life at No.7: Annie was a snob who insisted on lessons for Lucille in deportment and elocution. However, with the Walkers working in the bar every evening Lucille had more freedom to listen to her records and read magazines, although her tastes grated on Annie: 'Manfred Mann – The Rolling Stones – Cilla Black – and a gentleman called Wayne Fontana with the Mindbenders. Those names are engraved on my memory to my dying day. I never closed my eyes once last night.' Lucille was a keen singer herself and won first prize at a local talent show for her version of the Mary Wells hit 'My Guy'.

At sixteen Lucille fell for the manly charms of Borstal boy Ray Langton. He was in his early twenties and exactly the sort of youth who horrified Annie Walker – rough and ready with a coarse tongue and wicked eyes. Lucille couldn't believe he was interested in her – and wasn't surprised later to learn that he was using her as a cover to steal from the Rovers and its neighbours. When she said she would tell the Walkers, he threatened her with sexual violence but luckily Harry's old friend Len Fairclough was on hand to give him a sound beating.

A couple of years later Lucille fell in love again, this time telling everyone it was *the real thing*. Gordon Clegg was the object of her desire, the son of the local shopkeeper. In Annie's eyes, he was a much more suitable catch: polite, well-mannered and training to

be an accountant. The only thing against him was his youth: he and Lucille were only eighteen. When Gordon's mother, Maggie, and Annie both refused to allow the couple to see each other, the youngsters eloped, heading for Gretna Green. However, the train was delayed at Preston so they returned home. Although the act convinced their elders that they were serious about each other, Annie couldn't accept that Lucille would ever settle down. The result was that Lucille determined to prove she would make the perfect wife, and a full church wedding was planned for Easter 1969. The banns were being read and Lucille had bought her wedding dress when Gordon

When her parents got at her and when homework got too much, Lucille could always rely on Ena Sharples for a supportive ear.

admitted the idea of marriage frightened him. He jilted Lucille and ran away to London. She tried to hide her heartache by throwing herself at her boss, bookie Dave Smith, a man older than her father. She was perfectly safe, though, as Dave was smart enough to recognize the pain behind her defiant attitude. He took her out for a meal and made a pass at her to force her to face up to reality. She broke down and sobbed for her lost love, as Dave held her in an avuncular embrace.

Lucille suffered two great losses while she was living at the Rovers. First, her father

Harry, was killed, crushed under a van while over in England for Elsie Tanner's wedding, and then gentle Jack Walker died of a heart-attack. Lucille was left alone with her auntie Annie and, with no one to act as a buffer, life between the two women became one great battle.

Although naturally bright, Lucille was lazy, which annoyed Annie. She shunned further education or a career structure for a succession of dead-end jobs in shops and factories where she had an active social life and no responsibilities. Annie was horrified when she took a job as a go-go dancer at the Aquarius,

'Now listen here, young lady' – Lucille closes her ears as her father Harry lets rip with another lecture.

a rival pub, but Lucille hung on to the job by threatening to write to the brewery saying that Annie didn't approve of the entertainment they endorsed.

Although at the centre of the swinging sixties, Lucille escaped the influence of free love until 1974 when she lost her virginity to Danny Burrows, a garage mechanic, with whom she set up home. Lucille delighted in Auntie Annie's outrage until she discovered Danny had a wife and child and then she had no qualms about running back to the Rovers. Shortly afterwards Gordon Clegg returned to the Street. The sight of him brought back all Lucille's memories of pain and she fled to Ireland for an impromptu holiday with Concepta. Once there, she decided never to return.

Character Name:	TRACY LYNETTE PRESTON
Date of Birth:	24 January 1977
Husband:	Robert Preston (1996–)
Parents:	Ray and Deirdre Langton. Adopted by Ken Barlow

Much of Lucille's story was repeated twenty years later in the life of another Weatherfield girl, Tracy Langton Barlow. Like Lucille, Tracy lost a parent, had a step-parent and abandoned further education for shop work. She was as fascinated by the sounds of the early nineties as Lucille had been by those of the sixties and stunned the

The generation gap causes Tracy to believe Deirdre doesn't understand what it's like being a teenager in downtown Weatherfield.

residents with her fashion sense, just as Lucille had. However, while Lucille was thwarted in love, Tracy found true romance in the arms of a carpet-fitter.

Tracy was born in the year of the Queen's Silver Jubilee, 1977, and won a bouncing-baby competition when just three months old. Her family lived at No. 5 Coronation Street until father Ray, who had treated Lucille so badly, deserted his wife and child for a new life in Holland. After he left, Tracy and her mother lodged at various locations until Deirdre married Ken Barlow and Tracy moved into the back bedroom at No.1 Coronation Street. Ken adopted Tracy and for a while she had a secure family environment.

The Barlow family was split apart in 1990 when Deirdre threw out unfaithful Ken and Tracy found herself in the middle of an emotional tug-of-war, with both parents using her to score points against the other. These were bad years for Tracy – no security at home, suffocated by her mother's possessiveness and exams at school, which were made all the worse for Ken's being appointed her form teacher.

Tracy had always admired the way her mother had fought against the odds to bring her up, but all that changed when she learned that, years before Ken's infidelity, Deirdre herself had had an affair with businessman Mike Baldwin. Tracy blew up. She told Deirdre that she was a hypocrite, that if she had forgiven Ken as he had forgiven her they could still be a happy family: 'You threw him out over that girlfriend. And I know he wanted to come back. And he begged you. And I begged you. And you wouldn't. But he'd forgiven *you*, hadn't he? So why couldn't you? You're a lousy rotten cow and I hate you!' A little later, Tracy made a drunken pass at Deirdre's boyfriend, Doug Murray. Deirdre was livid and slapped her daughter's face, but was grateful that Doug hadn't taken advantage of her.

After failing her exams and getting a job in a florist's, Tracy decided she had had enough of Ken and Deirdre's feuding and left home to move in with a twenty-two-year-old delivery-man, Craig Lee. Deirdre washed her hands of Tracy but Ken was appalled that his sixteen-year-old-daughter was living 'in sin' with a guitar-strumming, spaced-out no-hoper. Both parents were relieved when they split up, but by then Deirdre had married a twenty-one-year-old Moroccan and Ken had made the local hairdresser pregnant. Mortified by her parents' behaviour, Tracy moved to London, where she met Robert Preston, a Manchester lad living in the south. They returned north for their registry office wedding, where Tracy shocked her relatives by marrying in a second-hand dress with Doc Marten boots.

Character Name:	SHARON GASKELL
Date of Birth:	24 March 1965
Parents:	Geoffrey and Karen Gaskell

Sharon Gaskell was fifteen in 1982 when she first arrived in the Street. The only girl in a household of criminally minded boys, she was a tomboy more interested in a tool-kit than a doll's house. She arrived as Len and Rita Fairclough's foster-daughter at No. 9 and was pleasantly surprised to discover that they were very easy-going. After only a couple of weeks with them she begged her social worker to allow her to stay at No. 9 rather than return to her long-term home: 'I ain't going back there. I wanna stay with Rita! The daughter, Pam, don't like me. She thinks I'm a real scrubber. I'll finish up dotting her one. Honest. I mean, she offered to teach me to play the guitar!'

Len was delighted when Sharon showed an interest in his building work and helped him in his firm. Rita ran a small newsagent's and put few restrictions on Sharon, seeing herself at the same age in the reckless teenager. However, when she was sixteen Rita had become pregnant by a local boy and she was determined that a similar fate wasn't going to befall Sharon. During Sharon's sixteenth birthday party, her boyfriend, Steve Dunthorne, tried to lure her up to the Faircloughs' bedroom but Len and Rita were able to interrupt just in time. Rita had to stop Len punching the boy as he threw him out of the house. It was through Rita that Sharon learned that her body was her most precious possession and that she must treat it with respect.

Rita kept a wary eye on Sharon as she blos-somed into an attractive young woman but she failed to pick up the danger signals that Sharon was falling in love - unfortunately with garage mechanic Brian Tilsley, who was married with a young son. Sharon used any excuse to see him, from a punctured bicycle tyre to baby-sitting. While looking after his son Nicky, she stole a photograph of her hero and put it in a locket around her neck and once, when Brian drove her home late at night, she built up the courage to snog him, telling him that she loved him.

Brian was flattered by her attention and did nothing to curb it, which led Sharon to believe he loved her too. In her mind the only

Rita and Len came to parenthood late and then they were landed with a troublesome teenager rather than a baby.

Jenny refuses to listen to reason as Alan and her surrogate mother Rita try to explain why she can't start a singing career.

obstacle was his wife, Gail, so Sharon squared up to her rival. However, Gail refused to discuss it and went straight to Rita, who told Sharon to stay away from Brian. Sharon hit back, reminding Rita of her own past and how she had lived with a married man. That earned her a slap in the face but when Brian, prompted by Gail, told her that he didn't love her and never would, Sharon dissolved into tears and ran back to Rita for comfort. When Len was told of what had occured, he was all for 'sorting Brian out', feeling completely out of his depth in female matters.

Living on the Street became unbearable for Sharon. She couldn't cope with seeing Brian all the time so when the chance came of a job as a kennel-maid in Sheffield, she took it, saying a sad farewell to the Faircloughs, who were now living in the house that she had helped Len to build, No.7 Coronation Street.

Character Name:	JENNY BRADLEY
Date of Birth:	15 February 1971
Parents:	Alan and Pat Bradley

Rita Fairclough's second foster-daughter was Jenny Bradley, a fourteen-year-old who came to live at No. 7 after the death of her mother in a car crash. Her parents had divorced eight years previously, and Rita was asked to care for the girl until she could be reunited with her father, Alan. At first Jenny refused to speak to Alan, accusing him of having abandoned her but slowly, with Rita's help, Alan won her confidence and the pair moved into a flat on Ashdale Road.

Jenny was interested in a singing career and was grateful for Rita's advice and for setting up an audition with theatrical agent Alec Gilroy. Alec thought the youngster had talent, but Alan refused to allow his daughter to work in seedy nightclubs. Jenny resented her father's attitude and with Rita's support she entered, and won, a talent competition in Rochdale. She travelled to it in Rita's car, borrowed by her boyfriend Martin Platt. Although she was only sixteen she insisted on trying to drive part of the way home but couldn't control the vehicle. It ploughed into a field, overturned and Martin was knocked unconscious. Petrified, Jenny told the police that Martin had been driving at the time of the crash, and Alan accused him of nearly killing his daughter. Jenny was grateful when Martin corroborated her story but she had to tell the truth to stop Alan thumping Martin. Humiliation followed when Alan marched them to the police station to confess.

Unlike most of the Street's teenagers, Jenny decided to stay on at school for A levels. Alan and Rita were now an acknowledged couple and the three lived together at No. 7. Jenny's head was full of romance and, at her suggestion, Alan planned a surprise wedding for Rita. He told Rita that they were attending a friend's wedding and it was only when they arrived at the registry office that she discovered she was to be the bride. Jenny was upset when Rita refused to go through with it and rowed with Alan for tricking her.

For a while it looked as if Jenny would do better in the marriage stakes than her father. She went grape-picking in France with Martin but then stayed on longer than originally planned: French medical student Patric Podevin seduced her with his Gallic accent and deep blue eyes. He proposed and a delighted Jenny returned to England with her fiancé. On hearing his daughter's news, Alan was prepared to have Patric run out of the country for child stealing but when he met the young man he was forced to change his mind: here was an intelligent, polite, charming student, who understood that Jenny was too young to marry. Patric suggested that they

remained engaged for two years while he completed his degree, to which Alan agreed, but Jenny accused him of wavering in his love.

Before returning to France, Patric gave Jenny a diamond engagement ring and vowed to remain true to her. She was thrilled to wear it around school and boasted of her future as Madame Podevin. But her love for Patric didn't stop Jenny wanting to have fun in Manchester, and when her friend Lisa Wood's boyfriend made a pass at her she allowed him a passionate kiss. Unfortunately Lisa saw it and promptly ended their friendship. She also told Patric about the kiss and that Jenny took off his ring when she went out at night. Patric was heartbroken and broke the engagement.

Jenny's A level studies, in English, chemistry and biology, suffered as she underwent a turbulent final year at school in which Alan attempted to murder Rita, went on the run from the police, was caught, imprisoned, released and finally killed by a tram. Jenny did not know who to support, injured Rita or desperate Alan. She felt sorry for Alan in prison but ended by blaming Rita for Alan's death. Somehow, though, she passed all three subjects and began a course in environmental studies at Manchester Polytechnic, but had a nervous breakdown in her first term. It was Rita who brought her out of her dark tunnel, expressing love for her and helping her to come to terms with her father's death.

Rita moved out of No. 7, allowing Jenny to live there with a succession of fellow students. However, Jenny grew bored of academic work and was asked to leave college due to her poor attendance record. She then appalled Rita and housemate Angie Freeman by embarking on an affair with married dentist Robert Weston, twelve years her senior. Rita warned Jenny that Robert was just using her, but Jenny felt vindicated when he walked out on his family to be with her. She gladly left Coronation Street behind her and set up home with him.

~

"Don't tell me about my life! Don't tell me what I could do with it! Everybody but me's had a go at at my life so far and it hasn't been much fun!"

Jenny Bradley

~

Newly-weds Leanne and Nick nearly ended up in the divorce courts when he used her as bait to trap his father's killer.

Character Name:	TOYAH BATTERSBY
Date of Birth:	27 May 1982
Parents:	Janice Lee and Ronnie Clegg Les Battersby (step)
Character Name:	LEANNE ANIKA TILSLEY
Date of Birth:	2 July 1981
Husband:	Nick Tilsley (1998–)
Parents:	Les and Babs Battersby Janice Lee (step)

The two teenagers to hit the Street most recently are the youngest members of the dreaded Battersby clan, Leanne and Toyah. On arrival at No. 5 in 1997 they already had a string of convictions between them for assault, shop-lifting and threatening behaviour – not bad for a fifteen- and sixteen-year-old. The girls aren't actually sisters: Leanne is Les's daughter and Toyah is Janice's, but they've been together so long that that doesn't seem to matter.

Toyah seems to drift through life in a bewildered state, like a rabbit shot with a tranquillizing dart. As soon as she set foot on the Street she marked her card by lifting Bill Webster's electric drill and giving it to Les at a house-warming party. When, later, Bill confronted the family, Toyah was happy to play along with Les's explanation that she was undergoing psychiatric treatment for kleptomania. She seems to spend each day stating varying degrees of hatred against school, boys, parents, Leanne and herself. Whenever there is a family problem, Toyah pleads 'It ain't my fault!' but in early 1998 she took an active role in standing up against something that she recognized as wrong and fought Les over the planned development of the Red Rec. However strong her passions for the fight, though, they did not stem from deep eco-warrior feelings but from her obsession with Spider Nugent, the lad next door determined to save the world, who taught her to put trees before buildings.

Leanne left school with no qualifications and no expectations for a rosy future, fully aware that her only assets were her attitude, developed on the streets, and her body: 'That's me. Good laugh, good snog, bit obsessive – and thick.' She had no idea that only a short while after moving to the new house she would find a love that caused her to adjust the way she felt about everything. As soon as she saw Nick Tilsley she was bowled over by his good looks and tight T-shirts. Here was the son of the same Brian who had driven Sharon Gaskell to passionate despair, and Nick, now sixteen, had inherited all his father's physical attractions. The only obstacle to the young couple's love was Nick's tight-lipped mother, Gail, who branded Leanne a back-street tart and refused to allow her precious Nick anywhere near her. Nick wouldn't listen to her and the couple set up a secret love nest at No. 4, an empty two-bedroomed house on the Street. Gail worried that Leanne would trap Nick by becoming pregnant, which made Leanne ponder why her own mother didn't seem bothered what she got up to or who with.

Shortly after Nick's seventeenth birthday Leanne and he eloped to Scotland. They married in Gretna Green registry office and returned to Weatherfield as man and wife. Gail was horrified but there was nothing she could do about it. Later on in 1998, the marriage nearly ended after Nick grew obsessed with his father's murderer, Darren Wheatley. When Wheatley was released on parole Nick pushed Leanne to contact him, pretending to fancy him. Wheatley turned up and was

attacked by Nick who wanted to kill him. Leanne was horrified that Nick could put her through such an ordeal.

Having now put all this behind them, Leanne is trying hard to show that she intends to be a good wife for Nick, and has persuaded Rita to employ her at the Kabin. Who knows, perhaps Rita can instil in her new assistant the values she bestowed upon Sharon and Jenny?

Toyah's infatuation with eco-warrior Spider caused her to free a turkey, sabotage a supermarket and chain herself to trees.

125

> *"The purpose of football is to score goals, right? Well, it's daft. You've got two teams on the field and they're both kicking in opposite directions. Why don't they both kick the same way? Then they can score as many goals as they like."*

RAQUEL WOLSTENHULME

They come from different walks of life, are educated to various degrees and pass through the job market with little thought of a career until they hit thirty. They don't understand their Independent sisters and stop to coo into the prams pushed by Struggling Mothers. When they are teenagers, their motto is 'party, party, all the way' but when their energy flags they face a crossroads: marriage to a nice lad in a badly paid job, or life as an outgoing party girl – or Gad-about. They never achieved much at school, apart from lessons learned behind the bike shed, and they tend to drift through life always on the verge of a giant giggling fit, pulled up short whenever life slaps them in the face. For the past thirty-eight years Silly Young Things have arrived, hung up their film star and pop posters, cracked their gum and stared dreamily out of the window at the boy down the Street.

Character Name:	DOREEN
	CAROLE
	LOSTOCK
Date of Birth:	1 February 1941
Parents:	Jack and Amy
	Lostock

Sheila and Doreen debate what to do on Saturday night – the flicks, the Palais, the Rovers or a night in washing their hair.

The first to hit the Street came in a couple, factory workers Sheila Birtles and Doreen Lostock, commonly remembered as the 'barmcake girls' as they were always in the Corner Shop at lunch-time

with long lists of orders. They had only one topic of conversation: boys. Talk of the Palais, the bowling alley, the flicks and work was punctuated with remarks such as 'Ohhh, he was loverly', 'Ohhh, I could eat him on a buttie', 'Here, kid, I think they've clocked us' and 'Did you see his eyes? Ohhh, to dream of.'

Of the two, Doreen was the more upfront, or 'mouthy', as Elsie Tanner put it. A lively girl, she was popular with the menfolk, who envied her boyfriend Billy Walker. Billy's mother Annie had an altogether different view of Doreen: 'No girl can have a bust that size and remain level-headed.' However, that didn't stop her employing Doreen part-time behind the Rovers' bar. Doreen took the job to compensate for having to spend her days sewing on buttons at the raincoat factory. Girls of Doreen's class, leaving school with no qualifications, were expected to become factory fodder, and carrying out this monotonous work provided no stimulus to Doreen. She was smart enough to know it was a dead-end job and when the foreman started groping her she resigned. She kept on the bar work and could also be found propping up the counter at Snapes Café on Rosamund Street, operating the coffee machine and getting fresh with teddy-boys.

In an attempt to do something with her life she persuaded her best friend Sheila to join her in renting Florrie Lindley's bedsit over the Corner Shop. The move coincided with yet another career change for Doreen who became junior assistant at Gamma Garments, run by Leonard Swindley and Emily Nugent or, as Doreen called them, 'the undynamic duo'. In the world of mayhem that was Gamma, Doreen often believed she was the only sane person working there. Swindley and Nugent seemed to create havoc every time they served a customer, ordered stock or changed a window display.

Despite all her attempts to ensnare a man, Doreen had terrible luck with dating. She

found the local lads boorish, only interested in a fumble in the back row of the Luxy. A keen reader of romantic fiction, she longed to be swept off her feet by a handsome seafarer, but they were thin on the ground in Weatherfield. When she did land a date, Doreen tended to frighten the lad off, either with her wisecracking or her dissatisfaction with her looks: 'I'd like to wear one of them new with-it wigs but if we do a bit o' snoggin' it might fall off.'

Lusting after adventure, Doreen gave up on Gamma and the flat, and volunteered for the WRAC in a bid to see the world. She waved farewell to Weatherfield and set about learning to drive tanks.

Character Name:	SHEILA CROSSLEY
Date of Birth:	23 April 1940
Husband:	Neil Crossley (1966–)
Children:	Danny (1964)
Parents:	Dick and Marge Birtles

The realization that reliable Jerry loved her came too late for Sheila.

Doreen's dippy friend Sheila had more luck with boys. She was quieter, happy to listen to a lad talking about himself. Soon after moving into a flat she started to date builder's apprentice Jerry Booth, although she set standards for her suitor: 'Make sure you put some aftershave on. It makes all me toes curl up.' Their dates consisted of trips on his tandem or sitting on a park bench holding hands, and for a while Sheila was happy. Eventually, though, she decided he was too wet, especially compared with Neil Crossley, a self-assured older man, who had replaced Swindley as manager of Gamma Garments. Doreen warned Sheila that he was a wolf, but Sheila allowed her romantic heart to believe Neil's talk of never-ending love and engagement rings as he steered her towards her bed. When Sheila's other friends tried to warn her that Neil was no good, she believed they were all jealous: 'I'm not married to Jerry Booth, yer know! I'm me own boss an' I'll do what I choose, never mind what anybody says! I'm not goin' to rot in Coronation Street – I'm not goin' to stay 'ere like the rest o' you. I'm 'aving somethin' different – an' nobody's goin' to stop me neither. So you can get out of 'ere an' mind yer own business. You silly old cow!'

When he was uncovered as a petty crook, Neil left the area, owing money to local businessmen and telling Sheila she was 'nothing special'. She was crushed by his rejection as she had discovered that she was pregnant. Unable to face the disgrace of a child out of wedlock, Sheila turned on the gas and swallowed a handful of pills. Yet even death was denied her, as neighbour Dennis Tanner smelt the gas and broke a window to rescue the unconscious Sheila. She was taken to her parents' home in Rawtenstall and was soon forgotten by the residents. Yet her memory stayed alive in Jerry Booth's heart: when he married typist Myra Dickenson he asked Dennis Tanner to be his best man, in recognition of his having saved Sheila's life.

Three years later, Jerry was annoyed to be set up on a blind date at a nightclub. He was all ready to walk out when he discovered that Sheila was the date. Unable to bring up her son, Danny, alone, she had been forced to have him fostered and had decided to return

to Weatherfield. She wanted to find the only man who had ever loved her for herself in the hope that he would accept Danny. Elsie Tanner gave Sheila a room at No.11 and she took a job operating a welding machine at the PVC factory across the Street.

It was 1966, the height of the swinging sixties, but Sheila wanted to settle down. While her workmates were dancing and sitting on fellers' knees, Sheila encouraged Jerry to show his feelings for her. As always Jerry was slow to declare himself and Neil Crossley re-entered Sheila's life. He was stunned to discover he was a father but, keen to shoulder responsibility for the first time in his life, he proposed to her and the pair eloped to Sheffield, leaving Jerry wondering what had happened.

Character Name:	AUDREY FLEMING
Date of Birth:	19 May 1951
Husband:	Dickie Fleming (1968–70)
Parents:	Arthur and Freda Bright

Sixteen-year-old Audrey Bright was the envy of all her schoolfriends when, in the summer of 1968, she eloped to Gretna Green and married her boyfriend, eighteen-year-old apprentice Dickie Fleming. As a wedding present, Dickie's despairing father gave him the money to buy the dilapidated No. 3 Coronation Street. There was nothing left for luxuries such as a sofa, or a carpet, but the newly-weds were thrilled with their very own love nest. Audrey left school and took a job as a petrol-pump attendant on £5 a week, becoming the main breadwinner.

The happiness at No. 3 didn't last long as the novelty of marriage wore off: the romance of winning the race to be first married in her class had left Audrey a struggling housewife,

~

"Make sure you put some aftershave on. It makes all me toes curl up."

SHEILA CROSSLEY

~

while her darling Dickie snored in bed, and hung around the house at weekends as he had no money to go out. Within weeks Audrey was looking on in envy as her friends larked about and had fun, while she sat in darning socks.

Dickie was a weak lad and was happy to leave the decision-making to Audrey. He had no strong views on anything and Audrey discovered she had married a bore. Dissatisfied, her eye lit on rugged Ray Langton. His reputation as a womanizer made him all the more appealing and Audrey went out of her way to make sure he knew she was interested.

Unwittingly Dickie played into her hands by inviting his 'pal' Ray to lodge with them in an attempt to boost their income. Ray was quick to take advantage of his friend's generosity and amused Audrey by teasing him: 'You stick at technical college, mate. No worries. Nice even pace. Temperamentally you're

suited to it. You wouldn't thrive on chance.' Audrey made her attraction to him blatantly obvious: she talked to him while ignoring her husband, served him the best food and put Dickie down whenever she could. She hated having to share Dickie's bed, yet became frustrated that her strict upbringing wouldn't allow her to become Ray's lover. The local busybodies got their teeth stuck into the unusual relationship, some sympathizing with Audrey but most feeling that she should stick with her husband.

The situation reached its climax during a Street outing to Windermere. Audrey sat holding hands with Ray on the coach and decided that the time had come to cement their relationship. As he led her off to a lakeside copse Dickie sprang into action, grabbed Ray and thumped him. The two brawled until separated by their neighbours and on the way

Ena Sharples tries to give Audrey a word of wisdom, breaching the 55-year age gap between them.

home Audrey sat next to Dickie refusing to speak to him. The tension lasted until suddenly the coach crashed into a tree. Ray was thrown through the windscreen which left him paralysed from the waist down.

With Ray in a wheelchair, Dickie agreed to let him stay on at No. 3. But Audrey lost interest in Ray and objected to having to look after an invalid – that was, until he regained the use of his legs and decided to marry local girl Sandra Butler, who had declared her love for him when he was wheelchair-bound. As soon as Ray and Sandra had set the date for their wedding Audrey threw herself at him again, swearing love and begging him to cast off Sandra: 'Don't tell me to go away and grow up, Ray, I don't want to. Not any more. I grew up too fast with Dickie. We're standing here and it's like electric between us. You can almost see it . . . touch it. And there's nothing we can do, is there, Ray? I don't love Dickie. I don't think I even respect him any more. And I'll always love you.'

When he heard about this episode Dickie packed his bags, but this had little effect on Audrey, compared to the knowledge that Ray didn't want her in his life. Unable to continue living so near the man she said she loved, Audrey packed her own bags and returned to her native Preston.

```
Character Name:   PATRICIA
                  MARLENE
                  (TRICIA) HOPKINS
Date of Birth:    5 March 1958
Parents:          Idris and Vera
                  Hopkins
```

The 1970s versions of Doreen and Sheila, living above the shop flat, were Tricia Hopkins and her giggling friend Gail Potter. Gail matured, married and is today living in the Street as Mrs Platt. Tricia, however,

had a shorter stay, between 1975 and 1976. She was the only daughter of the Welsh Hopkins family who rented the shop from Gordon Clegg. Tricia moved into the bedsit with her best friend Gail when the rest of her family did a moonlight flit. Gordon was glad to see the back of the troublesome family but agreed to allow the two teenagers to stay and run the shop until a buyer could be found.

Tricia was a terrible businesswoman: she allowed pounds' worth of credit to local lads she fancied who ran up huge bills then disappeared. Tricia would shut the shop for hours over lunch to dance with the boys in the back room. She was a big fan of Radio Luxembourg and David Cassidy, and dreamed of the day Prince Charles would come in for a tin of oxtail soup and fall for her big hazel eyes: 'You can get rubbish blokes, there's plenty of them rubbin' about. Good stuff's in very short supply. Sort of feller who picks you up in a long red sports car. An' brings you flowers. An' says, "Tonight the world is yours – anywhere." An' you pick a dead posh restaurant an' it's all soft lights an' violins an' that.'

Where men were concerned Tricia was gullible and easily flattered; she had no qualms in going out with anyone who showed an interest. For months she had a crush on Ray Langton, although he looked upon her as a silly little kid. On the pretence that she wanted a shelf built in the flat she lured him upstairs and surprised him with a passionate kiss. He responded, unaware that Gail was hidden behind a curtain with a camera. The photograph became Tricia's most treasured possession but any thoughts she had of romance were ruined when he married Deirdre Hunt.

Tricia took against Deirdre immediately and started spreading rumours that Ray was two-timing her with a blonde checkout assistant. Deirdre put a stop to her malicious tongue by thumping her and giving her a black eye.

When Gordon discovered how the shop was being run, he sacked both Tricia and Gail, who used their life savings to enrol on a modelling course – run by a con man who disappeared with the money. Then Tricia decided to make the best of her 'cultured' voice and took a job selling showers over the telephone – which meant having a phone installed in the flat, a real boost to her social life. The job didn't last, though, and she was soon back behind the counter of the shop, working for new owner Renee Bradshaw.

Renee demanded high standards but Tricia was content to sit around doing nothing and expected others to wait on her. When Renee gave the girls notice to quit the flat, as she had plans for it, Gail found alternative accommodation but Tricia left the Street to return to her family.

Character Name:	RAQUEL CATHERINE WATTS
Date of Birth:	26 May 1966
Husband:	Norman Watts (1995–)
Parents:	Larry and Eileen Wolstenhulme

Fifteen years separate Tricia Hopkins and Raquel Wolstenhulme, and during that time women came out of kitchens to take control of their lives, run large organizations and entered No.10 Downing Street, but all this appeared to have passed Raquel by. She dreamed of marrying Mr Right and of standing on the doorstep with her two children, 'Blake and Tiffany', to kiss her husband goodbye as he set off to work each morning.

The Corner Shop flat gave Tricia and Gail freedom from their parents even though their plans for fast living and the high life never materialized.

But it was impossible to find Mr Right.

As a child Raquel had always looked up to her father, Larry. Her mother suffered from depression and endured so much criticism from her husband that she blotted out thirteen years with alcohol. Growing up in their council house with her sister Bernice, Raquel took on her mother's role, cooking and keeping house.

Picked on at school for her tallness, it came as a surprise when, at fifteen, the boys in her class voted her the most desirable girl. Suddenly her legs were admired and she basked in her new popularity. Boyfriends came and went over the next few years – Raquel fell instantly in love with each one and was heartbroken when she realized the lads were only interested in her body. It was when she opened her mouth that she let her lovers down: her father had told her she had no brain so Raquel had never pushed herself to acquire any knowledge: 'The only top mark I ever got at school was for attendance.'

Raquel first appeared on the Street in 1991 wearing a swimsuit and a sash as 'Miss Bettabuy Weatherfield'. Bettabuy was the name of the supermarket where she worked on the tills. Her boss was Curly Watts and, in the hope of promotion, Raquel made herself available for him. She was startled to discover that, while he found her attractive, he was interested in more than getting her into bed. When he set about wooing her, Raquel bolted for safety, taking up with a photographer who promised to turn her into a star.

Five months later she was back in Coronation Street, weeping on Curly's shoulder: the photographer had only been interested in sex and her father had thrown her out after finding some pictures of her semi-naked. With Curly's help she took a job as barmaid at the Rovers and moved in as Des Barnes's lodger at No. 6. At least, that's what she told the neighbours. In reality she spent only one night in the spare room.

In just a few months Raquel had found a home, a job and the two men who would dominate her life for the next four years. Des was a love rat who lusted after Raquel but offered no commitment. He applauded her naïvety and lack of intelligence and cast her aside when he felt there was a chance his ex-wife wanted him back. Raquel moved into the Rovers, and alarmed landlord Alec Gilroy: 'I think she might be moulting; there's hairs everywhere. I opened the fridge this morning and I found her tights in there. And the scent! Between her and Bet my nasal passages are in rags.'

At work she was adopted by Alec's wife Bet, who decided she was too vulnerable to be out in the real world. Bet looked on as, time after time, men cheated on Raquel, and saw no point in teasing her as some of the regulars did: 'It's like pulling the wings off a butterfly.' Bet represented the mother figure Raquel had always lacked, who took an interest in her, celebrated her success and was there with a shoulder to cry on when she needed one. Their relationship threatened new barmaid Tanya Pooley, who fought to discredit Raquel in Bet's eyes. She grew jealous of all the attention Raquel received, not just from the boss but from all the regulars, male and female. It seemed to Tanya that everyone loved Raquel. Knowing that Raquel was hoping to build up her modelling career, she left a message on her answerphone inviting her to a bogus modelling assignment. Raquel spent a cold, humiliating evening waiting for a photographer to turn up. When she discovered Tanya was behind the cruel trick, she was stunned when the other girl told her what she thought of her: 'I'm sick of you looking down your long bony nose at the rest of us. Going on about how you're not really a barmaid, you're really a model. Where in fact what you really are is an over-madeup tart. And that's all you'll ever be.'

Encouraged by Curly, Raquel tried to

"The only top mark I got at school was for attendance."

RAQUEL WATTS

educate herself. She tried to read but lacked concentration so took to watching documentaries on television. The problem was that, no matter how carefully a theory was explained to her, she could never seem to get the hang of it. She once tried to explain sexual attraction: 'If you take a mirror and stick it up your nose – like dividing your face – well, if you look into another mirror you can sort of make one big face out of half of your face, and it's different left and right. One of them's more what your face would be if you were a man and the other's more what it would be if you were a woman, if you weren't one already. So, when you fall for somebody what you're seeing – now, hang on a minute 'cos this bit's complicated – you see the face made up of the halves they'd be if that person were the same sex as you are. So your brain is imagining (although you don't know this), and if your brain is seeing that person as being the sort of person that you think you are yourself then you

fancy that person and it's as simple as that!'

When Des Barnes asked Raquel to move in with him again she felt certain the arrangement would lead to marriage. He gave her the freedom to decorate the house and plan the garden, and she went ahead with an eye to having children running in and out and maybe a cocker spaniel lying on the sofa. She planned her wedding day, down to her bouquet, 'peach roses and white freesias', and was thrilled to be given an assignment modelling wedding dresses. The photographer was pleased with the pictures and gave some to Raquel as a memento, which she left lying around in the house, but Des failed to pick up on the hint. It wasn't until she had lived with him for six months that Raquel made the sickening discovery that he was two-timing her with Tanya. When he stormed out of the house one night Raquel trailed him through the streets and into Tanya's flat, where she confronted Tanya in bed with her boyfriend.

Curly tries to work out how and when his wife changed from an empty-headed doe into an ambitious career woman.

135

Horrified to hear him refer to Tanya as 'my girl' Raquel fled to the Rovers and Bet, who moved her back into the pub.

Raquel was also comforted by Curly who, after a decent interval, proposed to her. Although Raquel didn't love him, she had always been fond of him, so she accepted. Deep down, though, she knew she was marrying Curly to escape Des and that this was not fair. The couple threw an engagement party, which was wrecked by Des who proposed to Raquel himself. In desperation she told both men that she couldn't marry either of them.

The party had been at the start of 1995 and for that whole year Raquel was on an emotional rollercoaster. Her modelling career dried up and she once dated Curly's boss, Leo Firman, who lured her into the deserted supermarket and tried to rape her in the stockroom. This brought her closer to Curly but she was still too attracted to Des to commit herself to him. Des, however, continued to see Raquel as a harbour in which to moor whenever he was battered by the sea of love and encouraged her to believe they might have a future together.

Eventually, after spending a night with Des, Raquel saw herself through his eyes – the willing girl across the street who was conveniently there when needed. 'I'm so stupid. I thought Des really, truly, wanted me. I thought he was serious. And so I told myself he was different, and we could make it work . . . and it wasn't what he wanted at all. What he wanted was the use of me. I never learn! And now I feel cheap, and dirty, and second-hand and, more than anything, so stupid.' Deciding that someone must protect her from Des, she proposed to Curly. They married almost immediately, and in secret so that Des couldn't put her off the idea. Before the registry officer ceremony Raquel sat in the toilet, crying for her romantic wedding dreams which had come to nothing.

Being married to Curly wasn't hard; he was undemanding, she knew he would do anything she asked and was keen to have children. But Raquel noticed that she had changed: the silly little thing had matured into a weary woman. She gave up working in the Rovers and took courses in aromatherapy and beauty treatment. She cut her long hair to shoulder-length and the tight little dresses made way for trouser suits. Finally the squeaky, high-pitched tone she had cultured as a teenager (men seemed to like it as it went with the defenceless blonde look) was dropped for her natural voice. It was a relief to have got Des out of her system but Raquel was sad that she had married a man she did not love. Curly remained devoted to her but she took a job in a beauty salon in a Kuala Lumpur hotel, trying to kid herself that after her year's contract was up she would return.

Character Name:	MAXINE HEAVEY
Date of Birth:	10 November 1975
Parents:	Graham and Di Heavey

Maxine Heavey is as hopeless in love as Raquel was. In fact, the first man she fell for on the Street was Des Barnes. She threw herself at him but he was only interested after he'd had a drink and was feeling sorry for himself. Maxine had attended Weatherfield Comp along with Fiona Middleton and when a vacancy arose in the hair salon where Fiona worked Maxine took it. She had set her heart on a career as a dancer but once installed at the salon she found that chatting to customers and looking at her reflection in the mirrors came naturally.

Although Fiona is now her boss the pair remain the best of friends, with Fiona fully aware of her assistant's limitations: 'No wonder you've not got jet-lag, you haven't got the imagination, have you?' Maxine would be the first to admit she isn't very bright but she had learned early on that she could rely on her looks to get what she wanted in life. At the moment she figures she's too young to worry about the future, marriage and responsibility. She's out to have fun and live life to the full.

Romance, though, has been pretty disastrous. Mechanic Tony Horrocks bored her, Des Barnes used her, she had one drunken night with Curly Watts she's trying to forget, and butcher's lad Ashley Peacock had the audacity to drop her for a homeless single mother. Her most recent romance with Greg Kelly has also had its share of bumpy rides, mainly due to his father Les Battersby's interference. She lives at home with her parents, because they charge her little rent which leaves more money for clothes and nightclubs. Now that Fiona is a mother and can't go out so much, Maxine worried: 'All the decent fellers go round in pairs and I can't keep them both happy can I?' Audrey Roberts offered to go out with her, but the thought of being seen with her appalled Maxine. At least, she figured, *she* still had youth on her side.

Fiona and Maxine went to the same school and grew up the best of friends.

> ## *"Hilda Ogden's the biggest gas-bag since the Graf Zeppelin!"*
>
> ### ELSIE TANNER

There's a type of woman who delights in hearing of the misfortunes of others. She jams her ear to a closed door or squints with determination through a key-hole. Inquisitive, quick-tongued and sometimes vicious, she's of the sort who hung round the guillotine during the French Revolution, knitting as the blade dropped. These are the original fish wives, the vultures who devour a person's good name. But behind the sharp tongue is always a vulnerable woman, often cast aside by the children she nurtured, and married to a man who has had all the spirit drained from him by his critical wife. Life has dealt these women a bad hand, and it seems that their only pleasure comes from passing on the titbits of information they glean in the market-place. And, of course, what they don't know they make up. As Martha Longhurst once indignantly shouted: 'I'm not going to stand here being insulted for saying what everyone else is thinking!'

Character Name:	MARTHA LONGHURST
Date of Birth:	2 September 1896
Husband:	Percy Longhurst (1919–46)
Children:	Lily (1925) Harold (1926)
Parents:	Jack and Mary Hartley
Date of Death	13 May 1964

' 'ave you 'eard about Kenneth Barlow? Well don't tell Ena but...' Minnie listens in as Martha disects a neighbour's love life.

Martha was the first dedicated gossip in the Street. She was Ena Sharples' shrew-like friend, always following two steps behind the great woman, with a dewdrop at the end of her nose. Ena was a master gossip herself but even she used Martha to find out all the details of an intrigue or romance before she berated a resident on their behaviour.

Martha's house on Mawdsley Street backed on to No.11 Coronation Street, giving her a bird's-eye view of Elsie Tanner's back door and all the men who entered at night. She'd rented the tiny house since her marriage to Percy Longhurst in 1919. He was a weaver who lost his job and spirit during the Depression, while Martha struggled to bring up the children, Lily and Harold. Harold drowned as a toddler and Percy died of consumption, leaving Martha to take cleaning jobs to feed Lily. As soon as she could Lily married Wilf Haddon and disappeared to classy Oakhill. Martha hid her hurt at Lily's desertion and swanked about her daughter's lifestyle: 'Our Lily's Wilf is 'avin' a new roof put on the garage to make way for the conservatory. Did I tell you about the conservatory? Oh, it's shop-designed, yer know.'

Cleaning at the Rovers was a good place to pick up the beat of the local drums and find out what was going on. As Martha scrubbed the floor, she listened to Annie and Jack Walker as they mulled over what had been said by their customers. If she learned anything spectacular Martha finished quickly and ran like a whippet for Ena's door. Sometimes the gossip she brought was so red-hot it got her into trouble. Len Fairclough's reaction to hearing her comment on shopkeeper Florrie Lindley's love life was typical: 'You want to watch what you're saying. What's the matter? Aren't Elsie Tanner and me enough for you to talk about without dragging poor Florrie into it? You're always repeating things aren't you? Especially after you've added your own little bits to it. Have you never heard of the law of slander?'

While helping Ena clean the Mission Hall she found an old love letter stuck behind a radiator. As she read it Martha's imagination ran riot: it was from a man named Jack,

thanking a woman for nights of passion. Knowing that Ena's husband had been Alfred, Martha was thrilled to discover her moralizing friend had had a lover, and spread the word that Ena had been unfaithful. Her remarks were finally overheard by Jack Walker, who quietly requested the letter to be returned to its rightful owner – him: Annie had lost it when the residents had been evacuated to the Mission following a gas scare.

Never having ventured further than Blackpool, Martha was thrilled when the Haddons invited her to accompany them on holiday to Spain, although she knew they'd only asked her as a cheap child-minder. The day she was given her passport coincided with a party at the Rovers and she dressed up to show it off. Her joy was short-lived, however, as sitting alone at a table in the snug bar she had a heart-attack and died. Her friend Ena laid her out, organized the funeral – and crossed Lily at the funeral tea: 'I've known you since yer bottom showed through yer bloomers, Lily Longhurst-that-was. You only wanted to use her. You know it, God knows it, and I think she even knew it herself.'

Character Name:	HILDA ALICE OGDEN
Date of Birth:	2 February 1924
Husband:	Stan Ogden (1943–84)
Children:	Irma (1946)
	Trevor (1949)
	Tony (1951)
	Sylvia (1952)
Parents:	Arnold and Florence Crabtree

Martha's job at the Rovers did not stay vacant for long. Next month it was filled by newcomer Hilda Ogden. Hilda was built much like Martha – a small, bird-like woman who darted to and fro, listening, mouth gaping, to the conversation of her neighbours. Her hair was encased in curlers, to ensure that she was always ready to go out somewhere smart. Unfortunately she was seldom asked out anywhere other than Jackson's chippie. A turban to protect her hair and a pinny to keep her skirt clean completed Hilda's daily wardrobe.

She had married her husband Stan after falling over him during the black-out in the war and had brought up four children while he worked away from home on lorries. When she couldn't cope with everything the two youngest children went into a home, leaving Hilda with Irma and Trevor. In 1964, in an attempt to keep the family together, Stan gave up driving and bought No.13 Coronation Street.

Hilda worked like a steam engine, at the Rovers and a host of other locations during her twenty-three years at No.13, while Stan fought hard to avoid all work. Throughout her married life Hilda carried her husband and, in moments of despair, despised his lack of drive, holding it responsible for their meagre existence.

Like Martha, Hilda lost both her remaining children, although neither died. At fourteen Trevor was revealed to be a thief and ran off to London on money stolen from the neighbours, while Irma married as soon as she could but bought the shop next to the Ogdens'. Hilda was proud that her daughter had moved up in the world but furious when she refused her credit. After her husband died, Irma caused scandal by keeping company with a succession of unsavoury men, and Hilda was confronted with juicy gossip about her own daughter. When she overheard her boss Annie Walker discussing Irma, it was too much for her: 'You've been lookin' at us all evening, tittle-tattle written in big letters right across yer eyeballs. What our Irma does is her own business. It's not 'er fault she's attractive an fellers wanna take 'er out. I've never 'eard

GIFT OF THE GAB

As queen of all Street Gossips, Hilda Ogden's nose pressed up against more doorways than Bet Lynch's back. During her twenty-four years on the Street she gave many pearls of wisdom to her neighbours, only they never seemed to listen.

- **On cleaning:** 'Folk seem to think shifting muck's easy, but it isn't. It's an art.'
- **On romance:** 'Anyone caught trying to undo my tiny buttons is going to get his mucky paws slapped.'
- **On training men:** ''Ave you tried mekin' his belly suffer? It works wonders wi' my Stan - three days o' burnt dinner an' no drippin' in the pantry an' he's like putty in me 'ands.'
- **On looks:** 'I were fourteen when I first decided me face didn't suit me.'

that fellers queued up to take your daughter out. And why? Because she's like her mother, that's why, got a face like a pan scrubber.' Eventually Irma made a new life for herself in Canada, but the final insult came in 1973 when the Ogdens tracked down Trevor. They turned up on his doorstep, only to find that he was married with a son and had told his wife that his parents were dead.

Luck hardly ever shone on Hilda. What little she had was normally followed by more ill-fortune than before. In 1965 she made the thrilling discovery of £25 stuffed inside a cigarette packet on the Rovers' floor. Rather than hand it in, she splashed out on a knitted two-piece outfit and then discovered that the money belonged to family friend Charlie Moffatt. He had collected it in his role of insurance man and now faced the sack. Hilda was forced to visit the pawn shop with her treasures to repay what she'd spent. Stan once promised to take her to Paris for her birthday but they spent so much time in the duty-free shop that they missed the flight. Another time, on hearing of a TV detector van roaming the area, Stan tried to hide the set but

dropped it, just as Hilda came home with a licence. Even the inflatable chair she bought from the Better Homes exhibition sprang a leak and deflated. Finally Hilda insisted that Stan change their door number from 13 to 12a. To mark the occasion she roasted a leg of lamb but on stepping outside to admire the new number Stan had screwed on, she locked them out of the house. By the time Stan had broken in, the lamb was burned, and they were told that the council wouldn't let them change their number.

Hilda was devoted to Stan, and hated the role life had cast her in: 'We're just a joke to everybody in this street, aren't we? Either a joke or somebody to level diabolical accusations at. Well, I'm fed up of bein' the clown. I want to play Juliet for a change.' Only on one occasion was she tempted by another man but not even a kiss was exchanged. He was park keeper George Greenwood, who befriended her and invited her to share tea and biscuits with him in his shed. After she took an interest in his budgie he bought her one, which she kept in the same cage as his. Although she wasn't having an affair, Hilda felt that she was being unfaithful to Stan as she sipped tea and shared the events of the day with George. Eventually, the guilt was too much and she ended the friendship. Three years later George re-entered her life when he judged a local flower shop. It was one of Hilda's most embarrassing moments as Stan had entered a bloom stolen from the park, which George identified as one of his most prized flowers.

When she first met Stan, Hilda thought he looked just like Clark Gable and to her he was always the handsomest man on the Street. She came to believe that every woman who smiled at him was his mistress. She once rose at 4.30 a.m. to follow him on his milk round, suspecting him of stopping off to entertain some floozy. When she saw him go into a house she pounced, only to discover the occupant was an eighty-year-old woman whom kind-hearted Stan kept company over break-fast. Elsie Tanner at No.11 was a definite floozy in Hilda's mind, and she often worried about Stan being led astray by her feminine charms. She was mortified when Stan gave Elsie driving lessons, especially when they were stranded all night on the moors. When they returned, Hilda confronted Elsie in the Street and accused her of getting her nails into innocent Stan. Elsie retorted: 'I might be old, Mrs Ogden, but I'm not so old that I have to scrape the bottom of the barrel and chase after great lumps o' lard like your husband.'

Elsie, of course, was no real threat to the Ogden marriage but Mrs Clara Regan at 19 Inkerman Street was, and Hilda was badly hurt by the gossip that linked Stan to the infamous widow. Although he always swore innocence Hilda was certain Clara enter-tained him, and kept watch on the house. When she discovered Clara had a regular boyfriend who was a professional wrestler, she warned him that a certain Stanley Ogden had been seen in Clara's company then sat back in the knowledge that Stan wouldn't be wander-ing her way again. Hilda's jealousy knew no bounds and on one occasion she even lost Stan his job. Wary of his working for ice-cream baroness Rose Bonarti she reported him for trading without a licence.

While Hilda viewed Stan as an unfortu-nate, easily led astray, he saw her as an open purse to scrounge off and exploit. Since she was a child Hilda had always thought she had psychic powers and was thrilled when Stan set her up professionally. Even she was impressed

Hilda where she felt best – at a door with her ear jammed against the keyhole.

when her predictions started to come true. What she didn't know was that Stan ensured that anything she told a client came to pass. The game was up, though, when Hilda told Valerie Barlow she was going to have another child, and Stan had to admit defeat.

Although Stan constantly let Hilda down – allowing the house to become infested by mice in her absence, getting into trouble with the police over a donkey kept in the backyard, losing jobs and treating her badly in front of his mates – she stood by him. When he was accused of being the local Peeping Tom, Hilda confronted his accusers in the Rovers and spat on the floor as she told them what she thought of them: 'You're a bunch of filthy scum the lot of you. Scum! There's not one of you fit to lick my Stan's boots! A maggot wouldn't stop 'ere with you lot. You're like a disease!' When the real culprit was caught Hilda demanded apologies before allowing Stan back into the Rovers.

Hilda was a mistress of the art of gossip-mongering. As shopkeeper Renee Bradshaw put it: 'In darkest Africa they use a set of drums. Here we've got Hilda Ogden. I suppose that's civilization.' From her vantage-point at No.13 she could keep an eye on the whole Street by standing on the sideboard in the front parlour and peering over her nets. She was also next door to siren Elsie Tanner and was well versed in the art of listening through a glass against the party wall. Elsie was often a victim of Hilda's swoops: she would open a back door at random, call out, 'It's only me,' and barge in on the pretext of borrowing sugar or lard while looking out for evidence of marital discord. Elsie often complained to Hilda about her borrowing, but not after 1980 when Hilda came round for some sugar, found the house full of smoke and Elsie unconscious on the sofa. Hilda dragged her to safety.

Hilda was a woman of principle – on learning that Mike Baldwin had moved a woman into his flat she refused to clean it until he gave her £1 a week extra. She had clearly defined views and was upset by shopkeepers who denied her credit or documentaries on Channel Four that showed sex-change operations in graphic detail. She was proud of her scenic 'murial' and her flying ducks. Indeed, as she once explained to Percy Sugden: 'I've come in 'ere, more times than I care to remember, cold, wet, tired out, not a penny in me purse, and the sight o' them ducks an' that murial, well, they've kept my hand away from the gas tap and that's a fact.'

When Stan died in the winter of 1984 Hilda surprised the residents by saying that she had hundreds of happy memories to live on. But life without Stan was empty and she found it hard to get out of the habit of nagging an empty chair. She tried taking in lodgers, but they had no wish for her to run their lives and the world became a lonely place. Vera Duckworth was horrified when her son Terry left home to lodge with Hilda. When he moved out of the back room Kevin Webster moved in, to be later joined by his wife, Sally.

When her employers, the Lowthers, decided to retire to the country, Hilda helped them pack away the silver. During this they were disturbed by thugs, who knocked Hilda unconscious, but Mrs Lowther died in the attack. Hilda became frightened of the world and locked herself away inside No.13 with her cat Rommel, until Dr Lowther offered her a granny flat in his new cottage in Derbyshire.

When Hilda left the Street on Christmas Day 1987 she had commented on, judged and gossiped about each of the residents who waved her a fond farewell. She had stayed longer than Elsie Tanner, Annie Walker and Len Fairclough, and found that the newer generation wasn't so interested in her tittle-tattle. Besides, these days, everyone kept their back doors firmly locked.

"In darkest Africa they use a set of drums. Here we've got Hilda Ogden. I suppose that's civilisation."

Renee Bradshaw

Character Name:	VERONICA
	(VERA)
	DUCKWORTH
Date of Birth:	3 September 1937
Husband:	Jack Duckworth
	(1957–)
Children:	Terry (1964)
Parents:	Amy Burton and
	Joss Shackleton

Nowadays Veronica Duckworth has gone up in the world. She has her name over the Rovers' door and wears posh frocks. It appears that the Vera of old – loud-mouthed, gossip-mongering Vera – has been replaced by a woman able to clear a bar full of punters with an icy stare. She's still interested in gossip – 'So have you not got any searing tales of sordid sex to tell us? No? Oh, well, Betty can serve you, then' – but she's not likely to be found with her ear flapping in the ladies' toilets.

Vera's story runs along lines similar to Martha's and Hilda's. She grew up not sure who her father was, married Jack after meeting him at a fair, and had a son, Terry. The Duckworth marriage was punctuated by discord, and by the time the family moved into No. 9 Coronation Street in September 1983 they were a dysfunctional lot clinging together because they had nowhere else to go. Vera's life consisted mainly of factory and warehouse jobs (she was once voted Miss Candle), and making ends meet with fraudulent insurance claims.

At work Vera had a reputation as a trouble-maker with a big mouth, and it was as such that she first appeared in the Street, fighting the management at the Mark Britain Warehouse over the retirement age. After the warehouse burned down Vera joined her old friend Ivy Tilsley in working for Mike Baldwin at his denim factory, which started up on the gutted site. Vera and Ivy worked side by side and kept an eye on the clock. Ivy was a more conscientious worker than Vera, who viewed her job as a means to an end but she enjoyed the company, too, and led the daily debate and gossip. Vera saw no point in keeping marital rows private and aired everything with the girls, seeking their opinions and tearing Jack's character and reputation to shreds.

Once Ivy was made up to supervisor, Vera called upon the length of their friendship to get away with as little work, and as much chatting, as possible. She continued to be a disruptive influence: as far as Vera was concerned Mike was the demon employer. When there was talk of him employing Japanese work techniques, she led the girls in making a life-size effigy of him and attacking it with a broom. She befriended the factory cat and fought Mike when he planned to get rid of Cleopatra after she spilt coffee over his paperwork. To ensure the cat's safety, Vera enrolled her in the Union and was speechless when Mike split her bonus with the cat, for its keep.

At one stage Elsie Tanner had been supervisor in the factory but when she returned, hard up, on the same level as the others, Vera commented on how the mighty had fallen. She disliked Elsie but the older woman proved more than a match for Vera, or Rentagob as she called her. When an important order was cancelled due to Elsie's relationship with a buyer, Vera led the girls in sending her to Coventry. Elsie acted as if nothing had changed, talking to the girls even if they refused to answer. Eventually she insulted Vera to her face. Vera was so indignant that she let loose a string of obscenities at Elsie before she realized she had spoken to her.

Home life was just as turbulent for Vera. Once Terry spelled out how much the constant arguing affected him: 'How am I meant to grow up well-adjusted wi' you pair as role models? Him bone idle and drunk, an' you with a gob like the Mersey Tunnel.' Vera was proud of Terry and his good looks, and had

"So have you not got any searing tales of sordid sex to tell us? No? Oh well, Betty can serve you then."

VERA DUCKWORTH

high hopes for him, which were shattered when he ran off with one neighbour after making another pregnant. He soon ended up in prison.

Despite all their ups and downs, though, the Duckworths have been together for more than forty years, making theirs the longest surviving marriage in the Street. It's been a relationship built on mistrust and swapped insults: 'You know why I stay wi' you? Pity, that's why. Cos I know if I left yer no other woman would look at yer!'

The Duckworths actually separated once for seven months and Vera dated a series of men, including Rovers' cellar man Fred Gee. He shocked the pub's landlady, Annie Walker, by entertaining Vera after hours but Annie spoilt their fun by insisting on acting as a chaperone. Vera returned to Jack but continued to see other men behind his back. A regular feller was a boiler-stoker called Harry, and she roped in friends to provide her with alibis. This backfired once when she asked barmaid Bet Lynch to cover for her. Bet agreed but didn't let on to Vera that while she was sitting on Harry's knee, Bet was having a night in with Jack. When Vera discovered Jack's infidelity she flew at Bet in the Rovers, calling her a back-street trollop. But Bet rose to the occasion with her passing shot: 'I don't know what you see in him, Vera. It's not even as if he's got hairy shoulders!'

Bet was instrumental in another Duckworth spectacle in the Rovers. She attended a video-dating agency and was stunned to see Jack on offer, with a fake husky accent, calling himself Vince St Clair. She sent Vera along to view the same tape and arranged for her, as Carole Munroe, to have a meeting with 'Vince'. Vera donned a red wig and a figure-hugging dress to wait for Vince in the Rovers and when he turned up she turned on him with her handbag.

As the years went by, Vera began to pick up on the warning signs that Jack fancied his chances again: 'He's had more baths than Cleopatra. Usually it's one a week if you're lucky. I tell you, he's on heat and I'm seeing none of it.' When she found out that he had tried to get barmaid Tina Fowler into bed she cut all his trousers in half so he couldn't leave the house. Then she went for Tina but Tina said she could never have an affair with an old lech like Jack and had only gone out with him for a laugh. Vera threw a pint of beer at her: '*Nobody* treats my husband as a bit of a joke! That's what they all think round here. Duckworths – village idiots, good for a laugh!'

When Baldwins' was pulled down Vera took a job at Bettabuy supermarket where her mouth got her into trouble again. Supermarket manager Reg Holdsworth ran a 'fill a trolley' competition and Vera was furious when shopkeeper Rita Fairclough won. Vera insisted that as Reg fancied Rita he had fixed the competition – and was suspended for spreading rumours.

Terry caused Vera a lifetime of heartache in just a couple of years, which started when he brought his pregnant girlfriend Lisa Horton to meet his parents. Vera took an instant liking to Lisa, seeing her as an honest working-class lass. She was thrilled when the couple married, although the service was spoilt because Terry was handcuffed to a prison officer. When Lisa gave birth, Vera was with her in the delivery room and delighted in her grandson Tommy, but the happy family was devastated when Lisa was hit by a car and killed in the Street. Vera gave up her job to look after Tommy until Terry had completed his sentence for GBH, but two days after his release Terry sold Tommy to Lisa's parents, insisting that Vera was too old to bring up a child. Jack thumped his son and threw him out but Vera refused to think bad of the lad and clung to the thought that he'd done it to help her. A few years later when he turned up with Tommy in an attempt to fleece the Hortons again, Vera wasn't so forgiving. She

threw away his photograph and altered her will: 'Why can't this family be like any other family? There's nothing goes right in this family. Everybody's always up in arms. Everybody's killing each other, and arguing and walking out. I don't think I'm meant to be happy, ever.' During one of his later visits, Terry left Vera's friend Tricia Armstrong pregnant. Their son, Brad, was born in the Rovers' back room and lived close enough for Vera to visit.

For once good fortune smiled on the Duckworths when Jack's brother died, leaving enough insurance money for them to buy the tenancy on the Rovers. Vera was made licensee and it was the proudest day of her life when her name was put over the door. At first she feared the pub would prove too much for her and Jack – they'd come to it so late in life – but, in a rare moment of tenderness, Jack made her see that at long last they were due some respect.

At times Vera considers changing the name of the pub to reflect her own heritage and royal connections. After her mother Amy's death she had discovered that a man named Joss Shackleton was her natural father. She took him into her home, delighted to have a father – although Jack thought he was a trickster looking for a cosy billet – and was thrilled when he revealed he was the illegitimate grandson of King Edward VII. Since then, Vera had harboured dreams of being recognized by her royal cousins, of a dukedom for Jack and the royal coat-of-arms being erected on the outside of the pub. If this was ever the case, though, then she'd have to lose the characteristic that always drags her down – as Jack once said: 'Learn to keep your mouth shut. Learn to control that tongue of yours! Nobody else has to say what they think – why should you?'

Vera gives Jack a lecture on spending the housekeeping again. Although they've now gone up in the world she still keeps a sharp eye on the petty cash.

JEAN ALEXANDER

~

"The door to Coronation Street was left open and I've been told I can always go back any time I want. But now I've managed to play a few different characters I don't want to resurrect Hilda again."

JEAN ALEXANDER

~

Jean Alexander began life in a house similar to those in Coronation Street. She was born to Nell and Archie, at 18 Rhiwlas Street, Toxteth, Liverpool, in 1926, with an older brother, Ken. Jean's childhood was happy and she grew up in a close, loving environment. Her first taste of the theatre was during family visits to the Pavilion Theatre, where she watched variety acts and pantomime.

After winning a scholarship to Liverpool's St Edmund's College, Jean discovered her acting talents through participation in school plays. At fifteen she was taken to her first Shakespeare performance and saw John Gielgud in *Macbeth*. By the time she was seventeen Jean had decided to become an actress. She took elocution lessons to get rid of her accent and joined an amateur company.

She also took a job as a library assistant and her acting ambitions were put on hold for five years. It was an unhappy period as she longed so much for the stage.

In 1949 Jean broke free from the library to join the Adelphi Guild Theatre, a touring company based in Macclesfield. Her first professional appearance was in Somerset Maugham's *Sheppey*. When the Adelphi closed, Jean was taken on by the Oldham repertory company as an actress and wardrobe mistress. Then she moved to the Southport theatre where she met Eileen Derbyshire, the Street's Emily Bishop.

After leaving Southport to spend two years with the York repertory company, Jean finally made it to London, in early 1961, and landed her first television part, in a series called *Deadline Midnight*. Small parts in various shows led to a role in the BBC series *Television Club*, which lasted several months. Then in 1962 she travelled to Manchester for a two-episode appearance in *Coronation Street*, playing Mrs Webb, a local landlady, whose tenant had stolen a baby, Christopher Hewitt.

The beginning of 1964 found Jean starring in the television series *Badger's Bend* and that June she made her first appearance as the world's favourite char, Hilda Ogden. Jean took the job, anticipating it would last a couple of months. She stayed for twenty-three years making friends with cast members and fans alike. During that period she took only one other acting job, in a production of *Arsenic and Old Lace*, which played to a packed theatre in Oldham.

Laurence Olivier was a passionate fan of Hilda Ogden, so much so that he joined forces with Russell Harty and Michael Parkinson to form the Hilda Ogden Appreciation Society. Another fan was the late Poet Laureate Sir John Betjeman, who travelled to the Granada studios and insisted on having his photograph taken with 'Hilda and her ghastly husband'.

Jean had a special, close relationship with Bernard Youens, who played her screen husband. They had a magical working partnership that brought Stan and Hilda to life and made them the most popular couple on television. When Bernard died in 1984 Jean decided to carry on playing Hilda, but three years later felt it was time to hang up the curlers. She bowed out, on Christmas Day 1987, watched by 26.6 million viewers, in the most watched Street episode of its thirty-eight-year history.

Since leaving *Coronation Street*, Jean has been able to enjoy her Southport home as well as taking on the acting roles that have most appealed to her. She appeared in the film *Scandal*, playing Christine Keeler's mother, starred in a series of *Rich Tea and Sympathy*, and has found fame with a whole new generation as Auntie in the BBC hit comedy *Last of the Summer Wine*.

THELMA BARLOW

Thelma Barlow's life was touched by tragedy five weeks before she was born when her father Thomas died of pneumonia. His wife, Margaret, was left to bring up two children – baby Thelma and her elder sister – with the help of her widowed mother in the Middlesbrough family home.

As a child Thelma longed for adventure and, along with her sister, created an imaginary soap opera called 'The Nixons', in which they took on the roles of two wealthy daughters, living a life of romance and high jinks. After leaving school, she worked as a secretary for eight years, and joined an amateur dramatic group, where she developed her love of acting. Eventually she decided to take it

seriously and travelled to London in search of work. She landed a job with Joan Littlewood's Theatre Workshop in Stratford, then worked for a various theatre companies, including the Bristol Old Vic, the West of England Company and repertories in Liverpool, Birmingham and Nottingham.

In 1956 she married theatre designer Graham Barlow, and in 1960 her first son, Clive, was born, followed by James two years later. The family moved to Scotland and it was from their home in Lenzie, near Glasgow, that Thelma commuted for the first few years of her life on *Coronation Street*. She first appeared as Mavis Riley in 1971, proved a hit with the writers and viewers, was invited back in 1972, and a year later became a long-term member of the cast.

Thelma enjoys dressmaking, gardening, travelling, cooking and going to the theatre. She has undertaken ventures involving these interests, presenting gardening, cookery and

~

"Leaving the Street will be a huge wrench. I have made good friends and enjoyed the work immensely but I feel excited about the future."

THELMA BARLOW

~

149

travel programmes for television. In 1988 she took time off from the Street to return to the stage at the Bristol Old Vic, appearing in a production of *The Cherry Orchard*. She is an active member of the National Centre for Organic Gardening and in 1992 published *Organic Gardening with Love*.

In 1997 Thelma left the Street after playing Mavis for twenty-four years and is enjoying spending time with her grandsons, Thomas and Matthew.

AMANDA BARRIE

Aged just thirteen, Amanda Barrie started work as a chorus girl, and in those early days she still went by her real name, Shirley Broadbent, and was a long way from home in Ashton-under-Lyne. Expelled from school and

allowed to go her own way by her parents, Shirley's new home became the Theatre Girls Club, a hostel in the middle of Soho, London's red-light district. At night she danced at the Winston Club with Barbara Windsor, Fenella Fielding and Danny La Rue.

Amanda's theatrical career had begun at the age of three when she made her stage début at Ashton-under-Lyne's Theatre Royal, which was run by her grandfather, Ernest Broadbent. Ernest was devoted to the theatre and was responsible for the discovery, among others, of Jack Hylton and the Crazy Gang. Amanda remembers being dragged off a train by her grandfather when he spied silent-screen legend Buster Keaton at the station. Buster was encouraged to shake the little girl's hand for luck and she was late for school. Her first professional job was to sing 'The Fairy on the Christmas Tree' in *A Christmas Carol* and she was pushed by her ambitious mother Connie: 'When we went on holiday she'd pack my sheet music and tap shoes just in case there were any talent contests. I had to enter everything.' Her father, Hubert, an accountant, had hoped that his daughter would become a secretary, but she had a form of dyslexia and found academic work hard. After being expelled from two schools she enrolled at ballet school where she was 'chucked out once again' for attending the audition that led to her employment in Soho.

In the early days of television Amanda worked on variety shows such as *The Morecambe and Wise Show* and *Double Your Money* with Hughie Green. In the theatre she graduated from chorus girl to revues and then straight acting. At nineteen Amanda bid farewell to Shirley Broadbent as she decided the name wasn't suitable for a serious actress: 'I picked Barrie after J. M. Barrie as I love *Peter Pan* and felt I'd like Amanda because I am a devotee of Gertrude Lawrence, who always wanted to be called Amanda. However, I opted for Lynne Barrie.' Unfortunately,

there was already an actress with the same name so she flicked through H. G. Wells's *Rival Experiments*: 'One page was completely blank, the other had only one word printed on it "Amanda". I felt that it was Gertrude giving me a sign.' Years of revue work saw her dancing with Lionel Blair, having things thrown at her on stage by Spike Milligan, and Peter Sellers once sat on her knee, pretending to be a ventriloquist's dummy.

During forty years in showbusiness Amanda has been out of work for only one three-month period. She's had her name up in lights in the West End seventeen times, starring in shows such as *Stepping Out, Any Wednesday, She Loves Me, Noises Off, Donkey's Years* and *Absurd Person Singular*. Television credits include hosting the children's programme *Hickory House* and starring in *The Bulldog Breed*, a twenty-six-episode series made by Granada, which started the same week as *Coronation Street*. She has appeared in numerous films, including two *Carry Ons* – *Cabby* and *Cleo*.

Amanda married actor Robin Hunter, with whom she acted in a West End production of *Public Mischief*. The marriage ended thirteen years later, in 1980.

In 1981 Amanda made her début as Alma Sedgewick, working in Jim's Café and exploiting waitress Elsie Tanner. The character was a hit with the viewers, and over the next seven years Amanda popped up from time to time. Her mother Connie adored the programme and, in the hope that Amanda would be taken on long-term, continually telephoned the production office, assuming different voices and saying how wonderful the character was. In 1988 Amanda became a regular member of the cast. Since then Amanda has balanced two lives with care: in Manchester she lives in a flat near the studios and concentrates on learning lines, while in London she relaxes and indulges her passions for antiques and horse-racing.

ELIZABETH BRADLEY

Elizabeth Bradley was born Joan Abraham on 20 May 1922. She was brought up in Hampstead, London: 'My father was a civil servant and my mother stayed at home. I was very, very close to my parents, and there was also a lady who looked after me called Lily, who I really loved. My mother used to do a lot of work for the Free Church. She would make pounds and pounds of toffee and strawberry jam to order and sell it for the church, and Lily and I used to deliver it. We'd take it round in my pram – I loved doing that.' Elizabeth's parents, John and Gladys, took her to see her first pantomime when she was eight and it was then that she decided she wanted to act.

School was in a stately home called Wentworth: 'I was pretty badly behaved. My sister was the head girl and I was a terrible embarrassment to her. I used to torment her

"I love Maud's basic common sense. Although she is so old she understands younger people and I'm thrilled that she's a champion of the young."

ELIZABETH
BRADLEY

and she would get fearfully cross with me. She used to report me all the time.' While at Wentworth she was further inspired by seeing Dame Peggy Ashcroft's performance when she played opposite Laurence Olivier in *Romeo and Juliet*.

Her acting ambitions were put on hold at the outbreak of war. She left school and became a member of the British Red Cross. After nursing soldiers she trained at the Royal National Orthopaedic Hospital, specializing in the care of children. Throughout the rest of the war she worked in a London hospital where she tried to comfort patients during the bombing. The end of the war was a sad time for Joan as her father was killed three days before VE Day.

After the war, Joan took the stage name Elizabeth Bradley, borrowing her mother's second name and a name common in her father's family. She trained at the Webber-Douglas Theatre School and her first professional engagement was as the governess in

Emma, which played first at Buxton, then transferred to the Embassy in Swiss Cottage, London. When she was twenty-four, she met actor Garth Adams when they both joined the same theatre company – the Penguin Players at Bexhill. They married in 1950 and spent their honeymoon working on stage together in a production of *Vanity Fair*. Following the birth of her children, Johanna, Rodney and Bradley, Elizabeth gave up acting to be a full-time mother.

It was only after Garth died in 1978 that she decided to return to the stage full-time and since then has rarely been out of work. Much of her time has been spent at the National Theatre, including her much-acclaimed performance as Grandmother in *Billy Liar*, for which she was nominated for an Olivier Award.

Maud Grimes first appeared in *Coronation Street* in 1993 and since then Elizabeth has manoeuvred her wheelchair through nearly four hundred episodes. When not working in Manchester, she lives with her large extended family, including grandchildren Jessica, Tom and Daniel, in Hampstead, and spends happy hours watching the swans at the bottom of her garden.

MARGOT BRYANT

For a woman who lived to be ninety, little is known about the actress Margot Bryant. Speak to actors who worked with her and you'll receive a smile, a laugh and a recollection of how the woman behind timid Minnie used outrageous language simply to shock. She was a private person. She never married and devoted her life to cats.

Born in Hull in 1897, Margot's father was a doctor, and she developed her love of felines at an early age. As she said in a rare interview: 'Our back garden was a sort of mustering ground for cats. One cat used to call only

> *"People are surprised to discover I am nothing at all like little Minnie Caldwell. Well, all I can say is, why should I be?"*
>
> MARGOT BRYANT

when she was expecting kittens. Very sensible of her, I suppose. It's always best to have a doctor around at times like that.' Her childhood was secure and she was so close to her elder sister that when she decided to become an actress Margot dropped everything to follow her on to the stage: 'My first appearance was in the chorus of *Aladdin* at the Theatre Royal, Plymouth. I did lots of touring in the chorus of musical comedies although I could *not* sing a note!' If she couldn't sing, Margot compensated with her flair for dancing. In the 1920s she appeared in the West End in the Fred and Adele Astaire revue *Stop Flirting* before moving into straight acting.

At Manchester's Palace Theatre she featured in *Gay's the Word* with Cicely Courtneidge, and also worked on radio, including *Mrs Dale's Diary* in which she took the part of Violet Hitchins. Minor film and television roles followed before she was given the part of Minnie, an old woman bossed around by Ena Sharples in the snug of the Rovers. The part grew, and quickly became one of the most popular characters ever to appear on the Street.

The security of appearing in *Coronation Street* allowed Margot to indulge her passion for cats. Her best-loved was one known as the Earl of Hammersmith: 'To be honest, he isn't really an earl, his name is Sandy, but he's such a majestic cat I felt the title was justified. He's a bit of a bully too. Whenever I get home late at night, he waits up for me, and tells me off.' Another of Margot's passions was reading, especially biographies and travel books. Her greatest thrill was seeing the Pyramids for the first time: 'One of my most wonderful memories was a New Year's Eve party on a house-boat on the Nile. We could see the Pyramids standing there under a sky full of shooting stars, and in the distance the lights of Cairo were twinkling.' Margot was also dedicated to the theatre and often flew to New York to see shows on Broadway.

In 1976 Margot was forced to leave *Coronation Street* when she suffered severe loss of memory and underwent psychiatric treatment. A few months later she moved into a nursing home in Cheadle and lived there until she died at Cheadle Royal Hospital on 1 January 1988.

BEVERLEY CALLARD

Beverley Moxon was born and bred in Leeds where her father Clive worked as a baker. Mother was a concert pianist and Bev and her younger sister Stephanie grew up surrounded by music and dogs. She made her stage début at the age of seven when she acted in a school play, *Darins The Page Boy*, starting off as the understudy but taking over when the

teacher discovered she was better at acting.

On leaving school Bev took a job as a typist and became a member of the Leeds Proscenium Players. She had a short-lived marriage to Paul Atkinson, which left her mother to a daughter, Rebecca. Beverley longed to follow her passion for acting but, with a young daughter, couldn't enrole in a full-time theatre school. Instead she studied at summer schools.

Although Beverley never underwent any formal training in acting, she had the luck to be discovered while appearing in amateur productions. Her first television role was in *Lucifer*, which starred William Gaunt. Parts in *The Practice* and *Emmerdale Farm* followed. She made her first appearance in *Coronation Street* in 1984, when she played June Dewhurst, the wife of Brian Tilsley's best friend.

In 1988 Beverley married Steven Callard and their son Joshua was born in late 1989. When Josh was only six weeks old Beverley landed the part of Liz McDonald.

Beverley is also a trained aerobics instructor and has produced best-selling videos and books on fitness. She has a growing fitness business, which has spread across the country.

In 1998, Beverley announced her intention to leave the Street after nine happy years.

LYNNE CAROL

Lynne Carol's family have been actors since the days of Charles I and when she was born, on 29 June 1914 in a rented room above a bank in Usk, Monmouthshire, she was given a name appropriate to such a heritage: Josephine Caroline Gertrude Mary Faith. Her parents, Mina McKinnon and Charles Harber were both actors, and at just nine days old little Josephine made her stage début, carried on in her mother's arms.

Mina ran a 'fit up' theatre company, tour-

ing the country from village to village, fitting up the stage and performing. Josephine had two brothers, one of whom drowned in a fishing accident aged nine, and the other, James McKinnon, followed his parents on to the stage. Josephine was educated wherever she was while touring with the family and she spent much of her childhood playing children's parts in the family productions.

At the age of eighteen Josephine met actor Bert Palmer when he joined Mina's company. They fell in love and married in 1934. Their children, Janet, Michael and Robert, were all born into the same tradition. The Palmers decided to break from the family company and formed a comedy double act, enlisting together to work with ENSA during the war. The couple entertained the troops in Belgium, Holland, Germany and the far reaches of the Shetlands.

When the Palmers broke up their act to return to straight acting it was felt that Josephine should change her name. Initially she decided to split her second name into Carol Lyn but an actress already used a similar name so she reversed it to become Lynne Carol.

Lynne and Bert worked together in two repertory companies at the same time – at Lytham St Annes and at Blackpool's Royal Pavilion before Lynne decided to retire in the 1950s. At the time the family lived in Blackpool and while Bert found employment in the new age of television Lynne took in boarders from touring repertory companies. Among them were people she would work with on *Coronation Street*, such as Patricia Phoenix and Arthur Leslie.

Bert persuaded Lynne to take occasional work in television and pushed her to attend an open audition for a part in Granada's new drama series, *Coronation Street*. She landed the part of gossipmonger Martha Longhurst and first appeared in episode two.

When new producer Tim Aspinall decided

Lynne Carol and Bert Palmer raise morale during the war.

to shake up the programme by killing off a popular character he chose Martha, which devastated the whole family of actors. Lynne's friend Violet Carson threatened to resign if the death scene went ahead, but Lynne's professionalism ensured that she 'died' on cue.

After a successful run of stage plays, Lynne's career dwindled to the occasional television appearance. She had roles in the TV series *The Newcomers* and in Tony Warren's mini-series, *The War of Darkie Pilbeam* before becoming semi-retired: 'Martha's death left me typecast and unemployed. I was so bored. I never went out so I took a job in a local hotel. But even there people recognized me as Martha.' In 1966 Lynne's son, Michael, was

killed in an air disaster, and in 1980, just after she appeared in the film *Yanks*, her beloved Bert died. Lynne continued to live in the house in Blackpool she bought with her *Street* wages until her death in June 1990.

VIOLET CARSON

During the slum clearances of the mid to late sixties, rows of terraced houses all over the north of England fell to the demolition ball. One of the first of Manchester's cobbled streets to be flattened was Corporation Terrace, off the Oldham Road, and it was in this street, at No.1, that Violet Carson was

≈

"The trouble with playing in a popular television show for so long is that when you're out you're forgotten. When they killed off Martha Longhurst it looked sometimes as if they had also killed me."

LYNNE CAROL

≈

155

born in 1898. William Carson worked as a manager at a flour mill and, as Violet said to a journalist in the 1960s: 'There is one thing I shall never forget. Every morning at five o'clock hundreds of clogs used to clatter past our house. They were cotton-mill workers. The noise would last an hour, then stop. Those people worked very hard in what people now call the bad old days. It's a strange thing – some of them seemed very happy.'

William's status brought him in thirty-five shillings a week, giving the family more security than most of their neighbours. Violet and her younger sister Nelly both had music lessons, Violet on the piano, Nelly on the violin, and from an early age Violet entertained. At St Jude's church she played the piano with the Band of Hope and when she left school in 1918 she played for a silent-cinema orchestra, which comprised typically a piano, two violins, a clarinet, a double bass and occasionally an organ.

For ten years Violet pounded the ivories in cinemas in Central Manchester until, in 1928, she gave up working when she married a road contractor, George Peploe, in Manchester Cathedral. They moved into a house in Swinton, but after two years Violet was a widow: 'Those two years were about the happiest of my life. I was happy to give up the piano for the hurly-burly of married life. I loved washing dishes, cleaning floors and looking after the home. I often think now that I should have really been a housewife and not an entertainer at all.'

After her husband's death Violet returned to earning her living by the piano, performing at musical evenings and company dinners. She also sang, and combined her two musical skills in performing with the BBC Northern Orchestra, making her first radio broadcast in 1935. Between that broadcast and her first appearance as Ena in 1960, Violet appeared on thousands of radio shows, either playing the piano, singing or acting. During the Second World War she toured the country entertaining factory workers and servicemen, and for six years was the pianist on radio's popular *Have a Go* with Wilfred Pickles. The programme was music- and quiz-based, light-hearted and heart-warming, broadcast from a different location around the country each week. One broadcast that stuck in Violet's mind was when she played 'I Set My Love To Music': 'I thought no more about it until shortly afterwards I received a letter from a London woman who had been crippled in an accident. When she heard the music it gave her the courage to walk again. I think receiving that letter was the most moving experience of my career. It was frightening in a way. Unwittingly I had changed a person's life by just playing a piece of music.' After *Have a Go*, Violet appeared on *Children's Hour* and was an interviewer on *Woman's Hour*. She made the change from radio to television in 1960, when she played the Duchess of York for the BBC in *Richard III*.

After she finished the recording she heard that Granada were casting a new family drama series and wrote for an audition. The letter was never answered. Meanwhile, the producers of what was to become *Coronation Street* were in despair. They had seen hundreds of actresses for the part of Ena Sharples who, as Tony Warren had written the part, 'clutched her purse to a bony bosom'. None of the bird-like actresses they had seen seemed right and it looked as though Tony would have to cut the role. It was at that point that he remembered Violet from his days as a child actor on *Children's Hour*. She was asked to audition and landed the part straight away when she threw in an extra line. The scene required Ena to intimidate shopkeeper Florrie Lindley and to ask for some cakes: 'Are those fancies fresh? I'll have half a dozen - and no éclairs.' Then she added aggressively, 'I said, no éclairs!' The line was kept in the script and Ena Sharples was made flesh.

Violet also added a piece of costume, which even now, eighteen years since Ena last appeared, is still associated with the character: 'My hair was looking particularly pretty one day, and I absolutely refused to let the make-up girl ruin it. I asked myself what Ena would have done, rummaged in my bag and found a hairnet. As I put it on I could see Ena nodding back approval through the mirror.'

Although Violet was a well-known voice, Ena made her an international star. As early as 1961 she picked up two television awards as Most Popular Actress, and in 1965 went to Buckingham Palace to collect an OBE from the Queen. In March 1968, when visiting Australia, she was mobbed by 150,000 residents of Adelaide who threw rose petals at her. In 1971 she was voted Most Compulsive Female Character on TV, and in 1973 received an honorary MA from Manchester University. She had a floribunda rose named after her, and replaced Marlene Dietrich at Blackpool's waxwork museum. In 1973 overwork led to a breakdown and Violet dropped out of the Street for a year while she recovered. When she returned, her working schedule was scaled down to allow her more time to rest in her Blackpool home. She continued to play Ena until April 1980, when she became ill with pernicious anaemia and was forced to give up acting. She was looked after by her sister Nelly until her death on 26 December 1983.

In interviews given in the early sixties, Violet Carson often talked about leaving the Street and Ena, of hanging up the 'old bitch' and getting on with her career. But by 1972, when she'd been playing the part for twelve years and was herself in her early seventies, she had realized that Ena would be the one role for which she would be remembered, as she told *TV Times* magazine: 'I have almost given up any idea of having time to grow old, but though Ena may be everlasting, I know that I am not. Sometimes I feel as if I've been in *Coronation Street* for a thousand years. Yet its pull is as strong as ever. Ena still dictates my future so I shall go on. She's the boss.'

~

"As an actress I have been destroyed. That's the word to use and I use it quite fearlessly. Ena Sharples killed Violet Carson on day one of Coronation Street."

VIOLET CARSON

~

JANE DANSON

When she was fifteen Jane Dawson made the frustrating discovery that if she wanted to be an actress she couldn't keep her own name as another actress already bore it. Desperate to hang on to as much of her family identity as possible she changed the W for an N to become Danson.

Jane was born on 8 November 1978 in Bury, Lancashire. Her father, Jack, is a bricklayer and mother, Lynn, a care assistant. She has an older brother and sister, and a dog called Judy. After an early interest in acting, she joined Oldham Theatre Workshop where she trained for six years while studying for her nine GCSEs.

She planned a degree in theatre studies but left after eight weeks to take part in the BBC children's series *Out of Time*, which she worked on for six months. The programme was a success but Jane decided against appearing in the second series and, instead, returned to the north for Granada's own children's hospital drama, *The Ward*. She considers herself lucky: when *The Ward* finished on a Friday she started the next Monday on another Granada show, *The Grand*. Playing the part of rebellious chambermaid Monica Jones was the break of a lifetime for an actress in her teens. Not only did she play opposite actors like Susan Hampshire, Tim Healy and Mark McGann, but her role called for her to commit murder and to hang: 'I knew the basis of the storyline but had no idea it would grow as big as it did. It was really challenging.'

As is typical in the acting world, Jane went from the dizzy heights of *The Grand* to rolling around in mud having rotten vegetables thrown at her during the filming of her small part as a wench in the BBC's acclaimed production of *Tom Jones*. After this she went through a depressing period, attending audition after audition and not being picked for any parts. Even *Coronation Street* turned her down. The part she sought then on the Street was that of Zoe Tattersall, the single mother taken in by the Malletts, but she was unsuccessful. However, casting director Judi Hayfield recognized Jane's ability and told her that she was ideal for another part, which at the time was top secret. It was, of course, Leanne, the elder daughter of the Battersby clan, who would take the Street by storm.

Like all other members of the cast, Jane gets her fair share of fan mail although many of the letters she receives are from young girls telling her how lucky she is to be kissing Adam Rickitt: 'Every interview I do for the papers or magazines I get asked, "What's it like to kiss Adam?"! And then in one interview he was quoted as saying it was boring kissing me!' What viewers don't realize is that when the kissing goes on thirty people are watching behind the cameras, and scenes have to be recorded time and time again. After all that, kissing just becomes part of the job.

ELIZABETH DAWN

Born on 8 November 1939, in Leeds, for the first twenty-five years of her life Liz Dawn was known by the name she was given at birth, Sylvia Butterfield. Her father, Albert, was an engineer and her houseproud mother, Annie, looked after Sylvia, her elder brother, Albert, and her sister, Maisie, while holding down a job in a tailoring factory.

Young Sylvia was educated at Corpus Christi School where she took advantage of her height and tried out for Leeds City Girls netball team. On leaving school she had a variety of jobs, ranging from working in the same tailoring factory as her mother, to cinema usherette and assistant at Woolworths.

At eighteen Liz married her first husband and had a son, Graham. The marriage didn't last, and in 1965 she wed for the second time, to electrician Don Ibbotson. The couple are still happily married and have three daughters, Julie, Dawn and Ann.

In 1966 Liz had her first brush with *Coronation Street* when she met actor Philip Lowrie, who played Elsie Tanner's wayward son Dennis, at a holiday camp. She had her photograph taken, sitting on his knee.

Don encouraged his wife to follow her interest in show-business, feeling that she had a great voice that would go down well in the local clubs. To Liz's amazement he was proved right and she landed bookings straight away. Overnight she became a professional singer. When it came to a stage identity, she reversed her eldest daughter's name, Dawn Elizabeth, and created one of the best-known names in the show-business world.

Throughout the sixties and seventies Elizabeth Dawn became a top name on the northern cabaret circuit. She made her acting début in 1972 in a Cadbury's commercial, closely followed by a part in Barry Hines's play *Speech Day*. She quickly worked out how to adjust her performance from stage to television: 'If you're singing and you're going up on stage in front of five hundred people you've got to grab their attention and sell yourself. But in television you don't have to please anybody but the director. So long as he said it was all right that was fine.'

Her first acting job for Granada was in the comedy show *How's Your Father?*, which led to Vera Duckworth in Coronation Street. The character appeared in only a couple of episodes in 1974 but the writers of the popular *Wheeltappers and Shunters Social Club* in the next studio saw Liz's Vera and employed her as their regular waitress on the show. Back on the Street, though, Liz had made a lasting

"It was my idea that Vera should have curly hair as I didn't want to look like everybody else. I thought I couldn't be red as Pat and Barbara were red-heads"

ELIZABETH DAWN

EILEEN DERBYSHIRE

The actress who has the honour of being the longest serving actress in any continuing drama series in the world is far removed from the archetypal Soap Queen associated with the likes of Joan Collins and Linda Grey. Cultured, quietly spoken, a woman who keeps herself to herself and who remains popular with all her colleagues, Eileen Derbyshire shies away from interviews, personal appearances and the usual show-business razzmatazz. Rather, she is wary of and embarrassed by fame: 'Once I was driven through a Welsh mining village in an open Rolls-Royce. People were hanging out of windows and they literally carried out invalids on chairs to see me pass. That is very dangerous stuff and could easily go to your head. I'm always glad that I had a solid background and that fame didn't happen to me when I was a young girl.'

Eileen was born in Urmston, near Manchester, the younger daughter of civil servant Frank Derbyshire and his wife, Edna. The family home was filled with music and from an early age Eileen and her sister Joan learned to appreciate the arts. While Joan went to art school Eileen favoured the theatre and trained as a teacher of speech and drama.

Aware of the precariousness of the theatre, Eileen's parents insisted she studied shorthand and typing as a back-up. She took office work, but her heart still ached for the theatre. Her acting career started one day when she hopped off a bus after passing Chorlton repertory theatre. Acting on impulse she went in, asked for an audition and was taken on as an actress/assistant stage manager. As well as acting on stage Eileen had a long, enjoyable career in radio, making her first appearance as a teenager in the BBC's *Children's Hour*.

Eileen toured the country with various repertory companies, acting in varied roles, many of them character types, such as old

"It's strange, but people talk to me as though I am Emily – they apologize if they swear and, if they offer me a drink, it's always a sweet sherry."

Eileen
Derbyshire

impression on the team of writers, and the character of Vera was written back into the scripts. For the next nine years Vera appeared on and off until, in 1983, Liz Dawn became a long-term member of the cast.

In 1989 Liz made a single 'I'll Be With You Soon' with William Tarney, her screen husband Jack Duckworth, and five years later cut another, 'Passing Strangers', this time with comedian Joe Longthorne. Although her time is mainly taken up with *Coronation Street*, Liz also does charity work. She has raised thousands of pounds for hospitals, children's charities and breast-cancer appeals. In 1998 she achieved two lifelong ambitions: she received a Ph.D. from Leeds University and had an audience with the Pope.

drunks or eccentric charwomen. All stood her in good stead for her creation of timid Emily Nugent, when she first appeared in episode fifteen of *Coronation Street* in January 1961. In fact, the character had already appeared in the third episode but when the part was enlarged Eileen was cast to carry on Miss Nugent, and on and on.

In the spring of 1965 Eileen married engineer Tom Holt, and the following year took a break from the Street to give birth to her only son, Oliver. Her family home continued to fill with cats and dogs, and at one stage in the mid-seventies seven of the former and five of the latter lived at Eileen's cottage.

Eileen values her privacy and guards it well. In many respects she is similar to Emily in preferring a quiet lifestyle. She confesses to being in love with Italy and enjoys travelling there. One obvious difference between Eileen and her screen sister is the difference in their sense of humour. While Eileen is often portrayed as having little or, at times, none, Eileen is renowned as the wit among the cast.

As for the future, Eileen has no idea how long she will continue in *Coronation Street* and admits to not being ambitious, although she would be interested in appearing in films playing eccentric old ladies' parts in the ilk of Irene Handl.

BETTY DRIVER

Born in Leicester on 20 May 1920, Betty moved to Manchester two years later after her policeman father, Frederick Driver, was relocated. Home was respectable and middle class, but Betty's childhood was short-lived.

At the age of nine she made her first stage appearance after her parents took her to a theatre and she won a bottle of toffees for being the loudest singer in the audience. Betty's mother Nellie had always craved a show-business career, and when Betty showed

potential, she decided to channel all her ambitions into getting her daughter on the stage. Along with her younger sister Freda, Betty was tutored personally by Nellie and taken around the local parks every Sunday to sing on bandstands.

Betty turned professional at eleven, singing in variety all over Manchester: 'I used to go to school in the mornings, rehearse in the afternoons and then sing at night.' Under Nellie's guidance, Betty toured the country, staying in down-at-heel lodgings and attending a different school each week. Everything revolved around Nellie's determination to turn Betty into a star – no holidays, no hobbies, no rest.

161

Nellie persuaded the manager of London's Prince of Wales theatre to employ Betty in his revue, singing five times a day. In 1935 she made her first record 'Jubilee Baby' and shortly afterwards she was invited by Gracie Fields's manager-husband Archie Pitt, who launched her to the stardom Nellie had always longed for, as the lead in his tour of *Mr Tower of London* with Norman Evans. Nellie was delighted as Gracie Fields was her favourite singer and she chose all Betty's songs in the same comic style. Betty hated singing them, though, and in an act of rebellion Freda burned all the sheet music, freeing her sister to concentrate on the ballads she loved.

The great impresario C. B. Cochrane lifted Betty from *Mr Tower of London* for his West End hit *Home and Beauty* at the Adelphi Theatre. In 1938 she made her film début as the heroine of *Penny Paradise*. At the outbreak of war, Betty continued to sing, making hit records such as 'We Mustn't Miss The Last Bus Home', and teaming up with Henry Hall and his orchestra for seven happy years. Throughout the war she and Hall entertained troops all over the world with ENSA. As well as touring, Betty appeared in the popular BBC radio programme *Henry Hall's Guest Night*.

Betty continued to make successful records such as 'The Sailor With The Navy Blue Eyes', 'I'll Take Romance' and 'You Don't Have To Tell Me', the latter being taken from her second film *Facing the Music*, which was followed by her last film, *Let's Be Famous*.

It was while recording her own radio programme *The Betty Driver Show* that Betty met guitarist Wally Peterson. She fell in love and married him, giving up her career to live with him in his native South Africa. After Wally had worked through Betty's savings, the marriage collapsed; she returned to England and Freda, with just seven pounds to her name. The sisters then ran a country pub with their father.

In 1964 the call came for Betty to audition for the part of Hilda Ogden in *Coronation Street* but Betty turned it down as she didn't like the idea of being tied to curlers and aprons. Instead, she took a role in the Street comedy spin-off *Pardon the Expression*, sharing top billing with Arthur Lowe. It was during the filming of a stunt in which she had to flip Arthur over that she sustained a back injury, which forced her to leave the show and retire from television.

Betty's back recovered during the five years that she and Freda ran the Devonshire Arms in Derbyshire. One customer was H. V. Kershaw, the then producer of *Coronation Street*, who commented that if Betty was pulling pints there she might as well be doing it in the Rovers. In the summer of 1969 Betty made her début as Betty Turpin and has been stuck behind the Rovers' bar ever since.

Betty's second career has tended to overshadow her first, and fans are often amazed to hear of her success as one of Britain's top dance-band singers. Over the twenty-eight years she has spent in *Coronation Street* she has been given many honours, including having a peachy-pink rose named after her. She has legions of fans but her greatest is still Freda, the sister with whom she still shares her home. In the words of the song, there never were such devoted sisters.

VICKY ENTWISTLE

Victoria Entwistle was born on 15 September 1968 in Accrington. Her father Alan was an insurance manager but now runs a couple of newsagents' with his wife Maureen and Vicky's brother Martin.

At school Vicky turned to acting as an escape: 'I wasn't very sporty and I didn't want to do PE. I realized that if I did drama I wouldn't have to do PE. Then I discovered it was a laugh so I decided to carry on doing it.'

"I love being part of the family on Coronation Street. I think they'll have to shoot me to get rid of me."

BETTY DRIVER

After doing A Levels, in English and sociology at Blackpool College, she trained at the Drama Centre in London.

Vicky's first professional work was at Colchester's Mercury Theatre in *Night Must Fall*, playing Dora the maid 'done wrong' by the villain of the piece. Then, as work was scarce, she took a position as usherette at the Strand Theatre, a job to which she returned over two and a half years between roles: 'I'm very good at ripping up tickets and selling programmes!'

Vicky's parts have tended to be downtrodden, hard-working women, struggling against the world. Her first television appearance was in *Against All Odds*, a BBC drama documentary based on the life of a brother and sister separated for fifty years. She toured with the Hull Truck Theatre Company, playing a teenager looking after a friend dying of leukaemia:

'The most amazing thing is when you're on stage and you know things can go wrong at any minute, so that's a thrill as you're on edge all the time. And then having the ability to make people laugh and cry their eyes out at the same time.' The relationship between actor and audience is important to Vicky and that is the thing she misses, working in television: 'I love *Coronation Street* but you don't get that hit, that thrill, there's no audience and no atmosphere. As much as the crew appreciate what you're doing it's still not the same.'

Coronation Street's casting director, Judi Hayfield, saw Vicky in the Hull Truck play and the decision was made to try her out for a big part in a family still being planned. She appeared in three episodes as Janice Lee – the character's maiden name – before Judi broke the news that she was going to head up the new Street family, the Battersbys.

~

"I'd read about this new 'family from hell' on Coronation Street but when I was told I was going to be a mother on the show I assumed it was for another family. Then the casting director said, 'No, Vicky, you are the mother from hell.'"

VICKY ENTWISTLE

~

GAYNOR FAYE

"She's a Mallett by name, and mallet by nature. She comes in like a sledge-hammer."

GAYNOR FAYE

Gaynor Kay Mellor was born in Leeds on 26 August 1971. Her mother is the internationally famous writer Kay Mellor, and her father, Antony, runs a day centre for the disabled. The Mellors have always lived in Yorkshire, and it was in the back garden of the family home that Gaynor and her elder sister Yvonne started to act, performing plays written by their mother. Gaynor was soon bitten by the acting bug and at school she proved a hit as Dorothy in *Gregory's Girl*, entering to a drum roll, which she enjoyed.

While studying for A Levels in theatre studies and English language, Gaynor earned her Equity card by taking part in an

alternative pantomime, playing the heroine Sharon Christmas who saved Father Christmas from kidnappers. After her exams she took the unusual and far-sighted step of setting up her own theatre company, Not Quite Hollywood, with her best friend, Faye. At the same time she borrowed her friend's name to create her stage name. The teenagers toured around venues in Yorkshire, acting in two-handers written by Kay.

Gaynor's big break came when she was cast as Gwen Taylor's abused secretary Crystal in the BBC drama series *The Sharp End*. She had to dye her hair blonde for that part, and kept that and her blue contact lenses to audition for a part in her mother's play *In All Innocence* at the West Yorkshire Playhouse. She didn't reveal to anyone that she was Kay's daughter and was thrilled to get the part on her own merit. It was while she was at the Playhouse that Gaynor first met Ian Mercer, the actor who would eventually play Gary Mallett.

The call to audition for Judy Mallett came at the right time for Gaynor: 'I always said I didn't want to be in a soap as I didn't want to be in anything that was long-running. However, I'd been jobbing it for six years and I'd been on tour and had done a lot of one-off dramas, and needed to settle for a bit. And if you're going to be in a soap you might as well be in the top one!' The audition reunited Gaynor with Ian, although they didn't read together. When she was told she'd got the part Gaynor was celebrating her birthday and had a party planned. Knowing she had been successful made the party go with even more of a swing and she invited Ian to the bash.

Since moving into the Street as a long-term character Gaynor has been able to put down more secure roots in Leeds. She is also involved in her mother's film company, Rollem Productions, but has still to achieve her ambition of acting in one of Kay's films, in a part especially written for her.

JULIE GOODYEAR

Born in Heywood, Lancashire, on 29 March 1942, Julie Goodyear was brought up over her parents' (Alice and William), public house called the Bay Horse Hotel. William and Alice married when Julie was seven and Alice had divorced her first husband, Julie's father, George Kemp. As she grew up in the warm family environment of the pub, Julie looked upon William as her true father and continues to do so to this day.

Educated until she was sixteen at Queen Elizabeth's Grammar School in Middleton, Julie became interested in acting after appearing in school plays. Her first job, however, was at the aviation firm Avro, where she worked as a shorthand-typist and met her first husband, Ray Sutcliffe. They married in 1959 and a month after her eighteenth birthday, in 1960, Julie gave birth to a son, Gary. Unfortunately the marriage fell apart; Ray went to Australia, which forced Julie to support herself and her baby. She won a Miss Britvic competition, and enrolled at a Manchester modelling agency.

Julie proved herself to be a hard worker and her career took off. She moved from the catwalk to work as an extra in television; her first job was in *Scene at 6.30* with Bob Grieves. She wandered around in the background of programmes such as Granada's *Pardon the Expression* before getting her big break in May 1966 when she was cast as Bet Lynch, the trouble-making welder at the PVC factory on *Coronation Street*. Although the part only lasted six weeks, she impressed Pat Phoenix, who helped her get a job with the Oldham repertory company and it was there that Julie learned the fine arts of acting and discipline. Roles followed in *Nearest and Dearest* and *The Dustbinmen*.

When June Howson took over as producer on *Coronation Street* in 1969 she remembered Julie's performance in the Granada drama series *Family at War*. Julie recalled: 'She asked me if I would be interested in becoming a regular member of the Street cast. I really didn't take the question seriously because it was my dream and sometimes when dreams come true you find it very hard to believe that it's happening.' Bet was reintroduced into the programme in May 1970 and remained for twenty-five years and 2002 episodes, of which Julie is very proud.

While her screen character searched for love among the menfolk of Coronation Street, Julie, too, struggled to find Mr Right. In 1973 she married businessman Tony Rudman, and

> *"Many women can identify with Bet. I know from the letters I get. They often go through their lives not finding Mr Right."*
>
> JULIE GOODYEAR

was escorted to the Bury church by her son Gary and soldiers from the King's Own Border Regiment, who formed a guard of honour with fixed bayonets. The cast of *Coronation Street* attended the wedding and thousands of fans blocked the road outside the church. What they didn't see were the events at the reception: Julie's new husband walked out of the room and never returned. The marriage was annulled.

Julie married a third time, to American airline executive Richard Skrob, but their work commitments meant that the couple were seldom together. The marriage ended in divorce and, a few years later, he died of leukaemia.

In 1979, Julie was diagnosed with cervical cancer. It was detected during a routine smear test and caught early enough for the cancerous cells to be removed. As soon as she was well enough, she launched an appeal for funds for Manchester's Christie Hospital, and in 1983 the Julie Goodyear Laboratory was opened. Since then she has continued to campaign and urge women to have regular smears. Tragically, her mother died of cancer in 1987.

As the character of Bet became more flamboyant, Julie took delight in her new role as grandmother with the birth of Emily and Elliott to Gary and his wife. She valued her time with the family and decided eventually that the time had come to give Bet up and spend more time as Julie.

The press had a field day with the news that she was quitting the Street and, rather than take another job straight away, she sensibly turned her attention to the farm she had bought and started to turn it into a home. Although she left *Coronation Street* three years ago, it was only at Christmas 1997 that she decided she was ready to take on another role and become a hit as Mrs Twankey, slapping her thigh in Liverpool's Royal Court production of *Aladdin*. Julie made history in the pantomime as until then the part of Twankey had only ever been played by a man.

On 20 February 1996 Julie was awarded the MBE for her services to drama and television.

SANDRA GOUGH

Sandra Maria Gough was born in Newton Heath, Manchester, on 2 August 1948, where her parents, Tom and Jeanne, ran fruit and vegetable stalls at local markets. She was a natural mimic and spent her childhood putting on shows for the family in which she impersonated the likes of Al Jolson and Hylda Baker.

Sandra began her acting career in radio at the age of ten, after she had written to the BBC to ask for a part in *Children's Hour*. She worked on several radio plays, including a

> *"I grew to hate playing Irma Barlow. Everybody I met treated me as if I were her and didn't want to know Sandra Gough."*
>
> SANDRA GOUGH

children's serial called *The Whittakers*. Then, at thirteen, she moved to London to train professionally at the Ada Foster School in Golders Green, returning north two years later to join the Oldham repertory company.

As well as acting, Sandra cashed in on her looks by becoming a model. She posed for the *Daily Mirror*'s 'Daughter of Jane' and for romantic comics, as well as modelling clothes on the catwalk.

After working with Manchester's Library Theatre Company for a year she decided to give up acting and instead took work in shops. However, the lure of performing brought her to Granada Television and bit parts in local programmes. In 1964, she made her first appearance as Irma Ogden in *Coronation Street*. Her bubbly personality and wit shone through on the screen, and in less than a year a whole family had been built up around Irma.

After playing Irma for five years Sandra left the show as her character emigrated to Australia. In real life she also left the country, taking bar work in Spain. She married Miguel Mayor in 1970 but the marriage was later annulled. During her absence, the Street office was flooded with letters from fans, demanding the return of the popular character. Sandra came back to England, and when the Street producers offered her the chance to play Irma again she agreed, and stayed for a further two years, this time behind the Corner Shop counter.

Sandra made her last appearance as Irma in 1972. Since then she has worked on various television and radio shows, even joining another soap, *Emmerdale*, to play the highly acclaimed Nellie Dingle. She spent six years living in Australia and New Zealand, where she married her second husband, Maletai Falealli.

She now lives in Leeds, and spends as much time as she can working for Oxfam, Amnesty International and Pet Rescue, looking after distressed puppies.

ANGELA GRIFFIN

Angela Griffin grew up in Leeds on a huge council estate in Cottingley. She was born on 19 July 1976, and has two older brothers, Kenny and Stephen. Her father, Desmond, went to live in America when she was four and her mother, Sheila, worked at the local Cadbury's factory. Sheila later met Wallace Hippolyte, and together they encouraged Angela to follow her passion for acting.

Angela joined Leeds Children's Theatre when she was six, then moved to the South Leeds Youth Theatre. At school, instead of studying PE and craft, Angela took lessons in the performing arts. She was taken on from school to appear in two television shows for Yorkshire Television, *Under the Bedclothes and Just Us*. Those roles led to a part as a heroin addict in *Emmerdale*.

~

"When I started in the Street the first person I saw was Kevin Kennedy and my heart nearly dropped into my toes. It was Curly! And I had just walked into the same room as him. For people my age, he is a TV icon."

ANGELA GRIFFIN

~

167

"The most convenient thing about being in the Street is that you know where you've been and what you've been up to because you read about it in the papers the next day."

MADGE HINDLE

At Intake High School in Leeds, doing A Levels in English, psychology and theatre studies, Angela planned to study psychology at university. However, while working at Burger King, raising money to supplement her grant, she landed the part of Fiona in *Coronation Street*.

The security of having a long-term contract in a long-running programme has meant much to Angela, allowing her to buy a house in Leeds and a car. She was voted Best Newcomer in the first National Television Awards, and over the last year has won acclaim for her acting during one of the strongest storylines ever seen in the programme. Still in her early twenties, Angela, like Fiona, has even greater heights to look forward to.

MADGE HINDLE

Lancashire lass Madge Hindle was born in Blackburn, where her teenage friend was Russell Harty. As a child she loved frequenting the local cinema, and her family had regular seats at the town's Grand Theatre. In 1966 her mother, Edith Railton, became mayor of the town and Madge served as her mayoress.

Madge trained as a teacher and taught in a Manchester school for a number of years, but had always been interested in acting and had frequently worked with amateur companies. Then her friend Alan Bennett wrote a new television series *On the Margin* and asked her to be one of the characters in the series. Comedy writers Vince Powell and Harry Driver, who had met while working on scripts for *Coronation Street*, saw Madge's performance and made sure she was cast as 'Our Lily' in their new programme, *Nearest and Dearest*.

Roles in television programmes such as *The Wild West Show*, *Porridge* and *The Cuckoo Waltz* led to Madge being cast as shopkeeper Renee Bradshaw in *Coronation Street* in the spring of 1976. Bill Podmore had taken over as producer and had directed Madge in *Nearest and Dearest*.

Working in the Corner Shop was exhausting for Madge and she struggled to cope with a vicious till, which snapped shut on her whenever she used it. As she was used to working mainly in comedy she had to adapt quickly to Renee's storylines, which were mainly dramatic and involved traumas of one kind or another. In 1980, after four years on the show, Madge was written out when Renee was killed in a horrific car crash.

Madge lives in an old farmhouse in the Yorkshire Dales with her husband of thirty-six years, Michael Hindle. She has two daughters, Charlotte and Frances, and four granddaughters, Florence, Martha, Daisy and Chloe.

TINA HOBLEY

Growing up in London Tina Hobley's favourite television programme was *Coronation Street*, and out of all the colourful characters the one she most loved to watch was Elsie Tanner. At that point she had no idea she would follow in Pat Phoenix's footsteps as a national red-headed sex symbol. It isn't just the red hair that the two actresses have in common: both had Irish mothers and Tina, like Pat before her, suffers from an acute sense of insecurity.

Tina grew up in Hampstead, in London, where her parents, Harry and Kathleen, ran market stalls and grocery shops. She was born on 20 May 1971 and was a quiet, shy child.

In an attempt to bring her daughter out of her shell, Kathleen enrolled Tina in speech and drama lessons with a local woman who taught her throughout her teenage years, helping her to win awards at festivals. After being educated in Catholic schools, Tina was unsure what to do after A levels in sociology, theatre studies and English literature. Eventually she took a year out and travelled to America where she worked for five months as a nanny. She turned down a place at Leicester University to read theatre studies, and instead enrolled at the Webber-Douglas Academy.

While many drama graduates wait months or years for their first job, Tina walked straight into a television role as a saucy waitress in *All In the Game*. The script called for her to appear in a swimming-pool scene. When it came to the location Tina was horrified to discover she had to play the scene naked: 'It took three shots of brandy to get me to take the dressing-gown off – I had no idea, they'd not warned me about it at all! I was devastated!' For a while afterwards, it seemed that she was locked into a cycle of playing saucy parts on television and she was relieved to be employed for three seasons by Colchester's repertory

company. A role in David Renwick's first play, *Angry Old Men*, followed, playing another saucy part.

Touring in the Middle and Far East with Derek Nimmo's company finally allowed Tina to shrug off her saucy characters. She had been back from the tour only a few days when she auditioned for the part of Samantha, fighting off a roomful of blonde hopefuls to become the new Rovers' barmaid.

In the summer of 1998 Tina left *Coronation Street* to pursue other ventures, including marriage to draughtsman Steve Wallington.

~

"I grew up on the Street and loved it. When I was seven I won a fancy dress contest dressed as Hilda Ogden."

TINA HOBLEY

~

DOREEN KEOGH

Growing up in her Dublin home, Doreen Elsa Veronica Keogh had a passion for dressing up and putting on plays for her siblings, Hilda, Dermot and John. Her father, John, worked for an animal-feed company but it was her mother, Alice, who encouraged her daughter to work on the stage. She had been an award-winning Irish dancer, and helped Doreen by sending her to elocution lessons where Doreen shone by winning fourteen medals.

At the age of seven Doreen started attending school at the Holy Faith Convent in Clontarf where she outraged the sisters by stating her choice of career: 'All the nuns asked us what we wanted to be and the others were all saying, "I'm going to be a nurse," or "I'm going to be a teacher," and then they came to me and I said, "I'm going to be on the stage," which caused consternation!' It was while she was still at school that Doreen made her first professional appearance on stage, at the Gate Theatre, walking on as a page in *Twelfth Night*.

"I have nothing but good memories of working on Coronation Street and I have hundreds of them to look back on."

DOREEN KEOGH

To ensure she had something to fall back on in life, Doreen's parents insisted she took a business course when she left school. Doreen rushed through it, eager to embark on her acting career, and by the age of nineteen was back in *Twelfth Night* at the Gate, but this time playing Olivia.

Sam Wanamaker cast Doreen as the juvenile lead in his production of *Purple Dust* and she quickly became established as one of the most used Irish actresses, appearing in BBC radio productions. She made the transition from radio to television in the late fifties and was asked to audition for *Coronation Street* after appearing in a successful play for Granada Television.

Originally, Concepta was to appear in only six episodes but after only two weeks' playing the character Doreen was asked to stay on for the rest of the scheduled ten-week run. Four years and 323 episodes later she finally decided to break with Concepta. She left the Street on a Friday and the following Monday started work on a spin-off *Coronation Street* play called *Firm Foundations*, touring the country to packed houses.

Doreen's time on the Street was packed with filming and personal appearances. As one of the original cast members, she remembers how stunned the actors were when they all attended a fund-raising evening in a local pub: 'The reception was astounding and the people who wanted autographs were actually tearing strips of wallpaper off the walls for us to sign the back.'

In 1989 Doreen returned to live in Ireland and for five years played the part of blackmailing snob Mary O'Hanlon in the Irish soap *Fair City*. When she told the producers she was leaving the show, Doreen remembered what it had been like to leave the Street and this time insisted that her character was killed off: 'If you're not killed off, people keep asking when you are returning.'

As well as being a stalwart of the Irish

stage, Doreen is barely off the television screen. She has worked on programmes as diverse as *Ballykissangel*, *Z Cars*, *Father Ted*, *Pie in the Sky* and the BBC series *Inside Out*. Her film career has been just as busy: she has appeared in *Some Mother's Son* with Helen Mirren, *Widow's Peak* with Mia Farrow, *The Lilac Bus*, *Lamb* with Liam Neeson, and the award-winning *Mercy*. She even flew to Hollywood for *Darling Lily* with Julie Andrews and Rock Hudson.

Doreen lives in the Irish countryside, in County Wicklow, with her husband of twenty-two years, Jack Jenner, and a menagerie of animals she has rescued over the years – four dogs, two donkeys and twelve hens.

ANNE KIRKBRIDE

In March 1998 Anne Kirkbride celebrated twenty-five years as Deirdre Hunt Langton Barlow Rachid in *Coronation Street*. During her time on the programme she has won awards for her performance and earned the love of millions of fans. Anne is also held in the highest esteem by her colleagues in the cast, who all supported her during her six months off screen in 1993, when she battled with non-Hodgkin's lymphoma.

Born in Oldham on 21 June 1954, to cartoonist Jack Kirkbride and his wife, Enid, Anne grew up with her younger brother, John, spending much of her time daydreaming and living in a romantic make-believe world. The family lived in a farmhouse on the edge of the Pennine moors and the rolling hills added fuel to Anne's vivid imagination.

At eleven, she joined the Saddleworth Junior Players, where her first acting role was as a tiger-lily. Encouraged by her father, she developed her interest in acting, and after leaving school with two O Levels, she joined the Oldham repertory company, starting there as a student, graduating to assistant stage

manager and finally becoming an actress. She was glad to leave stage management behind after a disastrous performance of *Snow White*, at a Saddleworth drama festival: 'I was trying desperately to stop a piece of scenery from falling down. The dwarfs, who were all grouped in the middle of the stage frantically holding the curtains together, saw the state I was in and leaped to my rescue – letting the curtains go. They swept apart giving the audience a lovely view of seven dwarfs and me clinging to the scenery.'

Granada's casting department spotted Anne in an Oldham performance and she was cast in the play, *Another Sunday* and *Sweet FA*. Then, aged eighteen, she was cast as Deirdre Hunt, the chirpy secretary at Len Fairclough's building yard in Coronation Street. It was only her second television part and she has remained with the programme ever since.

"I just wanted to be an actress, a good one. It never occurred to me I'd be famous and I don't handle it that well. I'm really a quiet, private person."

ANNE KIRKBRIDE

>
> ∼
>
> *"I don't mind if people call Coronation Street a soap. But if it is a soap it is the cleanest, brightest and the best."*
>
> BARBARA KNOX
>
> ∼

Coronation Street has certainly given Anne plenty of drama to get her teeth into, as Deirdre has survived three husbands, a daughter, suicide attempts and other domestic traumas. The programme also gave her a husband in real life: Anne met David Beckett when he was cast as Deirdre's boyfriend Dave Barton in 1990. Two years later the couple married and now live in South Manchester with their cat.

BARBARA KNOX

Nowadays, award-winning actress Barbara Knox is associated with glitzy occasions, and is seen as one of the country's leading actresses in a glamorous profession. She has come a great way from her roots in Oldham, where she grew up as an only child in a hard-working, working-class home.

As a child Barbara loved dressing up in her mother's ballroom-style dresses, pretending to be Ginger Rogers. She was fascinated by the glamorous world portrayed at her local cinema, and imagined herself in Betty Grable musicals. It was these films that first influenced Barbara into considering acting as a career. The harsh world of practicalities forced her to abandon her dreams. When she left school at fifteen she sat civil-service examinations and learnt shorthand and typing. A string of jobs followed – post-office telegraphist, office worker, shop assistant and, at one point, standing all day in a factory putting plastic caps on steel rods.

The acting bug never left Barbara, though, and she took part in amateur productions before being spotted by the director of Oldham repertory company. He was impressed by her talent and offered her a job. She stayed for nine years.

Barbara enjoyed a long career as supporting actress to various comedians on their radio shows. Ken Dodd, Mike Yarwood and Les Dawson all asked for her to work with them time after time, which she found very flattering: 'In comedy, timing's more important than anything. You have to be careful not to tread on comedian's lines or get in on their laughs. Once you have worked successfully with them they seem to like working with you again and again.'

When Ken Dodd moved his show to television Betty went with him. She appeared in many classic programmes of the 1960s, such as *Emergency Ward 10*, *Never Mind The Quality Feel The Width*, *The Dustbinmen* and *Family At War*. She also had a small part in the film *Goodbye Mr Chips*.

Barbara juggled her acting career with family life, but in 1969 after a serious illness she decided to retire from show-business to concentrate on home life. She was lured back, though, by Dennis Main Wilson, the BBC comedy producer, who cast her in a Comedy

Playhouse, *Don't Ring Us, We'll Ring You*.

Coronation Street first beckoned in 1964 when Barbara appeared in an episode as exotic dancer Rita Littlewood. Eight years passed before she returned, as the same character, and she has remained there ever since, going through a variety of name changes – Bates, Littlewood, Fairclough and Sullivan.

Originally Rita spent much of her time singing in nightclubs and in 1973 Barbara released an LP of her own, *On The Street Where I Live*. Since then her talent as a comedy actress has been fully exploited in many scenes between Rita and her assistant Mavis. She has also featured in some of the most dramatic – and traumatic – storylines in the programme's history.

In recognition of her considerable contribution, Barbara has been presented with the *TV Times* Best Actress Award and was voted BAFTA Actress of the Year in 1979.

SARAH LANCASHIRE

Sarah Lancashire first walked down Coronation Street as a little girl. Shown round by her father, script writer Geoff Lancashire, Sarah was befriended by Street legends Violet Carson and Pat Phoenix, little suspecting that one day she, too, would be classed as a classic Street actress.

Sarah and her twin brother, Simon, were born in Stretford on 10 October 1964, although when they were young the Lancashires moved to Oldham. She is the only daughter in a family of brothers, with John and James as well as Simon. Sarah has always remained close to her family, and sees her mother, Catherine, nearly every day.

As a child, Sarah had no ambition to be an actress; instead she was interested in writing. She left school after eight O Levels, and A Levels in English, theatre studies and general studies. She trained at the Guildhall School of Music and Drama and sang with a dance-band for six years. Wary of long gaps between acting roles, Sarah became a lecturer in theatre studies before spending a year in Bill Kenwright's West End production of *Blood Brothers*.

In 1987 Sarah made her first appearance in *Coronation Street*, as a nurse called Wendy Farmer who applied to be the Duckworths' lodger. The part was only for one episode and it wasn't until 1991, after Sarah had had her two sons, Thomas and Matthew, that she returned to the programme as Raquel Wolstenhulme. The character was an instant

~

"I went into acting not to become famous but because I enjoy exploring a piece of writing and talking it off the page."

SARAH
LANCASHIRE

~

hit with writers and viewers alike and she remained for five years.

In 1996, the same year the Royal Television Society presented her with its Best Actress award, Sarah decided to leave the Street to concentrate on other acting roles and to spend more time with her sons. Since then she has not stopped working, appearing in two series of *Where The Heart Is* and the BBC situation comedy *Blooming Marvellous*.

JENNIFER MOSS

The youngest member of the original Street cast was born on 10 January 1945. Her father, Reg, was a director of a mill, but her mother, Dora, who was a teacher of speech and drama, was very keen for her daughter to go on the stage.

Jennifer was educated at Wigan High School for Girls and planned a career in law. As a pastime, at the age of twelve, she started working for BBC radio in *Children's Hour*. She moved to television, appearing in a Sunday night drama, *June Evening*, and then, at the age of sixteen, she took the part of Lucille Hewitt, thinking the job would last for six weeks. She remained for fourteen years, growing up on the programme and struggling when the viewers continued to think of her as a young child.

When her beloved father died, Jenny's world fell apart and she started to drink heavily. In 1974 she was written out of the Street and has never returned. While that was the end of Lucille Hewitt's traumas, Jennifer Moss's nightmare had only just begun.

In 1968 she had married millionaire's son Peter Hampson. They had a daughter, Naomi, but were divorced after a year. Her second marriage, to motor dealer Adrian Glick, was an unhappy one due to his violence. They had two children, Sarah and Marcus, but Marcus died as a baby. Escaping from her husband, Jenny fled with the children.

Jennifer's third and fourth marriages were also dissolved but she had the strength to seek help and join Alcoholics Anonymous and has been sober for the last eighteen years. After finding sparse employment as a taxi-driver, she landed her first acting role in fifteen years in the radio soap *The Merseysiders*. Roles in *Bread*, *Help* (playing Steve McGann's mother) and *Hetty Wainthropp Investigates* followed, but Jennifer is now waiting for her considerable acting talents to be put to use once again. Now happily married, to her fifth husband, Steve Ramsden, she plays bridge and enjoys spending time with her daughter Naomi, son-in-law Ken Hewitt, and grandsons James and Christopher.

~

"The public have never forgotten Lucille and, in spite of everything, they still seem to have a soft spot for her, and for me."

JENNIFER MOSS

~

SUE NICHOLLS

The Hon. Susan Nicholls grew up in very different circumstances from her screen sister Audrey Roberts. While Audrey was dragged up in the back-streets of Manchester, Susan grew up in a comfortable home with her elder sister Judith. She was born in Walsall in the West Midlands on 23 November 1945. Her father, Harmar, became the Conservative MP for Peterborough, and eventually Lord Harmar-Nicholls, Euro MP for Greater Manchester South.

Home was always filled with music, and from an early age Sue learned to appreciate drama, visiting Wolverhampton's Grand Theatre often. Her paternal grandmother, who ran a public house, was expert at the honky-tonk piano – 'I learned old-time music-hall songs on my grandmother's knee' – and Sue inherited her mother Dorothy's rich signing voice. At the age of nine, she went to boarding school – St Mary and St Ann's, Abbots Bromley, where she passed seven O Levels and A Levels in German and French. She decided against going on to Oxford University and announced, to her parents' surprise, that she wanted to act. After failing to get into RADA, she spent a year helping out at her father's paint and wallpaper shop. The following year RADA accepted her.

After leaving RADA, Sue joined actor-manager Charles Vance's Group of Three and repertory companies in Wolverhampton and Weston-Super-Mare. In 1964, she auditioned for a new Midlands soap opera, *Crossroads*, but failed to get the part of hotel-owner's daughter Jill Richardson because she overdid her West Midlands accent (which was odd as it was her own accent!). Instead she was given the part of waitress Marilyn Gates. *Crossroads* made Sue a household name, and she remained with the show for four years, during which time she released a single 'Where Will You Be' after singing it on the programme. The record was a hit, staying at number seventeen in the charts for eight weeks.

Sue left *Crossroads* to concentrate on her singing career, but never achieved the same chart success. She embarked on a career in cabaret, and took her solo act all over the country. She returned to the theatre in a variety of popular plays and pantomimes and worked on classic television shows such as *The Duchess of Duke Street*, *Dixon of Dock Green* and *The Professionals*. The early seventies found her playing against Hylda Baker as busty Big Brenda in *Not On Your Nellie*.

During the 1970s Sue did two very different stints abroad. In Vienna she sang between strip acts at a nightclub, while in 1976 she toured America and Canada with the Royal Shakespeare Company in *London Assurance*, finishing with a six-week run on Broadway. Throughout the 1970s Sue found fame with younger audiences in children's television, appearing alongside a host of puppets in *Pipkins* and then as the ghost Nadia Poppov in *Rentaghost*. Then, she starred in another classic programme, *The Rise And Fall of Reginald Perrin* as the raunchy secretary, Joan.

In 1979 Sue made her Street début as Audrey Potter, and over the next five years she kept popping up to cause havoc in daughter Gail's life before she landed a long-term contract with the show and Audrey became Mrs Alf Roberts.

Sue married in 1993, becoming Mrs Mark Eden at Camden Register Office. The couple had met ten years previously at a party, and it was a happy coincidence that found them working together on *Coronation Street* when Mark was cast as Alan Bradley.

A couple of years ago Sue took a break from the Street to recreate her role of Joan in *The Legacy of Reginald Perrin*. While she's happy to carry on playing Audrey, she would love to appear in an old-fashioned stage musical such as *Hello, Dolly* or *Mame*.

LYNNE PERRIE

The news that a television actress had been sacked from the nation's top show because she'd had fat taken from her thighs and inserted in her lips made all the headlines in September 1994. Camera crews camped outside Granada TV and freelance photographers trained their long lenses through railings. Everyone seemed to be waiting for the same thing – that photograph or interview with Lynne Perrie who, years earlier, had been christened 'Poison Ivy' by the media. It wasn't because she had been axed or because she had been popular in the show that people were interested, it was because of the lips, and a photograph taken after the operation, in which they looked almost freakishly large.

While the nation debated the operation and the sacking, the two women who knew the truth about Lynne Perrie's departure from the Street remained silent. Executive producer Carolyn Reynolds had had to tell the actress that after twenty-three years Ivy was to go and not because of the change in Lynne's face but for more mundane reasons: 'For quite some time we had had difficulty in storylining Ivy. She seemed to go down very narrow routes in terms of stories. There was a lot of soul-searching and discussion, and eventually it was decided that it was time to move away from that character. So I met with Lynne Perrie and we had a long discussion about it and it was agreed that she should leave *Coronation Street*.' In her autobiography, *Secrets of the Street*, Lynne also recalls that meeting: 'I walked out of that office and a weight lifted from my shoulders. I felt light-headed. At last I was free.'

Anyone who has not met Lynne Perrie might well have difficulty with the notion of her having anything to be 'free' of; here was a rich actress, with fabulous dresses and jewellery, a lavish lifestyle and the nickname 'Champagne Perrie'. She was internationally famous and every door opened to her. However, behind all this was a sad, lonely woman, who had learned that both fame and riches meant nothing when weighed against the absence of love and family. After working at the studio each day, she would seek solace in the neighbouring private bar, drink to excess and let herself into an empty flat, just a stone's throw away from Granada.

It had all started on 7 April 1931, in the Yorkshire steelworking town of Masbro, Rotherham, when Lynne Perrie was born Jean

Dudley to bricklayer Eric and his wife, Agnes. The family were close-knit and Jean was brought up a Catholic churchgoer. She was happy and content and her parents were proud when, after having passed her eleven-plus, she went to Rotherham High School for Girls. On leaving school at sixteen, Jean started work as a trainee pharmacist at Boots the Chemist, and spent her nights singing with a local dance-band. It was while singing at a club that she met carpenter Derrick Barksby and fell for his tall, good looks. Desperate to keep him out of National Service, she contrived to become pregnant so that her father would force her to marry. The plan worked and Jean became Mrs Barksby in October 1950. Seven months later Stephen was born and less than a year after that Jean took the stage name Lynne Perrie (after Gordon Pirie, a Yorkshire athlete) and, with Derrick as her manager, launched herself into cabaret.

Throughout the 1950s and 1960s Lynne belted out numbers supporting groups such as the Beatles and the Rolling Stones. She sang in cabaret all over the country and in Africa, during which time a gulf grew between her and Derrick and she turned to a string of boyfriends for comfort. Her big break came in 1969 when Ken Loach cast her as the blowsy, mouthy mother in his film *Kes*. That led directly to *Coronation Street* and the role of Ivy, who to begin with, in 1971, was a minor character. In her book Lynne describes her first day on the set: 'My arrival at Granada studios in a brand new Mark 10 Jaguar didn't escape the notice of some of the regular members of the cast. I recall overhearing a bemused Betty Driver whisper, "They must be paying the talking extras well."'

Although she had no formal theatre or acting training, Lynne had a natural quality which she brought to the screen, and Ivy became an instant success. For the next twenty-three years the character grew in stature and Lynne Perrie slipped down the slope that ended with the lip operation. Too much time on her hands, more fame and money than she could stand, led her to long drinking sessions in Granada's club: 'By the time the rest of the actors started piling in, I'd be half cut. Of course, the intention was always to stay for just one or two drinks, but it never quite worked out that way . . . My reputation as the Granada lush had been born.' The drinking made her behaviour erratic and her health suffered. Added to this came the blow that her son Stephen was HIV. Lynne Perrie's life was a journalist's dream story but a tragic one.

Since Ivy left the show and was eventually killed off, Lynne has been reconciled with Derrick and has concentrated on her cabaret career. She now has time to devote herself to her family, and the courage to admit to mistakes: 'I don't try and make excuses for my life.'

~

"When I was told Ivy was to be written out I burst out crying – then I realized they were tears of joy. I felt like this great weight had rolled off my back."

LYNNE PERRIE

~

PAT PHOENIX

Regarded as television's number one sex symbol throughout the sixties and seventies, Pat Phoenix was an international star who, it was often reported, had a 'heart of gold', a 'love for people' and 'time for everyone'. These weren't just glib sentiments put about by PR agents or journalists, they were true, and when she died of cancer on 17 September 1986, fans around the globe mourned the passing of a genuine, lovable actress who throughout her twenty-one year period on *Coronation Street* merged with her screen character Elsie Tanner so far that it was often impossible to see where one ended and the other began.

Patricia Frederica was born on 26 November 1923 in St Mary's Hospital, Manchester – not in County Galway, Ireland, as she allowed journalists to relay romantically to readers – and brought up in Ducie Street. Her father, Tom Mansfield, flitted from job to job, and was exposed as a bigamist when Pat was eight. Her mother, a part-time mannequin named Anna Noonan, marched Pat out of the family home and away from her 'husband' of sixteen years, then married a decorator named Richard Pilkington whose surname Pat took as her own.

At eleven, Pat decided on acting as a future career and landed her first professional engagement at the BBC in Manchester on *Children's Hour* after sending in a monologue on the death of Lady Jane Grey to Auntie Vi – Violet Carson. Between school and radio performances, Pat struggled to live with her unsympathetic step-father, once nearly stabbing him to death for hitting her mother. On leaving school she found employment at Manchester Town Hall and joined the Manchester Arts Theatre, a semi-professional company, and acted in her spare time before joining the company full-time on tour as Judith in *Granite*. The part gave her the recognition she needed and, after touring for eighteen months, she settled down at Chorlton repertory theatre and featured in a Manchester film, *Cup Tie Honeymoon*, playing the wife of popular comic Sandy Powell.

Crossing the border to Yorkshire, Pat played Catherine Earnshaw in *Wuthering Heights* in Keighley, and married actor Peter Marsh. Her name was changed by theatre manager, Jack Dillam, to Frederica Pilkington, when he dyed her hair blonde and presented her in a touring play *A Girl Called Sadie*. When her marriage fell apart Pat attempted to revitalize her life by changing her name again. After reading Marguerite Steen's book *Phoenix Rising* she borrowed half of the title and kept it as her stage name for the rest of her life. The change seemed to work as she landed the lead in Joan Littlewood's production of *Fings Ain't What They Used To Be* at the Stratford Theatre, working alongside Richard Harris.

Forced out of the production through illness, Pat returned to Manchester and tried her hand at writing scripts for *Lennie the Lion*. It was 1960, and at Granada casting was under way for a new family drama series entitled 'Florizel Street'. Along with the rest of the actors in the north-west, Pat attended an audition and won the part of Elsie Tanner immediately, after refusing to remove her coat when asked to do so by Tony Warren: '"No" I said flatly. "You'll just have to guess at it, won't you?" I'd be damned if I would parade for them. I had been to too many auditions and lost too many good parts to take this lot seriously.'

Elsie Tanner made Pat Phoenix an overnight sensation and sex symbol. Part of her appeal was the way Elsie struck a saucy pose with her hand on her hip. The reason behind the stance was not character led but because Pat's left arm was an inch and a half longer than her right and sticking out her hip was the most comfortable way for her to stand. For the next two decades she ruled supreme as Queen of the Soaps and enjoyed international stardom. When she visited Australia in 1966 a crowd of fifty thousand awaited her, and when she was filming *The L Shaped Room* at Shepperton she had a larger following than Judy Garland, who was also there. She became the official pin-up for the *Ark Royal*, a columnist with *TV Times*, made a record, 'The Rovers Chorus', and had a racehorse named after her. In 1972 she married actor Alan Browning, who for two years had played her screen husband Alan Howard. Shortly afterwards they both left the Street to embark on a joint career in theatre, appearing in plays such as *Gaslight*. Unfortunately their success was limited and they separated. Three years later Pat returned to the Street, telling reporters that she was back 'where she belonged' as she had missed her friends too much.

For the next seven years Elsie Tanner was an integral part of *Coronation Street*, battling with Hilda Ogden, swigging gins in the Rovers and crying on Len Fairclough's shoulder. But, as her character reached retirement age, Pat grew upset by the way Elsie continued to bat her eyelids and fall into bed with unlikely Romeos. Her decision to quit the Street in 1983 made headline news and this time, Pat announced, she'd leave for good: 'Somebody stuck a sex-symbol label on me which I find very embarrassing. But that was never my intention – I have too many curves, which I have been trying to get rid of for years.'

A new career as agony aunt on breakfast television beckoned but Pat was soon back on TV, playing a seaside landlady in the comedy *Constant Hot Water*. Sadly, for her and her fans, illness cut short the rest of her career when she was diagnosed with lung cancer. Television cameras and photographs focused on the Alexandra Hospital in Cheadle for the last few weeks of Pat's life. She made her final public appearance in a wheelchair surrounded by flowers and teddy bears before she married for the third time. The groom at her bedside was the actor Anthony Booth, with whom she had lived for some years. It was a private wedding and a week later Pat died. At her funeral, at Manchester's Holy Name Church, her coffin was carried in to the sound of a Dixieland jazz band playing 'When The Saints Come Marching In'. Pat Phoenix went out of the world as she had lived – in style.

~

"I wanted to be a famous actress, but I'm not sure I wanted to be a national monument."

PAT PHOENIX

~

ANNE REID

Anne Reid was born in Newcastle, where she grew up with her three older brothers, her mother, Anne, and father Colin, who worked as a journalist. Anne's early ambition was to be a ballet dancer but she switched from dance to acting classes when she was sent to boarding school, Penrhos College in Colwyn Bay.

After leaving school Anne trained at the RADA before joining Bromley repertory theatre, as a dream girl in *Seven Year Itch*. Comedy sketches with Benny Hill followed, as did a part in *Twelfth Night* with the Regent's Park Company. In 1961 she took the part of Valerie Tatlock in Coronation Street, and remained with the programme for nine years.

In the summer of 1969 Anne took a break from the Street to go on a theatre tour in the play *Come Laughing Home*, which also starred the Street's Reginald Marsh and Bill Kenwright. The experience made her realize how much she loved working on the stage, and she decided that she had played Val for long enough. She asked to be written out and was killed off in January 1971. Four months after leaving the Street, she married Peter Eckersley, head of drama at Granada Television. After the birth of her son, Mark, she happily gave up acting to concentrate on her family, but after Peter's death in 1981 she decided to attempt a comeback.

Since the early eighties she has seldom been out of work, becoming a familiar face in various television shows, such as *Heartbeat*, *Hetty Wainthropp Investigates*, *Roughnecks*, *Medics*, *Peak Practice*, *Casualty*, *Boon*, *The Upper Hand* and is a regular in Victoria Wood programmes and comedy playhouses. She has also appeared in countless stage plays around the country, including *Wild Oats* at the National Theatre. She received rave reviews for her performance in the original production of Kay Mellor's play *A Passionate Woman*.

At long last the ghost of Val Barlow has been laid to rest, and Anne has found international fame through a totally different medium – as the voice of Wendoline in the animated adventure of Wallace and Gromit, *A Close Shave*.

TRACY SHAW

Whenever stylist Maxine Heavey fiddles with a customer's hair, chats about the weather or sips half a lager in the Rovers there's always a part of actress Tracy Shaw's mind that is a hundred miles away from Granada's Manchester studios. To understand the real Tracy is to picture her in her true setting, in the small Derbyshire village, Belper, where she grew up. Her father, Karl, was a probation officer until

he took over the licence of the local public house, the Talbot Hotel in 1990. He and his wife, Ann, worked hard to provide Tracy and her younger brother, Karl, with a secure environment and it is from her family that Tracy gets her confidence: 'My dad always says, "Blood's thicker than water" and no matter how many crises I have, no matter what happens, I always end up going back to them. They are always there for me, for love and advice, and they are my strength.'

Tracy was born in July 1973 and educated in Catholic schools around Belper. When not at school she spent as much time as she could indulging in her passion for dance, encouraged by her parents: 'My mum danced until she was about ten and I just followed the same way. I started dancing at three and I dedicated my whole life to it and thrived on it.' As far as Tracy was concerned, dance was her future but she was faced with a crossroads after leaving a B. Tech course in performing arts: 'For those two years I was dancing professionally but grew interested in acting. I'd always wanted to dance on a cruise and had an audition for a six-month contract on one, but then I also had an audition for drama school.' Deciding that acting had a longer life-span than dance, she opted for the latter.

Training at the Arden School of Theatre was a mixed blessing for Tracy. The school was connected to Manchester's prestigious Royal Exchange Theatre so she was able to watch performances and be taught by the company's directors and casting agents. However, the move to Manchester meant leaving her family behind. It was the first time the shy teenager had left home and, emotionally unable to cope, she suffered anorexia.

Just months after leaving drama school Tracy put her degree to good use when she landed a part in Granada's *September Song*. At the time, the Street's casting director James Bain auditioned Tracy for an unspecified role, that of a bubbly young girl who was to be a pal

for the established character of Fiona. 'It was the first interview that I'd gone to where I felt it was my part. You go in for so many and feel you haven't clicked, but the lines written for Maxine suited me so well and it all came together.' Another young hopeful auditioning for the role was Eve Steele who was later cast as the power-crazed Anne Malone. It's hard to imagine how the characters would have turned out if the actresses' roles had been swapped!

Almost as soon as she burst on to the screen in May 1995, Tracy fell into the lap of the tabloid press and every aspect of her life was picked over and commented upon. However, since the death of Diana, Princess of Wales, the lenses have stopped following Tracy and for this she is grateful. The different attitude in the press came to her attention when filming the *Coronation Street* video in Las Vegas: 'When we got out there the paparazzi in LA were there and they were taking pictures but our national press then pulled together to get back at them and wanted to do good press. This was a big turn around.'

One subject often brought up by the press is Tracy's eating disorder: 'Every time I lose weight the press bring it up again – whether

⁓

"I based Maxine on Marilyn Monroe because she does what she thinks men want her to do, but really that isn't what she wants. She just wants a bit of love and attention."

TRACY SHAW

⁓

I'm stressed or ill - and they print nasty pictures which make me feel worse about myself.' This attention does have one positive side to it as Tracy has found that hundreds of young girls have written to her, opening their hearts about the problems Tracy herself faced at drama school: 'They see me as an icon and many say they pull through because they have someone to look up to and share their thoughts with, but the downside is I haven't got time to respond to all of them, no matter how much I want to help. And I want to help so much as there's so little known about anorexia in this country.'

At the moment Tracy is thrilled to be part of the Street and recognizes that her time playing Maxine has taught her much about working as part of a team and she has grown in appreciation of the technical side of television. She hopes to work in films in the future but admits to having an on-going joke with Angela Griffin, who plays her best friend Fiona: 'We say we're still going to be there, sat in the Rovers, gossiping like two Hilda Ogdens, when we're sixty-two. Still on our own, never having any happiness with men!'

DORIS SPEED

Doris Speed always said she based her performance as Annie Walker on her own aunt Bessie, who used to lead the Speed family in Christmas charades and had a withering look. Doris was born on 3 February 1899 while her parents were touring in Hulme, Manchester. Her father, George, was a singer, and mother Ada an actress. Doris toured with her parents from birth, sleeping in dressing rooms while they trod the boards. She made her first appearance on stage aged three, as a flaxen-haired child singing a song about a golliwog. She got her first speaking role aged five as the Infant Prince of Rome in a Victorian melodrama. Travelling with her parents around the country, Doris had a sparse education, moving from school to school each week. At fourteen, she took a course in typing and shorthand, and soon after completing it she started work as a clerk at the Guinness brewery in Manchester. The money she earned helped pay the family rent.

For forty years, from 1918 to 1959 Doris worked at the brewery, slowly moving up through the ranks until she became assistant to the regional manager. She retired from Guinness when she was sixty and only then started to live out her lifetime ambition: 'Acting was all I ever wanted to do.' All the time she had been typing and filing over those forty years, Doris had used her mind to learn lines and remember moves for the hundreds of amateur and semi-professional shows in which she appeared as a member of the Unnamed Society and the Chorlton repertory company. By the time she retired from her first career she was a well-known stage and radio actress and made the move to television. In 1958 she made her television début in Granada's serial *Shadow Squad*, followed up by *Skyport* in which she played a tea-lady. Shortly

"Annie Walker is an insufferable prig but a vulnerable kind of woman at the same time. She is full of pretension, she is self-satisfied and thinks she is a cut above the rest. And if I ever met her in real life I would feel like saying, 'Stop acting like a silly ass' "

DORIS SPEED

afterwards she was invited to audition for the part of Annie Walker, written by Tony Warren, who had often seen her amateur stage performances and who acted with her on radio.

Although she later said she did not really want the role, Doris auditioned for the part: 'I was in Bristol at the time,' she recalled, 'and it seemed such a long way to travel. In the end a friend persuaded me and I took the milk train up to Manchester. I knew the part was mine as soon as I did the audition. It was just a feeling.'

For the next twenty-three years she played the part of Annie Walker to perfection, although she did not share the character's views on the world and society. 'Annie is a silly, vain woman and she stands for everything I am not. She is a staunch Conservative and I am a Socialist and democratic in the extreme.'

Doris lived quietly in the suburbs of Manchester with her mother, who died in 1972 aged ninety-seven, and never married: 'It isn't because I haven't wanted to,' she told a reporter in 1966, 'but perhaps I set too high a standard of the man I would like to marry. There are plenty of nice, pleasant men around, but the one who would make me give up everything, who would definitely be the boss, just hasn't turned up.'

With her mother Doris travelled around the world, enjoying the financial security the Street gave her: 'My parents had long periods out of work. They were never able to save money. Never had a real home of their own. They always hoped for the big chance, but it never came. When I first went on the stage it looked as if the pattern was to be repeated. Then came the Street. It's given me security, and a measure of popularity.' She received much acclaim for her performance, travelling to Buckingham Palace in 1977 to collect her MBE, and was presented with the Pye Television Award for outstanding contribution to television by her fan Sir John Betjeman.

Throughout her time on the Street Doris would not reveal her age and was heartbroken when a national newspaper printed a copy of her birth certificate, showing the world that she was eighty-four. She collapsed on set and was sent home. She never returned: shortly after the revelation thieves broke into her home and wrecked it while she hid in her locked bedroom.

Eventually she moved into a Bury nursing home and stayed there until her death on 17 November 1994. She died while sitting in a chair reading the novel *To Sir With Love* and smoking a cigarette.

JILL SUMMERS

Jill Summers was Phyllis Pearce. She was also the Portress, the Waitress and the Blackpool Tart. She was a sport, too. In a fantastic career that lasted seventy years she trod the boards all over the country, appearing in hundreds of revues, musicals, pantos and plays. With her broad Lancashire wit she made friends by the coachload and was always ready with a joke, funny story and witty put-down. Like many actresses of her age, the stage had always been present in her life.

*"I love working
on the Street,
it's a second
home and all the
cast are like my
family."*

JILL SUMMERS

She was born on 8 December 1910 in Eccles. Her mother, musical comedy star Marie Santoi, was playing at the Palace Theatre in Manchester and Jill, or Honor Margaret Fuller, as she was named, came from pure showbusiness stock. Father Alf was a tightrope walker, one set of grandparents were Shakespearean actors and her other grandmother was a bareback rider. Jill's mother died when she was just thirteen and Jill and sister Jose left school to work in a cotton mill before Jill went into service.

She escaped life below stairs by marrying and opening a newsagent's in Sale with her husband Jack. They converted one of the rooms into a hairdresser's and Jill chanced her arm at the art of coiffure.

After the break-up of her marriage, she joined her brother, Tom Moss, who had created a musical double act: 'I was the comedienne. We used to do duets together. One write-up said I had the panache of Beatrice Lillie and the voice of Gracie Fields.' It was Jill's ability to hit soaring notes that caused her voice to break and she was left with the gravel voice that became her trademark: 'I

must have overdone it on stage one night. When I hit a top A, I suddenly heard my voice crack. By the time I came off stage it had gone completely. I didn't cry or get upset about it. I just thought I'd have to change my singing style, and I became a contralto.'

At the outbreak of war, Jill joined ENSA. At this point she was still known as Honor Fuller and was asked to provide a stage name. At the time she was enjoying a gill of beer on a hot summer day and decided upon Jill Summers. She had joined ENSA as a singer, but an incident on stage sent her career spinning off in another direction: 'I went on stage one night during a concert, tripped up, came out with a mouthful and brought roars of laughter from the audience. That was when I decided to concentrate on comedy.'

After the war, Jill made comedy her career, appearing in pantomime and revue around the country. It was in the early 1950s that she first shared the bill with Bill Waddington who, years later, she would chase when he played Percy Sugden. In 1949, though, she had met a young doctor, Clifford Smith, when he and some friends heckled her performance: 'He was in a theatre box with a group of doctors. And they were heckling me. I was used to dealing with that sort of thing and I remember shouting back that I'd seen many a rotten egg in a box! The doctors enjoyed that, and after the show we met up. Cliff introduced himself to me and romance blossomed from there.' They married a few months later and he started to write sketches for his wife, which made her famous. In 1956 she starred in her own Yorkshire Television series *Summer's Here*, then toured the northern club circuit.

Before joining the Street as Phyllis in 1982, she took a minor role in 1972, as cleaner Bessie Proctor, for eight episodes. Other television credits include Deliah Hilldrup in *Castle Haven* and Michael Elphick's mother in *This Year, Next Year*. Phyllis Pearce was described as 'a grim battleaxe' and the part was designed to cause trouble for binman Chalkie Whitely. When Chalkie left the show in 1983, Jill thought her character would not appear again. However, she did return, in 1985, shortly after the death of husband Cliff.

From 1985 to 1996, Jill played the purple-haired sex-starved pensioner to great acclaim, especially among children who wrote letters asking to adopt her as a granny. Her time on the Street was punctuated by illnesses and heart complaints and she was eventually forced to retire after appearing in 512 episodes. For Jill there was always the hope that she would return, one day, to the studios and to her favourite part: 'I just love it. I'll go on until they shoot me!' Sadly she died on 11 January 1997, aged eighty-six.

GEORGIA TAYLOR

The young woman behind Georgia Taylor was born Claire Jackson on 26 February 1980, in Billinge, Wigan. Her father, Geoff, is a financial consultant, her mother, Caroline, a housewife, and she has a younger brother, David, who is still at school.

At only ten years old and still at primary school, Claire got her teeth into the role of Lady Macbeth when a progressive teacher decided to introduce the children to Shakespeare, even though the pupils didn't understand some of what they were saying. Claire enjoyed the experience and carried on appearing in school plays when she moved on to St Peter's High School.

Youth theatre followed, as did plays in local theatres, before Claire took her first professional job as a singer in Manchester's Palace Theatre production of *Joseph and the Amazing Technicolour Dream Coat*, which starred Darren Day.

Claire joined a local college to do A levels in English language, psychology and theatre studies but abandoned this when she was cast

as Toyah in *Coronation Street*, joining the cast in the summer of 1997 and changing her name. She is enjoying her time on the Street and hopes to use the programme as a stepping stone into other roles.

DENISE WELCH

When twenty-one-year-old Denise left drama school, the first thing she did was write to the producers of *Coronation Street* for a job. As the years went by she continued to write, at one stage suggesting that she could play Ken Barlow's estranged daughter Susan: 'I was the right age and she'd have had a Newcastle accent.' Now that would have been an interesting twist – Kevin Webster might even have become Ken's son-in-law!

Denise Welch was born near Whitley Bay on 22 May 1958. Her father, Vin, worked in the family business, Welch's Toffees, but indulged his passion for theatricals by acting in amateur dramatics and appearing as a drag queen for charity events. Vin had married his

~

"I'm enjoying playing Toyah now as she's developed from a sullen, sulky teenager. She's had no stable foundation on which to build her personality but now she's blossoming into a person in her own right."

GEORGIA
TAYLOR

~

185

~

*"It was probably
more exciting for
me coming into
this show than for
a lot of people.
I've been totally
addicted to it for
years. I've loved
the way it
balances comedy
and drama.*

DENISE WELCH

~

wife, Annie, when they were both young and at university and Denise was born into a bustling, partying household: 'I used to end up sleeping with five men when I was four – it was the beginning of my downfall.'

Denise fell in love with the sea at an early age, playing on the beach with her younger sister Debbie: 'Whenever I need to be alone I like to visit the sea. But I don't swim in it, I like to be by the sea, not in it.' The Welchs are a very close family and pull together in times of need. After the birth of her son, Matthew, Denise suffered from post-natal illness for two years. Her family were a tremendous support to her during that time. She returned her mother's support when Annie was diagnosed with cancer in the early nineties.

Educated at a convent and the local grammar school, Denise is the first to admit she was an average student and struggled through five O levels. She sat A levels in drama and history, and decided to teach drama. It was only when she had been accepted on a teacher-training course in Crewe that her drama teacher and her father convinced her that she had a natural talent that should be trained. As a result she was taken on at the Mountview Theatre School in London where she struggled with some of the techniques: 'I never saw the point in being a tree, or felt the vibes, I wanted to get on with rehearsing plays.' However, things picked up in her final year when the school toured Italy as a repertory company.

To get her Equity card, Denise taught movement and drama to students at the Watford Palace Theatre. She married actor David Easter, but after two years the marriage fell apart and Denise concentrated on her career. She made her television début in Tyne Tees Television's *Barriers* but mainly filled her time with radio and theatre work, the highlight of which has to be her tour in *A Bedful of Foreigners*, playing Simone the French stripper, whose final appearance on stage was as a nun in stockings and suspenders.

Denise married her second husband, the actor Tim Healy, on 18 October 1988. They had known each other for a number of years, through being connected with the Live Theatre Company in Newcastle. However, neither liked the other and told mutual friends, such as Robson Green, that they didn't like being in each other's company. However, during a dinner party they got talking and, in the best tradition, fell in love. Their son, Matthew, was born in April 1989, and it is clear that her family means everything to Denise: she brings Tim and Matthew into every conversation, a big smile breaking out when she mentions them.

For three years Denise appeared as Marsha, a soldier's wife, in *Soldier, Soldier*. After two years of playing such a domesticated character 'making tuna sandwiches',

Denise complained to the producers and Marsha was turned into a nightclub singer. It was a natural transition from singing on television to singing in a studio, and Denise was signed up by Virgin and recorded 'You Don't Have To Say You Love Me' at Abbey Road, with the Royal Philharmonic Orchestra as a backing group. The single reached number twenty-three in the charts in 1996.

Natalie first appeared in the Street in 1997 and soon became a hit with the viewers. Denise worked alongside the writers to present the character as more than just a man-stealing bitch. The initial hard work put into creating Natalie paid off, and she is now on a yearly contract, which comes as a relief: 'I'm quite settled here now, and it's been nice not to have that constant churn of "I'm going for this" and "She got it" and "It's down to me and somebody else". I used to thrive on that when I was in my twenties but now I have a family and Matthew is settled at school it suits my lifestyle to be as settled as I can be.'

SALLY WHITTAKER

Sally Whittaker was born in Middleton, near Oldham, on 3 May 1963. Her parents, Jenny and Bob, encouraged their daughter's ambition to be a ballet dancer. She went to classes and intended to go to a ballet boarding school at thirteen but changed her mind when she felt she couldn't stand the discipline. Instead she joined Oldham Theatre Workshop and realized that acting was for her: 'From the very first day I walked in there I knew that I wanted to be an actress. It totally changed my life.'

After leaving school Sally trained at the Mountview Theatre School in North London, and then worked in America touring in old-style music hall with the Abba Dabba Theatre Company. Back in England she was spotted by an agent when she appeared in pantomime in a London pub.

Roles with *The Metal Mickey Road Show*, *The Practice* and *Juliet Bravo*, in which she played a heroin addict, led to a number of auditions for *Coronation Street*. The first was for one of the Clayton daughters, who moved into No.11 in 1985, then there was Kevin Webster's posh girlfriend Michelle Robinson. Eventually, in January 1986, she made her Street début as Sally Seddon, a part that outlived the other two, and twelve years later she is still in the programme.

In the last few years Sally has taken three breaks from *Coronation Street*. She appeared at Bolton Octagon in *A Taste of Honey*, where she played Anne Reid's daughter. Sally lives with her husband, scriptwriter Tim Dynevor, and their children, Phoebe and Sam, in Cheshire.

~

"I'm always pinching myself and thinking, I can't believe that this is happening to me – I'm just a working-class girl from Oldham."

SALLY WHITTAKER

~

HELEN WORTH

Although her birth certificate states her full name as being Cathryn Helen Wigglesworth, her parents, Alfred and Gladys, took to calling their daughter Helen from very early on. She was born on 7 January 1951, in Leeds, but the family moved to Morecambe when she was two, and it was there that Helen grew up with her older brother Neville. Her parents ran a hotel, the Erindale, and she recalls being surrounded by show-business from an early age: 'During the summer seasons a lot of the performers from the local summer shows would stay with us, so I actually grew up with singers, dancers, musicians and comedians.'

When she was three a doctor recommended that dancing lessons might cure Helen of her habit of walking with her toes turned in, and she embarked on the start of her theatrical career. She was educated at a small private school called Mount Independent School for Young Ladies and it was there, taking part in Shakespearean plays, that Helen began to develop an interest in acting and dancing. She didn't have much choice as she was continually sent out of class for being naughty, and told to sit in the corridor where the headmistress kept a bound copy of Shakespeare's plays. It was a case of read the plays or be bored.

Helen made her first television appearance at the age of ten, reading an excerpt from a book on Granada's *Scene at 6.30*. She also appeared in a *Z Cars* episode, in which she had more lines than Glenda Jackson, but her big break came at twelve when she landed the part of Brigitta in a West End production of *The Sound of Music*. The job ran for nine months, during which time Helen lived with a chaperone, changed her name to Worth and became homesick: 'The first night I was so terrified that I threw up in the wings and had to be pushed on to the stage, but when I got out there the atmosphere was so wonderful that I was hooked, and the feeling has stayed with me all my life.'

Helen left school at fifteen and enrolled in London's Corona Stage Academy although she never actually finished her training; parts in the films *Oliver!* and *The Prime of Miss Jean Brodie* led to her turning professional before her sixteenth birthday.

Playing the part of a bean-pod in Northampton Repertory Company's pantomime *Jack and the Beanstalk* led to a full season with the company and a variety of roles. For the next few years Helen worked with repertory companies in Watford, Hornchurch and Richmond before landing a job with the BBC Radio Repertory Company. After further work on television she joined *Coronation Street* in 1975, playing teenage Gail Potter, even though at the time she was in her early twenties.

Helen has continued to play Gail through marriages, divorce, affairs, births and a variety of traumas. Off screen she runs two homes, in London and Cheshire, and spends her spare time fund-raising for the charity of which she is patron, 'When You Wish Upon A Star', which helps terminally ill children. She is also president of Ossett Albion Football Club, where her brother Neville is chairman.

ACKNOWLEDGEMENTS

The author would like to thank the following women for having to put up with questions and a tape recorder being stuck under their noses. Without their help this book could have been written but wouldn't be so accurate.

Jean Alexander	Gaynor Faye	Sarah Lancashire
Thelma Barlow	Janet Featherstone	Jennifer Moss
Amanda Barrie	Julie Goodyear	Sue Nicholls
Elizabeth Bradley	Sandra Gough	Lynne Perrie
Beverley Callard	Angela Griffin	Anne Reid
Jane Danson	Madge Hindle	Tracy Shaw
Elizabeth Dawn	Tina Hobley	Georgia Taylor
Eileen Derbyshire	Doreen Keogh	Denise Welch
Betty Driver	Anne Kirkbride	Sally Whittaker
Vicky Entwistle	Barbara Knox	Helen Worth

There is also one man who needs to be thanked,
Coronation Street's *creator:*

Tony Warren

Index